UPROOTED
BY WAR

UPR**OO**TED
BY **WAR**

APPALACHIAN R**OO**TS – B**OO**K THREE

JANICE C**O**LE H**O**PKINS

Ambassador International
GREENVILLE, SOUTH CAROLINA & BELFAST, NORTHERN IRELAND

www.ambassador-international.com

Uprooted by War

Appalachian Roots – Book 3

Printed in the United States of America

ISBN: 978-1-62020-562-4
eISBN: 978-1-62020-493-1

All Scripture taken from the King James Version, the Authorized Version.

Cover Design and Page Layout by Hannah Nichols
Ebook Conversion by Anna Riebe Raats

AMBASSADOR INTERNATIONAL
Emerald House
411 University Ridge, Suite B14
Greenville, SC 29601, USA
www.ambassador-international.com

AMBASSADOR BOOKS
The Mount
2 Woodstock Link
Belfast, BT6 8DD, Northern Ireland, UK
www.ambassadormedia.co.uk

The colophon is a trademark of Ambassador

Trees whose fruit withereth,

without fruit, twice dead,

plucked up by roots.

~ Jude 1:12b

CHAPTER ONE

A Look Back

WATAUGA COUNTY, NORTH CAROLINA - APRIL 1862

LEAH WALKED FROM THE SMOKEHOUSE just as Luke rode in from Boone. She smiled and went to meet him at the barn. Her husband had come home early, and as always, the day seemed brighter and she felt more alive with him near.

"We both have letters," he told her. "I haven't read mine yet."

She went to him, and he took her in his arms. They'd been married eight years now, and she still missed him even when he only went to Boone for the day.

He unsaddled his horse and put him in the pasture. They walked to the log farmhouse with their arms around each other. She felt his gaze upon her and looked into his eyes. A knowing of need and love passed between them that required no words.

They sat on the sofa in the sitting room and opened the letters. Luke's came from his father and hers from her sister, Ivy. Leah read:

> Dear Leah,
>
> My, how time passes. It's hard to believe Patrick has just celebrated his seventh birthday. He's our delight. Lawrence loves him as if he were his own.

I'm so afraid Lawrence is going to have to go off and fight in this horrible war. He has tried to stay out of it for my sake, but he hears the displeasure from the other plantation owners around. Many of them have already volunteered, including your half-brother, Paul. I think he wanted to get away from Hester Sue more than fight for the South. It's ironic how much like Mama Hester Sue has become, and you know how little Paul liked our mother. I guess he saw her as the typical wicked stepmother.

Lawrence and I want other children, but God hasn't seen fit to bless us with any yet. I know you feel the same way, only probably more so, since you lost the twins. At least you and Luke are as much in love as Lawrence and I, but I know you still grieve for your babies. You're the strong one, though. You always have been.

Lawrence is pleased Zebulon Vance is now governor, because he seems to be a moderate. Perhaps you and Luke like him, too, given he's from that part of the state. He does seem to support the Confederacy, but then, I guess he has to, since North Carolina seceded from the Union.

This new conscription law frightens me. Lawrence thinks he'll be exempt, since he owns more than twenty slaves. If not, he plans to pay someone else to take his place. Luke might be able to do this too. I know he probably wants to go to war even less than Lawrence.

I just want this war to be over. No one thought it would take over a year. The South has been winning most of the major battles, but I'm still frustrated that it's taking so long.

I know you must be surprised to hear me talk about politics. I've always hated them so and still do, but I also understand now how they affect our lives. Lawrence and I can't help but discuss what's happening around us. Of course, we talk about everything.

Well, here I go talking too much about myself again. Tell me all about what's happening with you. I'm sure the war hasn't affected you in the mountains as much as it has us here. Still, you're likely to be facing even more shortages at the store, and if it continues, the fighting might also come to you.

Write soon. I love hearing from you.

With love,

Ivy

After they'd read their letters, she and Luke exchanged papers, and read the other's. They always shared everything.

Dear Luke and Leah,

I'm not writing to you separately, because paper is getting too dear. This blasted war is worrisome in so many ways. I hope I'll be able to avoid being forced to become a doctor for the Confederate army due to my age. Surely they won't conscript a doctor in his fifties. I hear they are in desperate need of doctors, though, and I think that goes for both sides to some degree.

The prison here is getting to be an abomination. I've tried to help some of the poor soldiers held there, but I'm rarely admitted. There's too much paperwork and procedures involved with anything governmental. It's a crying shame. All of the citizens of Salisbury are encouraged to donate food, clothing, and supplies, however, and I think some of the la-dies have special privileges. In the past, Mrs. Berry has been allowed to take care of some of the sick in her home, but then, she lives right beside the prison. There have been es-cape attempts, and this has put everyone on edge. The guards are being harsher, and the citizens are more frightened and less willing to help.

I'm sorry to hear Mama's not feeling well. It's hard for me to see her slowing down, since she's always been so active. Seventy-one years is longer than most people live, especially in the rugged mountains, but I trust the good Lord will grant her more. She's such a vital part of this family and so impor-tant to us all. Please give her my love.

Frances and the children are well, but she's unhappy with this war. Aren't we all! She sees the North as the aggressor, and she's upset I don't fully support the Confederacy. She is threatening to take the children and visit her sister in Charlotte. Perhaps it would be better if she did. There's even more tension here now that we're supporting different causes.

If I do decide to send her to Charlotte, I would love to come to the farm for a visit. It's been much too long. The only problem is there's an extreme shortage of doctors here now, and I'm needed more than ever. I'll just wait and see how things are.

It seems we used to write each other more often. Let's begin to do so again. I need to hear from you, for I'm missing all of you terribly. I hope to hear from you soon.

Love,

Father

"Do you think the Confederacy will try to conscript you?" Leah asked Luke when they'd finished reading.

"They probably will, for I'm in the right age group. It's the first time I've ever wished I were a few years older. Lawrence may hear from them sooner, but I think he'll be exempt for now. If the war continues and many more soldiers are lost, I wouldn't be surprised if they don't try to take us all."

"What do you plan to do?"

"I may need to volunteer for the Union army to keep from being conscripted by the Confederates."

"Luke! No!" She leaned over into his arms.

"It's not what I want, darling. You know it's not. I can't stand the thought of leaving you, and I hate to fight against the South, but I don't think I can fight for slavery."

"What about trying to pay for someone to serve in your place like Ivy said Lawrence could do if he wasn't exempt?"

"Three hundred dollars could leave us short on cash right now, and I'm not sure how long it would help. Father doesn't think this policy will be in place too long, and I tend to agree. The longer the war goes on, the more men they're going to need to replace the ones badly wounded and killed. Losses have already been pretty heavy, and they continue to mount. The Battle of Manassas had under a thousand killed, although over four thousand were wounded or missing. From the news coming in from Shiloh, there're almost twenty-five thousand casualties."

She nodded. "I still think it might be worth it . . . even if it just buys us more time."

"With the prices of the basic goods going up, we need to make sure we have enough for the necessities through the war. And the Confederacy could stop allowing men to pay for someone to fight in their place a few weeks after I paid, so I'm not sure it would be wise to even try."

"When would you need to leave if you do join the Union?"

"I'm not sure. I plan to wait as long as I can, but I dare not delay long. I'll try to leave everything as ready for winter as I can before I go. I'm hoping I can wait until next month anyway."

"I wish you could wait longer. It's going to be hard to see you leave."

"It'll be hard for me too. I don't feel good about leaving you and Granny here alone."

"We'll have a few weeks together then. I'm glad you told me, Luke." She gave him an impish smile. "Before you go, we'll have to try to make up for some of the time we'll be apart."

He gave a delighted laugh. "I like your way of thinking, Mrs. Moretz."

"I need some time alone," Leah told Patsy after breakfast the next morning. Luke had already started his chores. "Do you mind finishing up the dishes?"

"Not at all." Patsy smiled at her. "We're almost through anyway. Take your time."

Patsy had been Ivy's slave when they'd come to the mountains, and she'd stayed even though she could have left after Luke insisted she be given her freedom. Luke and Leah had never believed in owning people.

Leah dried her hands and quietly went out the larder door. Rarely did she need to be alone from Luke, but this was one of those times. He worried too much about her when she grieved. She guessed Ivy's letter had brought hard memories to the forefront again.

She walked straight toward the back of the house and the stand of trees in the distance. Soon she stood beside the graves. There were too many of them now.

The earliest belonged to Luther, Luke's great-uncle, who'd fallen to his death while out hunting. The next one held Christie Cagle, Granny Em's youngest sister. Granny Em and Edgar had two sons who'd been killed. Edgar's parents were there and so was Edgar. Emmie and Eddie, her twins, lay in the last grave, and they were why Leah had walked here today.

It had been several years, but the pain still hit hard. She'd become pregnant soon after she'd returned from helping Ivy in Anson County after their mother had died. She, Luke, Granny Em, and even Patsy had been delighted.

The pregnancy had gone rather well, although Leah's midsection had ballooned as her time approached. Granny Em was good with herbal medicines and had always helped deliver babies as well as had four of her own. They weren't worried.

Her labor began early in July. Leah thought it might be a little too early, but Granny Em said that wasn't unusual for the first baby.

Granny Em ran Luke out of their bedroom, but he insisted on leaving the door open. He pulled a chair into the hall and sat there what time he didn't pace.

"I'll stay out of the way," he said, "but I've got to know what's going on."

The first few hours were easy. Luke would come to the door every so often and smile at her in encouragement. Propped up in the bed, she liked seeing him.

After about ten hours, the pains became intense. Leah tried not to call out, because she didn't want to worry Luke.

"She'd do better if you'd close that door and go downstairs, so she could yell a little," Granny Em told her grandson.

"I can't, Granny," Luke said. He sounded almost as if he were about to cry.

"Let him come in," Leah told them. "I'll do better with him beside me."

Luke was beside her in an instant. He sat down on the edge of the bed and took both her hands in his.

"I love you so much, Leah. I hate to see you in so much pain."

Leah couldn't answer, because another pain hit. She gripped Luke's hands and clenched her teeth.

"It's okay," he said. "You can yell or scream. Do whatever helps you. I'll be okay now that I'm here with you."

She didn't yell out, but she let out some hefty groans after that. A baby made its appearance after what seemed like ages to Leah.

"It's a girl," Granny Em declared.

Granny Em cleaned up the baby and started to hand her to Leah when another painful contraction hit. She handed the infant to Luke instead.

"The pain's still severe." Leah moaned.

"It looks to me like there's another one coming," Granny Em told them.

Luke put the baby he held into the cradle and came to help Leah again. It didn't take long this time.

"This one's a boy," Granny Em told them. "One of each." Leah could hear the smile in her voice.

"Twins," Luke said to her. "Darling, this is wonderful." He wiped her hair back and kissed her forehead. "Thank you. I love you so much."

"I love you too," she whispered in a tired voice that didn't sound much like her.

"You must," Luke smiled tenderly at her, "if you can say that right after all this."

She smiled back as Granny Em placed the two babies by her side. The girl appeared to be looking around, but the boy still wailed with his eyes closed.

They'd already picked out names. It had been easy really. It would be Edgar for a boy, but they'd call him Eddie. They'd name a girl Emma, but call her Emmie.

The babies seemed fine at first, but neither took milk well. Emmie acted a little stronger than Eddie, but both babies were tiny. Luke and Granny Em stayed up all night tending to them, but Eddie didn't make it through the night. The thought of losing their son devastated Leah.

Luke held her and tried to comfort her, but she saw tears flow from his eyes on more than one occasion. Emmie lasted another day. Luke had been working on a small coffin and had dug the grave, so they buried them in the same coffin. After all, they'd been in the womb together for much longer than they'd lived.

Leah was inconsolable, but Luke tried, although he grieved himself. He held her often and spent as much time with her as the farm allowed.

"We'll have more children," he told her. "We'll always love and miss the twins, and although other children will never take their place, they'll keep us busy."

He did understand. She turned to him. She'd always loved him to distraction, but now they needed each other as never before. He'd become almost an extension of herself.

She had God too. He had been her mainstay for as long as she could remember. He, too, had comforted her, and gradually the intensity of the grief subsided, but it never completely left her.

Time had helped, but it hadn't brought other children. Leah prayed for a child every night and sometimes during the days. She knew God's timing was perfect, but she had a hard time being patient. She could now appreciate how Sarah and Elizabeth had felt in the Bible.

She stood before the grave with her arms folded so tightly she almost hugged herself. She stared at the plot with tears rolling down her face. She stood so lost in her thoughts that she didn't hear Luke when he came up behind her until he encircled her with his arms.

"Having a rough day?" he whispered over her shoulder.

She turned to face him. "A little, but it's not unbearable."

"Do you think there will ever be a time that it doesn't bring this much pain when you remember them?"

"I don't know, but I think it would help if we could have more children."

His eyes took on the mischievous gleam she loved. "Well, I'm trying every chance I get."

She laughed. "I love you so much, Luke. You've been wonderful through the pain – both during the labor and after they died. You're just what I need."

"As you're what I need." He pulled her into his arms.

CHAPTER TWO

Hawk

LUKE CAME FROM THE BARN to see a strange man riding up. They seldom had visitors here, unless someone needed medical help from Granny and Leah. This man's skin was dark enough to be an Indian, but he wore the shirt and pants of a white man although he had moccasins on his feet.

When he dismounted and walked toward Luke, Luke realized he was an old man. He had sat on the horse erect and had appeared younger at first.

"Is Emma here?" he asked.

"Hawk?" The thought popped out before Luke had a chance to catch it.

"Yes, and you must be Sarah's son." He smiled. "I'm so pleased to meet you at last. Sarah was always my favorite niece, and I've often wondered about you."

"Yes. Luke Moretz. I'm happy to finally meet you too." Luke extended his hand.

Hawk took it and pulled him into a hug. "It does my heart good."

"Granny's inside, but she hasn't been feeling well lately. We've been worried about her. Come. She'll want to see you."

"Are you sure about this?" Uncertainty covered Hawk's face.

"Oh, yes. I'm sure. She's told the family all about you. I know she's never forgotten you, and she always talks fondly of you."

A huge smile broke out on the Cherokee's face. "This is good."

They walked into the house and Luke introduced Hawk to Leah. Patsy still worked upstairs.

Hawk looked from Leah to Luke and smiled again. "I can see the love in your eyes. I'm happy for you. Where is your grandfather?"

"He died a long time ago . . . back in '51. Come, Granny is through here."

Luke led Hawk to Granny's bedroom. He tried to read the Cherokee's expression, perhaps a mixture of great anticipation and uncertainty.

"I thought I heard someone . . . Hawk!" Granny had recognized him immediately. She held out her hand for the man to come closer.

Luke looked at Leah, who had joined him at the door. She gave him a knowing smile. "Close it," she said. "Let them have some time alone to talk."

─────────────────────────

Hawk took Emma's hand and sat on the side of the bed where she indicated. She couldn't believe he was here. It had been so long.

"It's so good to see you, Hawk. I've thought of you often."

"You have never left my heart and mind."

"You speak English—very good English!"

"I learned it long ago. I began studying the winter after you left. I needed something to occupy my mind. You look wonderful."

"I look like an old woman."

"I'm older than you."

"How old are you? I never knew."

"I'm three years older than you."

"The same as Edgar."

"Luke told me that he's been gone for several years. Should I have come earlier?"

"Probably not. I think my heart needed time after Edgar died. I think it's now ready to receive you with gladness."

A look of surprise flickered across Hawk's face. He looked at her with guarded hope. "Is your heart ready to love me, Emma?"

"I came to realize I've always loved you, but I had been Edgar's when we first met. I had given my heart to him, and I never thought you were a choice for me. I always knew I had to come back. I'm sorry I couldn't love you enough to stay."

"Your honesty and loyalty made me love you even more. I understood. I didn't like it, but I understood. It was probably for the best. It would have been tremendously hard for you during the removal we now call the Trail of Tears. The Cherokee women who married a white husband were tolerated. Sheila and Connell were not taken from their land. The few white women who dared marry a Cherokee man were looked on with disgust and contempt. We would not have fared well at the hands of the soldiers on the forced march."

"How are Connell and Sheila? I haven't heard from them, since the first time Clifton and Sarah brought Luke here, and they came to see them. Sarah died after that, and they never came again."

"They've been dead longer than Edgar. A fever took them both at the same time."

"I'm sorry. They were good friends. What of you, Hawk? How have you been?"

"I've had a good life. You brought me many gifts, Emma. You came into my life and taught me what true love was. You sent me seeking for the One True God, I found Him, and I've never been alone again. You gave me the desire to learn English, and it's made it easier for me in the conquering white world. Your son filled my favorite niece's heart and brought her great happiness. Luke, your grandson, my grandnephew, seems to be a fine young man who is very much in love with a wife who loves him back. God has turned all things to good."

"I'm so glad you've found contentment. I've worried I might have hurt you."

"I did hurt when I had to walk away from you that morning. I ached for the want of you—not just a physical ache, but my spirit longed for you. However, I had expected it, because you'd never indicated anything else. But, how are *you*? I find you here in your bed? What's wrong?"

"My body is wearing out, and my spirit is tired." Emma looked away from Hawk for the first time and stared at the ceiling. "This war has me worried. I don't want to see Luke torn away to fight in bloody battles, but I'm afraid that's what will happen. I'm afraid for him and Leah." She looked back at him and smiled. "You look strong, though."

"I'm strong for a seventy-four-year-old man, but I'm no longer the young brave you met years ago. I was barely eighteen then."

"You seemed older. You were so steady and sure of yourself. You had the self-assurance of a born leader. I thought you were almost regal."

"I'd been blessed with strength and abilities early on. I became a leader among the braves, because no one could best me at hunting or fighting."

"Is that why you managed to take me from Sliced Arm? I seemed to belong to him at the first of my capture until you stopped him from assaulting me."

"That's right. He could have challenged me to take you back, and I thought he might at first, but we both knew I would defeat him. For this reason, he reluctantly gave in. I could have also taken him before the council for the way he attacked you in the forest near the village while you were under my protection, but I didn't want you to be so involved. I let him know I would do so; however, if he ever tried anything again, the council would have likely sent him away for good."

"Why did you come *now*—after all this time?"

"I'm not sure. I woke up one morning and had the urge to see you one more time. Sheila had once told me how to find your farm, so I packed my horse, told my niece and her family what I planned to do, and came."

"I'm glad you did."

"Are you, Emma? Are you really happy to have me here with you?"

"I am. Can you stay for a while? We have a lot of catching up to do."

"I might stay. We'll see."

A knock came at the door, and Luke came in. "Supper is almost ready and Leah sent me to see where you wanted to eat, Granny. We're assuming Hawk will eat with us."

"I think I might come to the table for a change," Emma told him. "You take Hawk with you and send Leah or Patsy to help me dress."

"Granny Em has told us so much about you, I feel I know you already," Leah told Hawk as they all sat around the table. "We've admired you and are so grateful for how you cared for her and kept her safe."

"I'm happy to hear she remembers me. I feared she'd have forgotten all about me." He glanced her way.

"Never," Emma told him.

Emma didn't know what was happening to her. She felt like laughing for the first time in weeks. Seeing Hawk had made her feel something she thought she would never feel again. She'd thought her time had finally come to join Edgar, but now she felt alive.

"Where have you been staying since the Cherokee were taken from their lands?" Luke asked Hawk.

"At first I lived with my sister, Sheila, and her husband, Connell. After they died, their daughter, who'd married a white man and didn't have to leave, took over their place, and I stayed with her. She had only two children."

They lingered at the table and talked even after everyone had finished. Emma watched Hawk closely. It seemed both strange and right to have him here.

"Do you feel like a short walk, Emma?" Hawk asked.

"I think so – if we don't go far. I feel stronger than I have in weeks."

"You ate better too," Leah commented as she and Patsy began to wash the dishes.

Hawk followed her through the front door. When they started down the steps, he put one arm around her waist and took her left hand in his other for support. He kept them there as they slowly walked across the road to the meadow.

He helped her to the large granite rock where she'd sat for Luke's wedding. He sat beside her and took her hand again. "I remember holding your hand like this on that final morning." He paused. "I still love you, Emma."

"I love you, too, Hawk." She looked down instead of at him when she said it.

He put his fingertips under her chin and gently lifted her face to his. "Enough to marry me now?"

She felt torn between the two answers this time. When he'd asked before, she'd known her answer would be no without pondering over it. Now, she didn't know anything.

"We're too old," she said. "There's not much time left for us."

"Why not enjoy our last days together instead of alone?"

"Let me think about it."

He laughed. "We don't have the time to do too much thinking. The more you think about it, the less time we'll have."

She looked into his eyes and found her answer. His eyes were the same as she remembered all those years ago. They were filled with love and longing.

"Do you love me enough to marry me?"

"Yes, Hawk. Yes, I love you enough to marry you."

"Will you marry me then?"

"I will."

"Oh, Emma." He pulled her into his arms. "Finally. After all this time, I'll finally have you for my wife. Do you have any idea how happy you've made me?"

"I think I might, because I'm pretty happy myself."

Luke, Leah, and Patsy all smiled at the news. Luke said he knew of a circuit rider in the area, and he would track him down and see if he would perform the ceremony.

"Do you think this is okay?" Emma asked. "I'm not being old and silly, am I?"

"No, Granny," Luke said and hugged her. "Love is never silly, and I think it is precious anytime we find it."

"Thank you," she told him.

They had their family devotion then. Hawk got his Bible and joined them. Emma could tell during the discussion that Hawk had studied his Bible with the same intensity he must have used in learning English.

Hawk spent that night in the guest room upstairs. Emma found him early the next morning sitting on the edge of the front porch.

She sat down beside him. "This reminds me of that morning you left your sister's house."

"At least I don't have to walk away this morning. You still move around pretty well." He smiled at her. He put his arm around her and pulled her closer.

"I seem to be doing better now that you're here. What are you doing out here so early?"

"Watching the sun rise and thanking God for all His blessings. Have you been happy all these years?"

"I have. It was hard when Edgar died, but I had Luke. He's more like my son than my grandson. I've had him since he was eight."

"Why did his father bring him here?"

"Clifton became so distraught when Sarah died, he didn't think straight. He met Frances and thought she would be a good mother for Luke. She was about ten years younger than Clifton and had never married. He married her when he still grieved for Sarah, and it turned out to be a big mistake. The woman hated Luke and began to mistreat him, so his father brought him here."

"Clifton and this Frances, they're not happy?"

"They have two children, a girl and a boy. Clifton says he's not unhappy, but he's not as happy as he could have been. He's re-signed to how things are. Part of the problem is that he had such a great love with Sarah, and he misses her so."

"Are you concerned about marrying me? Are you afraid the same thing might happen to you?"

"No, I've never even considered such a thing. I know you. I know what a good man you are. Frances is a petty, mean-spirited woman. You're nothing like her."

"And I have such a great love for you." His eyes sparkled at her.

"I love you deeply, too, and my love is growing. I never allowed myself to really love you as long as I had Edgar. Now I am."

"You'll find I've adopted many of the white ways. All our people have. I think we'll be very happy together."

He gently pulled her into his arms and kissed her. Emma felt unexpected emotions she hadn't felt in years. *Life is sure full of surprises* was her last thought before she lost herself in that kiss.

Emma and Hawk married the following Friday. The preacher had to be at a service across the county on Sunday.

Leah had pulled out one of Ivy's old dresses no one else had ever worn. The fabric still appeared strong, and after some alterations she had it ready in time. The light periwinkle-blue silk with ivory lace suited Emma.

They had the wedding in the meadow where Hawk had proposed and where Luke and Leah had been married. At this time of year, splotches of wildflowers splashed about the bright-green grass.

Only the five of them and the preacher attended. Luke led Emma out and handed her to Hawk. Hawk looked magnificent in his dark-brown suit. They said their vows and Emma realized he must have given his name as Hawk O'Leary. She hadn't even thought to ask, but it made sense, since his brother-in-law's surname had been O'Leary. Hawk slipped a wedding band on her finger. Where had that come from? Had he brought it with him? Surely not, since he'd indicated he hadn't expected this. After the short ceremony he walked her back to the house, where dinner awaited them.

"Would you like to walk with me in the forest?" Hawk asked her after they'd finished eating and the preacher had left. "We won't go far."

"Do you still have some of your Cherokee clothing?" she asked him.

"I do."

"We'll need to change clothes first anyway, so wear them."

He smiled in agreement and went upstairs to change. Emma went into her room and pulled out the deerskin dress she'd worn home all those years ago. It wasn't too stiff. She'd already checked, and it would fit, because her size had changed little over the years.

She got ready and opened the door, but she hesitated to go out until Hawk came. She didn't want to appear foolish to the others.

He came carrying the rest of his things. From a distance, he looked like the Hawk of old, except for his graying hair.

"I thought I would bring these down for later," he said as he set his things on the floor. He stood up and looked at her then. His eyes glowed.

"I remember the first time I saw you in that dress. You took my breath away. You still do."

"You gave me the deer hides to make it."

"I remember. Your other dress looked about to rip apart, and I knew you needed another—not that I wouldn't have enjoyed it when the other one completely fell to pieces."

She smiled. "I'd forgotten how you liked to joke and tease at times."

"Does it bother you?"

"Not in the least. In fact, I like it."

"Oh Emma, what fun we're going to have."

Emma led him into the woods. They didn't go far, just out of sight. They found a fallen tree and sat down on its trunk.

"When you captured me, I had been sitting on a log by the creek reading my Bible. My father had been drunk and got into a fight. He and Uncle Roy were running away, and Papa forced Mama to go with him. I refused to go because of Edgar. I expected him to come the next day, and I would've come back here with him."

"I had warned Sliced Arm to stay away from the whites, but he had great hatred for them. We came upon you accidentally, and when he took you I feared he would treat you roughly, especially after you cut his arm."

"You took very good care of me. Thank you, but why did you invite me to your blanket after you brought me the honey?"

"You must have thought of me some, because you have a very good memory. I didn't know you well then, but something about you drew me, and at eighteen years old my thoughts went to one thing. I hoped you liked me enough to comply. I apologize for what I tried then, but I began to see you in a different light after you refused me and told me you had a man to the east. I came to respect you, and my love for you began to grow."

"In the village, I always liked it that you often met me when I went to get water or gather herbs. I missed you when you didn't come."

"I wasn't sure, but I knew you often smiled at me, and you never sent me away. I felt drawn to you. I would have spent every hour with you if I could have done so without the others thinking you'd bewitched me. That would have even been okay, if I thought you'd stay, but I always knew you would leave me. I tried everything I could to get you to stay, but I knew you'd come back to Edgar as soon as you could. You had always told me so."

She looked down at her left hand. "Where did you get the ring?"

"Luke gave it to me as a wedding present. It had been his mother's. Is that okay? You don't mind Sarah wore it first, do you?"

"No, I am honored to wear her ring. I loved that girl like a daughter. I hope you and I will be as happy as she and Clifton were."

"I have no doubt of that on my part, because it's already true."

"Oh Hawk, I hope the Lord will grant us some time together now. I want a chance to explore this amazing love."

"Whatever time He gives us will be enough, Emma. I feel blessed for one day with you as my wife. I didn't dare hope for this when I came, because I didn't even know Edgar had passed away. I just felt I needed to see you one more time."

"Well, when our time here is over we'll all be together in paradise, won't we?"

"Yes, we will, and I'll get to see what was so special about this Edgar."

"No one is more special than you, Hawk. Edgar was just meant for my first love. I'm aware that I'd been given the love of two magnificent men. Now, I've also been blessed to love those two men in return. I'm overwhelmed by it."

He kissed her, and she became young again. Her heart melted into his, and a passion rose in her that had been dormant since Edgar had died. This was Hawk, the man who had protected her, kept her safe, and cherished her. This was Hawk, who loved her enough to send her back to the man who would make her happy. This was Hawk, who she could now love with her whole heart.

"I do believe you love me," he said after the kiss.

"With all my heart." She saw the question in his eyes. "It's the only way I know to love."

"I feared Edgar would always be your greater love."

"I think you both will be. I know you loved me enough to let me come back here, because that's what made me happy. I can't feel Edgar would love me any less now, so he would set me free to love you now that he's gone. I'd have done the same for him if I'd died first. I'd have wanted him to find as much happiness as he could."

"You are even more wonderful than I remembered."

She gave a delighted laugh. "Just you wait. You haven't seen anything yet. Come." She stood up and put out her hand. "I think it must be getting close to suppertime. We'd better get back."

They ate supper and laughed and talked with the family. Luke and Leah seemed quite taken with Hawk. Patsy just stared at him as if she didn't know what to think.

They held their family devotion, and Luke asked Hawk if he'd like to say the closing prayer. They all bowed their heads.

"Father in Heaven, we thank Thee for all our blessings, and they are many. We thank Thee most of all for Thy great love and grace. But we're also thankful for the love Thou hast allowed the members of this family to find in each other. I personally thank Thee for Emma, my wife, and for granting me my heart's desire. Continue to bless this family. Bring this terrible war to a speedy end and may Thy will be done. Amen."

Hawk and Emma went to bed after that. In some ways, it seemed strange to be taking Hawk into her bedroom for the night, but in other ways it seemed familiar and right. Still, she turned her back to him as she undressed.

"Emma, I'm older than you are. Don't turn away from me."

"Give me just tonight, Hawk. Let me be the shy bride for tonight, and I won't need it again."

Hawk turned out the oil lamp and felt for her in the darkness.

When Emma awoke, she found Hawk on one elbow looking at her. "Good morning, my wife."

Yes, it is a good morning, she thought for a moment and gave a chuckle.

"What do you find so funny?"

"I was just thinking how when we're young, we think we'll get too old to love as we did last night."

He smiled. "Even at this age, it was beyond anything I'd ever imagined."

"I didn't disappoint you then?"

"Are you serious? You thrilled me beyond words. I should have known you'd have great passion. It fits with who you are."

"You didn't ask me how I felt about last night."

His whole face lit up in a smile. "I didn't have to. You showed me last night."

"Have there been other women for you?"

Hawk paused as if stunned by her question. "What kind of question is that to ask your husband after your first night together?"

"I believe in complete honesty and sharing everything."

He breathed in deeply. "There were only a couple of other women before you. After I met you I wanted only you, and there's never been another. Why did you ask?"

"I guess I wondered if you had anything to compare with last night."

"Nothing I've ever known compares with last night. It went beyond just the physical. You touched my mental, emotional, and spiritual sides too. All parts of me came to know and love you in a new way."

"It's a shame you didn't speak English when I first met you. You're so eloquent."

"Let's not live with any regrets for the past. I've learned not to. Let's live in today. It's all we really have, and it's here we find our joy."

"Yes, my wise Hawk," Emma said as she moved closer to kiss him.

CHAPTER THREE

Off to War

"I THINK GRANNY HAS RECOVERED from whatever ailed her," Luke said to Leah after they'd finished milking.

"Hawk has certainly been good for her. I think the war had her depressed, and she needed a reason to get up and live again."

"The war has us all depressed."

"What's this about the war?" Hawk asked as he came into the barn.

Luke noticed the man didn't move fast, but he walked erect and easily with no sign of a limp or shuffle. He moved like a man fifteen or twenty years younger.

"We're worried the Confederacy will conscript Luke," Leah told him. "He plans to join the Union army before that happens."

"I'm glad you're here, Hawk. I won't be as worried about leaving the women now."

"Would that I were younger so I could really be a help, but I'll do what I can. That's what I came to talk with you about. I want you to let me take over the things I can do around here. It will keep me healthier in body and in spirit. I need to stay active."

"What did you have in mind?"

"Let me milk, gather the eggs, and feed. I'll also keep the tools sharpened and in good working condition. I can pick the vegetables and maybe do some short hunts. How does that sound?"

"You don't think that's too much?"

"Not at all. I might be able to help you with some other things, too, but I know I'm not up to the hard labor I once did."

"I gladly accept if you're sure," Luke told him.

"Granny Em told me something similar," Leah said. "She said she wanted to start cooking some meals again. She especially wanted to do this for her husband."

Hawk grinned. "I guess we're growing young again."

"You're good for Granny Em," Leah told him. "Luke and I are delighted you came."

"She's good for me, and I'm glad I came too." He turned and walked back to the house.

Luke and Leah picked up their milk buckets. "I think I'm growing to love Hawk too," Leah said. "He's so open and honest about everything. I don't know what I expected, but it wasn't this."

"Should I be jealous?" Luke teased.

"That's even sillier than when you got jealous over Sam Whitley just because I described him as 'good looking.'"

"You and my father have never let me forget that, either."

"You so seldom give me something to tease you about that I have to hold onto the ones I get. Granny Em said Hawk likes to tease too."

"I'm glad you warned me. I've never seen that in him, but maybe I will as we're around each other more. Grandpa teased too. He and Granny were always teasing and laughing. She used to say that's why he married her—because she liked his teasing."

"I guess it must run in the family, because I like your teasing too."

The days passed all too quickly. Leah worked alongside Luke as much as possible. The fact he'd have to leave soon tried to hang over her like a dark cloud, but she swatted it away. She vowed to enjoy the time they had and not let the future spoil the present.

Since Hawk now did many of the chores close to the house, she and Luke spent much of their time plowing through and hoeing the fields or gathering wood.

They joked and laughed and made whatever they were doing fun. Their nights were filled with an urgency and intensity that would make their separation even harder. Yet, they wouldn't have had it any other way.

"You were right when you said we would always live in a perpetual honeymoon," Luke told her early one morning as they lay in bed.

"Hm-m-m, isn't it marvelous? God blessed us richly when He gave us each other."

"We'll have to put great trust in Him to get us through the next few years."

"Do you think the war will last for years?"

"I don't think it's going to be won easily." He lay back and stared at the ceiling. "Both sides think they're right. They've dug in, and they'll be tenacious."

"Which side do you think will win?"

"I hope it's the North, but I really don't know. In my opinion, the South has better military leaders, tougher soldiers, and the will to protect her own land. The North seems to have more manpower, more resources, and their land isn't being ravaged as much by the fighting. Right now it seems pretty even, and that's the problem."

The next day, Raymond Blankenship rode by to tell Luke some men in the area planned to head to eastern Tennessee to join up with the Union forces so they wouldn't be conscripted by the Confederacy. Two of his sons were planning to be among them. His oldest son had already joined the Confederacy. "I jist don't know what this world's acomin' to," he said. "Hit jist ain't right fer brother ta be fightin' agin brother."

"I know what you mean," Luke told him. "When are your boys planning to leave?"

"In a couple o' weeks. Are you inter-rested in goin' too?"

"Yes, I think I'd better. I can't stand the thoughts of fighting against the United States and for slavery."

The next day, they had another unexpected visitor. Someone knocked on the door about eleven o'clock. Leah answered the door. A man in his early thirties stood on the porch holding his hat in his hand. With blond hair and bright blue eyes, he looked vaguely familiar, but Leah couldn't place him.

"Mrs. Moretz?"

"Yes?"

"I understand you are Ivy Morgan's sister."

"Yes, I am."

"May I come in just for a few minutes? I have some questions. It won't take long."

"Sure, come on into the sitting room and have a seat. Patsy, would you go tell Luke we have company. I think he's in the cabbage field."

"I'm Sam Whitley," the man began.

Leah almost gasped. Ivy had run away with Sam back when she and Luke were engaged. She'd ended up deserted, alone, and pregnant. Leah and Luke had found her, and Luke worked it out for Lawrence Nance to marry her quickly. Lawrence had loved Ivy and agreed to marry her, even after he heard she expected another man's baby. Lawrence and Ivy had been very happy, and when Patrick came along, the child just added to their happiness.

"I know I've made a lot of mistakes. I got involved with some counterfeiters and did some time in prison. The thing I regret even more, however, is how I treated Ivy. I really cared about her, although I was too self-centered at the time to recognize it. I know I treated her badly, and I wanted to check to see how she was doing."

Luke came in and introductions were made. Luke's face showed as much shock as she'd felt at first. At least the interruption gave her a little time to collect her thoughts. They would need to be careful here. Sam didn't know he had a son, and Leah didn't want him making trouble for Ivy and Lawrence.

"Mr. Whitley came to check on Ivy and see how she's doing now," Leah told Luke.

"And I wanted to apologize for my irresponsible behavior," Sam added. "I did care for Ivy. I was just too undisciplined and selfish at the time. We had an argument, and I abandoned her. That has haunted me for a long time, and since I was in the area, I wanted to check and make sure she's okay. I realize anything could have happened to her after I left."

"Yes, it could have," Luke said. "We searched for over two months to find her. When we did, we found her living in a deserted shack, impoverished, and irrational. However, things turned out fine for her. She's happily married and has a husband and son she adores."

"I'm glad to hear she's doing well now." Sam rose and shook Luke's hand. "Thank you for seeing me. God has forgiven me. Now maybe I can forgive myself."

"You don't think we should have told him about Patrick, do you?" Leah asked after Sam had left.

"No, the family is happy now. They don't need the kind of trouble another father for Patrick would cause. They're all better off without Sam knowing about Patrick."

"I know you're right, but I can't help but wonder, if that were your son, wouldn't you think you'd be entitled to know?"

"Well, Sam didn't ask if the child was his. If there's ever a time he needs to know about the situation, I trust God will send him back to us or let it be revealed to him in some way."

"Sam gave me quite a surprise when he told me his name."

"Not for me."

Leah could tell Luke was teasing by the way his eyes danced.

"I just thought he'd heard how good looking you thought he was, and he figured he'd come calling."

"Luke Moretz! You get worse all the time."

"And you love me all the more." He pulled her into his arms.

The dreaded day approached at breakneck speed. Luke would be leaving to join the Union army in a week, and it terrified Leah.

The one time she and Luke had been separated since their marriage had come when she'd gone to Anson County to help Ivy get over their mother's death. That time had been difficult, for she and Luke had been married only two weeks then. Leah knew this would be much worse.

Now, Luke would constantly be in harm's way. At any moment, he could be wounded or killed. How would she ever bear it? She prayed to God that He would not only keep Luke safe, but that He would also give her the strength to endure.

She didn't say anything to Luke about her fears, but he knew her too well. He must have known.

"You're apt to be facing dangers, too, Leah. You'll probably have marauders from both the Confederates and the Federals. This is war. Don't think twice about lying or pretending if that's what it takes to survive. God will understand. Show the Union soldiers the copies of my papers to prove we're Union. Use Patsy as your slave to convince the Confederates you're on their side. I have no doubt this war will get uglier the longer it goes."

"I'm sure I'll be safer than you."

"I'm not. At least I'll know who my enemies are. You may not. From what I hear, besides threats from soldiers, I'm afraid there may be lawless gangs terrorizing the women and old men left behind while their men go off to fight. Don't take anything or anyone for granted."

"You're beginning to scare me, Luke."

"That's good if it saves your life. Come with me. There are some places I want to show you."

He took her into the forest and showed her a large hollow place beneath a tree. She could hardly see it now, but Luke showed her how she could add some large twigs and leaves and completely hide it.

"Put your valuables here," he told her. "Include your jewelry, some money, and anything else we might need to save for later. I have most of our money in gold and silver. It will be good whichever side wins. I have most of it buried, and I'll show you where."

He led her up the side of a mountain. They wound around to a place Leah had never noticed.

"There are some natural caves here," Luke said. "We'll put some food stuff in here. You'll need to hide it from scavengers being called bummers. Both armies often send men to forage for food, and they'll take whatever they find. We'll have to enclose it well to keep it from the animals, but I don't think the men will find anything we put in here. You'll need to change it out or restock it every harvest."

"You've really thought this out and made plans, haven't you?"

"It makes me feel better if I leave you as prepared as possible. There's a larger cave down here near the base. Come, I'll show you. You can hide the horse and cows in here. I could build pens for the pigs and chickens, but I'm afraid they might make too much noise if they hear someone near and give the place away." He led her to the large cave. It looked plenty big. "I've already put some hay in the back, and I've fixed it so you can put these boards across the front. Then, if you scatter some large limbs around like this, it's completely hidden." Luke moved some limbs he had collected to show her what to do. No one would ever suspect there was a cave.

"How did you know all this, Luke? How did you know what we'd need to do?"

"I've read everything I could get my hands on. Even if the newspapers are old when I collect them, I pour through every one. Father's helped some too. He's written of the things he's seen in Salisbury and of things that have taken place elsewhere in the state."

"I'm impressed."

"Thank you, but you're the most precious thing in the world to me. I'll do anything I can to keep you safe. I want you here to come home to."

"And I want you to come home safe and sound."

He took her in his arms and kissed her. It seemed different, special standing here in the forest. No matter how many times he kissed her, his kisses still affected her. Her legs and knees still grew so weak she had to hold onto him for support. Her blood and heart started racing each other, and she had a hard time catching her breath.

He finally lifted his head, but he stood holding her in his arms. He rested his head on the top of hers as if he wanted to touch as much of her as possible. She leaned into his embrace. She loved him dearly and didn't think she'd be capable of walking back just yet.

Saturday, a horse and rider came up to the barn, and the man dismounted.

"Dr. Moretz!" Leah flew to his arms. "I am so glad to see you. What a surprise!"

"Well, that's quite a welcome. It's good to see you too."

"How did you know Luke planned to leave for the army Thursday?"

"I didn't, but I got your letter about Hawk. His story has fascinated me over the years. Sarah and I used to talk of him often. He was her favorite relative . . . apart from her parents. I had to come meet him."

"I'm so excited you did, and Luke will be happy to see you before he leaves too."

"As I will him. I'm certainly glad I came when I did. I would have hated to miss him. Frances and the children went to visit her sister in Charlotte, and with the cooler fall weather some of the sickness in Salisbury has seemed to abate, so here I am. For a month . . . if you'll have me."

"I'll have you as long as we can get you and as often as you can come."

"Well now, you sure know how to make an old man feel good. Is Mama still going strong?"

"She is. Hawk has given her a new lease on life." Leah led him inside. "Wait until you see them together. They're charming."

"Clifton!" Granny Em gave him a hearty hug. "This is a wonderful surprise."

"I should come up the mountain more often. I like the welcome I've received."

"Yes, you should." She turned around. "Clifton, this is Hawk. Hawk, this is my son, Clifton."

"I'm very pleased to meet you," Hawk said. "I've heard many good things about you, and I know you and my niece, Sarah, shared a great love."

"We did indeed. I miss her terribly still today, but it's a great pleasure to finally meet you."

Leah led them into the sitting room and ran to get Luke. He wouldn't want to miss this.

As he entered the room Luke heard his father tell Hawk, "I've always been bothered that you loved my mother enough to send her back to father so she would be happy, but you remained single."

"I remained single by choice. I never found another I could come close to loving as much as I had Emma, so I preferred to remain unmarried rather than have a poor marriage."

Father grimaced. "That makes a lot of sense. I wish I'd done the same."

"Emma told me your second marriage is not as happy as you wished."

"That's true, and things seem to get worse instead of better. I can't abide with slavery, and my wife is a strong supporter of the Confederacy. The war has caused a larger rift between us. She may choose to stay in Charlotte for an extended period of time. If she does, I don't think I'll encourage her to come home yet."

"Oh, Clifton," Granny said. "I'm so sorry."

"It's my own fault. I just wasn't thinking. I should have known it would be very hard, if not impossible, to find a love close to the one Sarah and I had. I would have been wise to have done like Hawk and waited. I can tell he and you are very happy now, Mama, and I'm happy for you."

"Thank you," Hawk said. "I wondered how you'd feel about your mother marrying me. I didn't worry that you would be prejudiced against the Cherokee, since you'd married Sarah. I did wonder how you would feel about having a stepfather."

"Since it's you, I'm delighted. I'd already accepted you from the things Sarah had told me."

"And I wondered if you wouldn't think I was too old," Granny said.

"Nonsense, Mama. You? Old? Never."

"Emma thinks about her being old more than anyone around her does," Hawk said with a sparkle in his eyes.

"I do not! I'm just being practical. I'm glad to be getting a day older each time the sun rises, and I hope they'll keep coming for all of us."

"I remember Father used to say the Good Lord needed to take him first, because Mama could do without him much better than he could do without her."

"He did say that, didn't he?" Granny smiled. "Maybe he finally got it right on some of his teasing."

"Mama, I can't believe you said that."

"Why not? Have you ever known me to mince on words or to fail to tell the truth? It doesn't mean I love your father any less. He's just in a better place now, and I'm left on earth to find my happiness as God chooses to send it to me. That just happens to be Hawk, and I'm thankful and counting my blessings. I've been blessed to love and be loved by both of them."

"Well said, Mama."

With six of them the work got done quickly. They'd probably already cut enough wood to see them through almost two winters, since Luke had been stockpiling it for a while, but they cut more.

Hawk took the men trout fishing, and they came back with enough fish for a big meal. The women fried it, and it turned out to be the best meal Luke had had in a while.

The few days were filled with activity, and they passed quickly. Suddenly, the night of the twenty-ninth had arrived, and Luke watched Leah prepare for bed. She looked like she fought to hold tears back, and he didn't feel much better. How would he ever be able to ride away from her? But he knew he had no choice. A small group of Confederate soldiers had already been seen in the area. They'd come to conscript more men. It meant he either needed to join the one or be drafted by the other. He'd be gone either way.

Neither of them could sleep. They pulled close, trying to savor each other enough to last through the separation. They knew it would be impossible, but they were compelled to try. Then they lay in each other's arms. Sometimes they talked, and sometimes they just lay there.

"Write to me," he told her. "It may take a while for your letters to catch up to me, and I might not always have a chance to answer you back, but keep the letters coming. They'll let me know you're all right, and they will do more to boost my spirits than anything else."

"I know it may be hard sometimes, but write me, too, when you can even if they are short. I also need to know you're okay."

They must have eventually dozed off wrapped in an embrace, for they awoke in the same position.

Leah shifted and put her head on his chest. "I want to be strong for you, Luke, but I don't think I'm going to be able to. I'm not that strong."

He stroked her hair. "You're a lot stronger than you think. Just because you're emotional and passionate doesn't mean you're weak. Tears are not just a sign of weakness. They can also be a sign of caring. I love you so much. Keep that in your heart and hold on to it. I plan to come back to you, but if something does happen, I'll be waiting for you in Heaven. Be happy, Leah. Love again if you can. If you can't, love God and serve Him. He'll be enough."

"You must know how much I love you. It's so much there're no words to explain. I'm going to be thankful for these years we've had. I'm going to expect to see you riding up again soon. There's no use to expect the worst."

"That's my girl. God will take care of us. We just need to grow our faith and our trust. We'll need an ample supply of both to get us through this war and back to our lives with each other."

―――――――――――――――――

Everyone started breakfast with a cheerful front, but it didn't last. Granny Em looked about as upset as Leah, and Dr. Moretz didn't appear much better. Hawk tried his best to help and support Granny Em.

"I'll see you all again as soon as this war is over," Luke said.

"If it lasts as long as we think it will, that might not be true," Granny Em said.

"Then I'll see you in Heaven someday, Granny," Luke said.

Granny Em just nodded, which was a sure sign she held back tears. Hawk reached over and took her hand in his, and she gave him a brief smile.

Leah packed Luke some food while he got his things together. He came in and they took it all to his horse.

He said good-bye and hugged each of the others first. Then, he came to Leah. He took her in his arms and held her a long time before he pulled his head back to kiss her. Neither of them cared the others were watching.

The kiss turned long and passionate, driven by a hunger born of urgency. In that kiss rested the uncertainty they'd had when Luke was still engaged to Ivy, but she'd run away. It held the passion they'd discovered on their wedding night. It reminded them of the despair they'd had when they were apart so Leah could take care of Ivy when she'd been in danger of losing her baby and herself. It spoke of the grief they'd shared after their babies died and the support they'd been for each other. But more than anything and through everything, it overflowed with love.

He mounted, turned, and looked at her as if he were memorizing her features. Love as well as tears filled his eyes. Then, he turned and rode away. When he had moved almost out of sight, he turned and waved.

Leah stood watching at the spot where he'd been long after he'd gone. Her face remained drenched in tears, and they wouldn't stop. Hawk and Dr. Moretz took Granny Em into the house, and Patsy tried to lead her, but she shook her head. She didn't know how long she stood there. She felt frozen in place, unable to move.

Hawk finally came to get her. He put his arm around her, and she sobbed on his shoulder. He didn't say anything for a long time. He just let her cry it out. When she finally stopped, he rubbed her back while he still held her.

"It'll be okay," he said. "You'll see. Time passes, and it takes care of things. Look at me. I waited fifty-seven years for Emma, but it was worth every minute. In this world there is great happiness and great sorrow. The lower you go into the valleys, the higher you can rise in joy. Your happy moments aren't over, Leah. Mark my words. You'll experience them again."

He couldn't have said anything that would have helped her more. "Thank you," she whispered and looked at him. He smiled and handed her his handkerchief as he led her inside.

Leah stayed in bed all day Friday. She rolled on her side and held Luke's pillow close to her body. It still smelled like him.

Patsy came up about ten. "They sent me to see if you're all right," she said. "They said you need to come down and eat something."

"Tell them I don't feel like eating, but if they'll send up some milk, I'll try to drink that. I couldn't sleep last night, so I'm tired. Tell them I'm fine, but I want to stay in here today. I'll come down tomorrow."

Patsy came back in about thirty minutes with what looked like a glass of milk. "Granny Em said this is some concoction Hawk made for you. It's supposed to keep your strength up."

"Thank you, Patsy, and thank Hawk for me. Just leave it on the bedside table."

Leah picked up the glass and smelled it. It smelled pretty good. She tasted it and smiled. She tried to figure out what he'd put in it. It looked and tasted like he had beaten an egg, added sugar and cinnamon, and filled the rest of the glass with milk. It tasted smooth, creamy, and sweet. She sipped it until she drank it all.

She took a nap and felt better when she awoke. She tried to guess where Luke might be and what he'd be thinking about now.

Luke felt his group had made good progress toward their destination. They'd stopped and camped for the night in a clearing. He looked appreciatively at the men. It had to be safer traveling together than if Luke had been alone.

After supper, he took out his Bible. It opened to a place on its own. There tucked between the pages he found the photograph of him and Leah taken at Ivy's wedding. Leah must have put it there for him to find.

Oh Leah, how I do love you and miss you already. He looked at the others, but they'd started bedding down for the night and paid him no attention. He felt silent tears slide down his face. He'd somehow managed to hold them back at the farm, although he'd felt them begin to pool as he looked at Leah one last time. Here, in the night with no one looking, he silently cried.

His tears were mainly for his wife, for having to leave her when he wanted to remain by her side to keep her in his arms, to protect her. But he also cried for himself. The future loomed with uncertainty, and the unknown is always a scary place filled with fear and foreboding. He knew the coming time would probably confirm what Ben Franklin had once said: "There never was a good war or a bad peace."

He'd told Leah tears were not a sign of weakness, yet he felt ashamed as he wiped them from his face. He'd also told her faith and trust were the answers. He needed a good measure of his own advice.

He held the picture and looked at Leah and him. She hadn't changed much in eight years. She was still the most beautiful person he'd ever seen. She had been from the moment he fell in love with her. She and he made a good couple and no wonder—they were perfect for each other.

He hugged the photograph to his chest. He knew it would be important to him over the long months ahead. How like Leah to care for all of him—for the emotional, mental, and spiritual side, as well as the physical.

He noticed she had placed the photograph to mark one of her favorite passages in Psalm 121: "I will lift up mine eyes unto the hills, from whence cometh my help. My help cometh from the Lord, which made heaven and earth. He will not suffer thy foot to be moved: he that keepeth thee will not slumber."

He needed those verses tonight. He needed to be reminded that God would take care of them, and with God helping why be afraid?

He read some more from Psalms, and when he started to close the Bible a letter fell out. Leah again. He smiled. He had quite a wife.

My dearest Luke,

Thank you for being the man you are and for being my husband. You have already brought me more joy than most women experience in an entire lifetime. You've shown me what love is all about.

I know you're probably missing me now, as I will be missing you. I'm less than half a person without you, because you always take the bigger portion of me with you wherever you go. I have no heart without you, because mine is grafted to yours.

Even though I miss you so terribly much, I'll be fine. I'll take care of the farm, while you're gone, so we can continue our honeymoon when you return. I look forward to that day.

I feel we married with God's blessing, so there's no reason to believe He won't continue to bless us. I hold to the promises that He will give good things to His children and that He will turn all things to good for those who love Him.

Go safely with God and with all my love forever.

Your loving wife,

Leah

He felt better. The photograph, the Bible verses, and Leah's letter had soothed him. Now, he wanted to get this war over with so he could get home.

Leah woke up before daylight on Saturday. She guessed she'd spent too much time in bed yesterday, but she'd needed the seclusion to be alone with her thoughts and memories. The clock said four o'clock. It would be at least an hour before anyone else began to stir.

She put on her wrapper and went to the desk. She'd promised herself she'd write to Luke as often as possible, and knowing it would take a while to get to him, she'd start right away.

She felt sure he'd already found the one she'd put in his Bible, because he would have had his devotion last night. Had he missed her as much as she missed him?

She thought of the photograph of them she'd tucked in Psalm 121. She hoped both had encouraged him. Luke tried to appear calm and unaffected, but he felt things as deeply as she did—another strong bond between them.

She picked up her own copy of their picture. The photographer had mistakenly made two copies for them, and Luke had decided to buy them both. Leah was glad he had. She'd probably wear her copy out before he got home, and Luke would be carrying his into all sorts of situations. Perhaps they should have gotten three copies.

She opened the desk drawer to get out some paper. The drawer brimmed full of paper. She smiled. Luke must have bought plenty so she wouldn't run low. She lifted a sheet and found a letter from Luke. The two of them thought very much alike.

My dearest Leah,

My heart overflows with love for you. You have been my greatest blessing. I think God brought us together, and He certainly knew what He was doing. He always does.

I'm guessing this will be the longest time we've ever been apart. It will be hard on both of us, but I know you'll do fine. You're like Granny in many ways, and she's always furnished much of the strength in our family. Both of you are capable, intelligent, brave, independent, and caring.

I'm glad Father will be with you at least three more weeks. Ask him to do anything. He loves to work around the farm, and he cherishes you. He would be so pleased if you would rely on him.

Hawk is amazing, too. I have never seen him as in his seventies, because he looks and acts about twenty years younger. He's so sturdy and wise. I've never met anyone quite like him, and he makes me wonder if my mother was natured anything like him. Hawk seems to have a very good understanding about what he can and can't do, so let him do whatever he wants. I see him mainly as a supporter, adviser, and protector for you. Lean on him when you feel the need. I've never met a man stronger in spirit.

I think Granny sees me as a son and you as her daughter. Her love for us has no end. Her gruff exterior hides a loving, caring nature, and she's solidly grounded. She'll be there for you whenever you need her.

Patsy also thinks the world of you. I think she almost puts you on a pedestal and thinks you can do no wrong. She quietly works in the background, but she's always been reliable and dependable. Since she is the youngest there, use her physical abilities and fitness to help you. Don't try to do everything yourself.

Finally, my darling wife, I leave you in the best hands of all. Rely on God. He has always been our strength and the center of our lives. We are His above all else. Never forget this, and let Him wrap His arms around you, pull you close, and keep you safe in the shelter of His arms.

With deep, undying love,

Luke

Leah reread the letter again. All of Luke's thoughts had been for her. He'd not once mentioned his uncertainties in heading to war, but they had to be there. She opened the ink, picked up her pen, and wrote.

My dear husband,

Thank you for the marvelous letter. What an encouragement! You're right. We are in God's hands, so why should we worry or be afraid? I'll try to remember that. I plan to keep your letter and read it again every time worry or depression wants to creep back.

I think I'll get better as time reveals what we have to face. My imagination often writes the unknown with disasters far worse than reality.

I stayed in our room and mainly in bed all day yesterday. I even did my devotion by myself. I felt so physically and emotionally drained, I needed the solitude to recuperate. Since I didn't feel like eating, Hawk made me a drink with milk to help me keep my strength up. Granny called it "some strange concoction," but it tasted quite good. I think it had an egg, sugar, and flavoring, besides the milk. I appreciate his concern.

I'm sitting here writing you early Saturday morning. I'm waiting for someone to get up, so I won't wake them too early. Then, I'll begin a day of work. Yesterday I needed to rest. Today I need to fill my day with activities.

I'll take all your advice and rely on the expertise of those around me. They are our family, and we're here for each other. We're so much stronger together than we are apart.

I'll be fine, Luke, so don't worry about me. I do have help and support here. You take care of yourself. You'll be basically alone, especially at first. Perhaps you can make some friends to help support you, too. Of course, we both know that the best One to take care of us is our Lord.

I think I hear someone downstairs, so I'll close for now. I hope I can get this in the mail and to you soon. I plan to keep writing, so you may end up with a stack of letters at one time. If you do, why don't you open and read one a day, so you will spread them out some. I will number them for you. May God put His hands around you and protect you from all harm.

All my love,

Leah

CHAPTER FOUR

Nightmares

SATURDAY, LEAH DID JUST AS she'd planned. She kept busy. She cooked breakfast and dinner. In the morning, she helped wash all the clothes and sheets. She made soap that afternoon, and between it all she dipped candles.

As they held their family devotion that night, it felt good to sit down. She hoped she'd be tired enough to sleep well.

Granny Em smiled at her. "You seem to be feeling better today."

"I am. Luke left me this wonderful, encouraging letter, and I'm taking all his advice."

"Smart woman," Dr. Moretz said.

"Humph," Granny Em said. "As if I didn't listen to both my husbands."

"Does she, Hawk?" the doctor teased.

"Actually, I think she does. Even though over the years she's gotten more outspoken and may seem gruff, she's still the sweet, loving girl I met all those years ago. I think she's always listened to me except when I wanted her to stay there."

"And which one did you love more?" Granny Em asked. "The young girl or who I am now?"

"She asks the hardest questions," he told the others. Then, he looked at Granny Em, his eyes softening. "The Cherokee brave in his teens loved the fifteen-year-old Emma better, but the man before you loves who you are now more."

"Hawk," Dr. Moretz said, "more than anyone I've ever met, you remind me of Solomon in the Bible."

Leah looked at Hawk. *How true!* Hawk was a wise man. Adversity must breed wisdom if reacted to in the right way.

Sunday turned into a cold, dreary day. The rain began around noon and fell steadily all day. Hawk and Dr. Moretz did the outside chores, and Leah stayed inside.

They had their morning worship time, ate their meals, read, and talked. Dr. Moretz and Granny Em played some checkers, and Hawk and Emma played chess.

"Connell taught me to play," Hawk told them. "I like the game, because it reminds me of strategies used in battle."

He proved to be a worthy opponent. Leah concentrated the most on this game of any in a long time. Hours later, Hawk won, but it had been a close game.

"You are very good," Hawk told her. "I've never played anyone better."

"I could say the same about you." She laughed. "After all, you beat me. Luke is also good. He and I stalemate more than either of us wins."

"I'm glad I have a worthy opponent for the cold winter days. I will look forward to them now."

The rain became a storm after supper and continued into the night. The wind hurled heavy raindrops against the windowpanes and tree limbs rustled and creaked.

Leah lay in bed and shivered. It had turned unseasonably cold. As she grew sleepier, she thought the large raindrops almost sounded like sleet scratching against the windowpanes, as if it, too, wanted to be inside in the warmth. She prayed for Luke and that he would be somewhere warm and dry tonight. She fell asleep still thinking of Luke.

Luke sank ankle-deep in mud, and icicles hung from his hat. He'd begun marching at first light. The enemy had to be close, because he'd heard picket fire all day yesterday.

The call to march came at daybreak, and with the sound of gunfire getting louder all the time, he guessed they were marching toward a fight. Rumors flew like blackbirds, but rarely did they hear any official information.

The mud pulled at his boots, and they grew as heavy as lead. It did no good to clean them off. They would be caked again before three steps. He felt sure mud even oozed inside them.

And, the cold! Even his bones and blood felt frozen. His feet and hands were numb, but the rest of him ached from the cold, and his face stung as if he'd encountered a thousand hornets.

Suddenly, shots rang out. An ambush! Bullets seemed to rain down from every direction even fiercer than the sleet and rain.

Men fell all around him, some with terror on their faces and some with so many bullet holes their blood gushed like fountains. Then the artillery fire began, and it turned even worse. Bodies exploded and body parts rained down almost as thick as the rain and bullets.

Luke worked without thinking. He fired, reloaded, and fired again. He wished he had more cover, but the open field they'd been marching through offered little. He tried to bend low and keep moving with his troops, but he had to stop to reload and to fire his rifle. The enemy mainly hid around the perimeter of the field, so they were protected.

He fell to the ground and fired from that position for a while, but he got up to run when he saw his fellow soldiers moving off toward cover. As soon as he stood, he felt it hit him in the stomach.

He'd taken a bullet, and the pain burned through him. He tried to clutch his belly and run. A shell exploded just in front of him, and in that split second he knew the shrapnel had put an end to his life on earth. *I love you, Leah!*

Leah woke up to the loudest scream she'd ever heard, and it didn't stop. It sent a terror through her she'd never experienced before. Dr. Moretz must have heard it too, because he rushed in, sat down on the side of her bed, and took her in his arms. His shoulder stifled the scream, and she realized it had been her own scream that had awakened her.

"It's all right, Leah," he said. "It's just a bad dream."

The dream. Leah remembered it then, and she burst into tears. It had been so real. She'd not only seen what happened, but she'd known Luke's very thoughts.

Hawk came rushing in. "What's wrong?"

"She had a nightmare."

Leah pulled back, so she could see Hawk. Both men looked so concerned.

"Was it about Luke?" Hawk asked as he came close.

She nodded. "I saw him killed."

"Leah, he hasn't even started fighting yet," Dr. Moretz told her as he smoothed her stray hair from her face. "He'll undergo some training first. I'm sure Luke's just fine and doing much better than you right now." His smile encouraged her.

Leah recognized the truth in what he said. It had been icy in her dream, and even with the storm, it wouldn't be sleeting this time of year.

She nodded again. "I'm okay, now. Thank you. I'm sorry I woke everyone. What time is it?"

Dr. Moretz glanced at the clock on the wall behind her. "About five thirty."

"I think I'll just get dressed then. I doubt if I could get back to sleep anyway."

"I'd better let Emma know what's happened," Hawk said. "I told her to stay there, and I'd come. I left her praying."

The men turned to leave, and Leah saw Patsy standing in the doorway. She came in after they left. "You want me to help you get dressed this morning?"

"Thank you. I'd like that." Leah still felt shaken by the dream and didn't want to be alone.

The next day, they'd just finished eating dinner when the men came. There must have been about a dozen of them on horseback, and the very look of them portrayed trouble. Hawk, Dr. Moretz, Leah, and Granny Em grabbed a rifle. Patsy picked up the old muzzle-loader.

"Doctor, you take the right window," Hawk called as he went to the door.

Granny Em already stood at the other window, and Leah joined her. They both looked out.

All the men looked dirty and rough. Some of them wore items that had once been part of a uniform, some Confederate and some Union.

"Deserters," she heard Dr. Moretz say.

"Hold it right there," Hawk called in a firm voice as he stepped through the front door. "What do you men need today?"

Leah realized her heart raced frantically, and she feared for Hawk's safety. In fact, all of them were in danger. *God, please protect us.*

Leah pulled back from the window to watch Hawk. He stood beside the partly opened door, where he could quickly duck back inside if need be. Leah had to admit, he looked like he knew what he was doing. He'd tucked the rifle under his right arm, where it could be easily raised.

One of the men sounded amused. "Looky thar, boys. We got us a Injun."

"An old Injun," another man added.

"I may be old, but I have been the greatest warrior my people ever knew. I may not be as good as I once was, but I can still drop about a dozen men before they take me. And that's not even counting the guns behind me. Now, which of you wants to be the first?"

Dr. Moretz raised his window at that point. Granny Em and Leah did the same. They stood with one on each side, away from the glass, and raised it together, so the deserters couldn't tell they were women. Three rifle barrels were pointed out the front, not counting Hawk's.

The men looked around and then at each other. They looked undecided. "Aw, come on, boys," one of them said. "This place don't look like it's got too much to take 'sides food, and we've already took enough of that this morning. We can always come back and take what they got later on." With that they turned and left.

Hawk came back in, shut the door, and stood his rifle by the door.

"You're absolutely amazing," Leah told him.

"You were magnificent," Dr. Moretz said. "You didn't look a day over fifty as you stood there defying them all."

"You were just as good as that young brave who rescued me all those years ago." Granny Em smiled at him. "I'm so proud of you I think my chest might burst open."

Hawk grinned at her. "This is good. A wife should be proud of her husband."

"Is what you told them true?" Dr. Moretz asked. "Are you the greatest warrior your people have ever known?"

Hawk's smile got bigger. "According to the old men and the tales they tell around the fire. Every time they speak of me, I get stronger and more talented. I refused to marry, because I didn't want the love of a woman to weaken me. The legends have me greater each time they're told."

"Well, we know the part about the woman is untrue," Granny Em said, "but I bet the rest of those tales have a lot of truth in them."

"Well, thank you for what you did for us," Dr. Moretz said.

"I told Luke I would protect you."

"You do that very well," Granny Em added, "and I speak from experience."

"Where's Patsy?" Leah asked. "The last I saw of her, she had Edgar's old muzzle-loader?"

"Well, I don't know," Granny Em said. "Surely she didn't go off and hide."

Just then Patsy came in through the larder door still carrying the old gun.

"Where have you been?" Granny Em asked.

"In the smokehouse. I wasn't about to let them take all that meat we worked so hard on."

"Patsy, we have some of it hidden," Leah said.

"I don't care. I feel like we're going to need all we can get and then some before this war's over."

Leah stood outside doing chores when the deserters returned. She ran to the barn and picked up the pitchfork. *Why didn't we put a rifle out here?* Three of the men came in and backed her into a corner. They looked even rougher close up than they had from horseback. She held the pitchfork in front of her, ready and alert.

"She's a beauty, ain't she, Art?" one of them said.

"She's a wildcat too," said a second. "And I like my women wild. The more they scratch and claw, the better I like it."

"I'm first," the third one said.

"We all need to rush her at the same time," Art said. "That pitchfork looks sharp."

Leah wondered where Hawk and Dr. Moretz were. Why hadn't they heard the riders and come to check on her?

"Ready, boys?" Art asked.

They lunged toward her.

Leah woke herself up screaming again, but she realized what had happened this time. Hawk knocked and came in. He held a faint candle in his hand. She sat up to light the lamp, but her hand shook so much she couldn't get it lit.

Hawk set his candle down, did it for her, and then sat down on the side of her bed.

"Are you all right?" He took her hand in his.

"I think so. Deserters were about to attack me in the barn this time."

"It must have stemmed from what happened today."

"Why is this happening, Hawk? I've never had nightmares before."

"You're probably under a lot of stress right now, and I know you're missing Luke. The mind is a strange thing. Whatever you hold inside will come out in one form or another."

"But, I'm not worrying now. I've decided to expect good things and put it all in God's hands."

"Really? That's easier to decide than to do. I did the same thing long ago, but I still thought of Emma all through the days and nights. Can you honestly tell me Luke isn't constantly in your thoughts?"

Leah looked down at the sheet and shook her head. She couldn't say that.

"Let me give you a little advice, Leah. Talk about Luke more. Talk about your feelings and fears. Once you voice them, they won't have the same effect on you. You could talk to any one of us here, we all love you."

"In the letter Luke left for me, he suggested you would be a good adviser and a strong support for me. You are both of those, Hawk. I'm so glad you came to us."

"I am too. Even without considering Emma, I feel much more at home here than I ever did with my niece and her husband."

He hugged her then, and she felt the strength of him. It went beyond physical strength. He had strength of character.

"Would you like me to have Patsy or Emma come stay with you?"

"No, I'm okay now. Thank you."

He smiled, nodded, and left.

Leah had never known any of her grandparents. With the exception of Granny Em, even Luke's had died before Leah came to the mountains. Hawk and Granny Em were the grandparents of her heart, and she could never have better.

After the morning chores were done, Hawk went out to follow some honeybees he'd seen. Dr. Moretz wanted to go, too, but Hawk said he'd prefer not to leave the women alone.

"Why don't we women get the loom going again," Granny Em said. "I think there's still enough wool we spun and dyed last year."

Leah knew Granny Em wanted to help her stay busy. They didn't usually weave until they were confined for the winter.

Leah strung the loom. Patsy still hadn't learned to do this part, but she did a good job of weaving once the loom got going. Leah had chosen a plaid pattern. They were her favorites. She got it started, and then Granny Em took over. Patsy liked to watch the pattern for a while before she worked on it.

"I like to hear the sound of the loom," Dr. Moretz said. "It has a comforting rhythm to it."

Leah started a stew for dinner while Granny Em worked. Afterwards, Granny Em went to watch the food while Leah wove. When the meal neared completion, Patsy took over and Leah helped put everything out.

"How long does it take to find a beehive?" Leah asked.

"I guess that depends on how far he has to go," Dr. Moretz answered.

"I'm getting a bit worried," Granny Em said. "I would have thought he'd be back for dinner anyway."

"I am," Hawk said as he came in through the larder. "I ended up tracking a deer I saw. I hadn't intended to do that. I killed him and dragged him back a ways, but I got tired and left him. I thought I'd get Clifton to go back with me and get him. We'll have to use most of it soon and heavily salt any we try to keep. In fact, it would be a good idea to dry a lot of it, since the weather will be getting warmer soon."

"Can we manage to carry it?" Dr. Moretz asked.

"I think so. I slit his throat so the blood would drain. If he becomes too heavy, we can take a rope, string him up where he is, and skin and partially butcher him there. I'd rather bring him on in if we can though."

"Well, let's eat dinner first," Emma said.

"I'm hungry," Hawk said with a smile.

Leah saw that Hawk and Dr. Moretz were able to bring the deer back to the farm. They cut off its head, strapped it onto a sturdy sapling, and carried it on their shoulders.

"It sure is heavy," Dr. Moretz said. "I'm glad Hawk dragged it part of the way."

"The leaf cover is so thick, I don't think the dragging damaged the hide at all," Hawk said.

"What are you planning to do with the hide?" the doctor asked.

"I'll store all the hides and furs," Hawk answered. "What we don't need, we can always sell."

They spent the rest of the day processing the deer. Hawk and Dr. Moretz skinned it and cut the meat into large portions. The women cooked some, salted a little, and dried much of it.

"You did a good job helping to cut the hide off the deer without damaging it," Hawk told the doctor.

"I guess that comes from all the surgery I've done."

The day had been a tiring one. They ate the leftover stew from dinner and went to bed as soon as they held their devotion.

"This has been a good day," Hawk said.

Leah ran and ran, but the man still followed her. She couldn't shake him. She crossed a creek and stayed out of sight as much as she could, but still he came. She could almost smell him in the wind. He must be a great hunter, and now she'd become the hunted.

She knew she could run faster than this man, so why couldn't she get away? He must be following her trail. How could she quickly flee and not leave a sign?

She heard the bullet whiz and almost instantly it hit her. An intense pain ripped through her chest.

Leah woke up without screaming this time, but her gown had become drenched in sweat. She lit the lamp and looked around. The brighter room helped ease her wariness. She'd been in the forest in her dream.

Someone tapped lightly on her door.

She pulled the sheet back over her. "Come in."

Hawk opened the door. "Are you all right?"

"Yes, I had another dream, but it wasn't as terrifying this time."

He pulled a chair close to the bed and sat down. "Tell me about it."

As she told him, a strange look came over his face. He let her finish her story, however, before he said anything. "Did you see yourself in the dream?"

"No, not really. I felt and sensed everything. I didn't see anything but the terrain in the forest and the man at a distance."

"This man, was he Indian?"

"Well, now that you mention it, I think he might've been."

"Leah, you were the deer in the hunt today."

"What does it mean?"

"I don't know." He smiled teasingly. "Remember, I'm like Solomon, not Joseph or Daniel."

She laughed, which helped dissipate the remainder of the dream.

"I think you're going through some changes in your life. I'm sure Luke's being gone is a main one, but there may be others . . . like my being here."

"But that's a good change."

He smiled. "It's still a change. I think these changes are making you extra sensitive. You need to talk about things just as we're doing now. That's the only thing I can think of that might help."

"It does seem to help when I talk with you."

"Then you need to talk with me more often. Come help me milk. We can even come up here if you need to talk privately when the weather is too bad to go outside. I don't think my wife would get too jealous." He laughed. "She's not that type, and she's too sure of me."

"How did you know to come?"

"I'm not certain. I slept soundly but suddenly awoke. I lay there for a minute, but something made me uneasy, so I decided to come and check on you. I knocked lightly, so I wouldn't wake you if you were still sleeping."

"Have you ever been this closely attuned to anyone before?"

"Only to Emma. But I think you are a lot like her, especially in her younger days. You seem more like her granddaughter than her granddaughter-in-law."

"I think so too. In fact, I never knew any of my grandparents, and I've been thinking you and Granny Em would fit the position nicely."

A huge smile covered his face. He reached out and gave her a gentle hug.

"I would be honored to be your grandfather," he said. "Sarah was the closest thing I ever had to a child. To have you for a granddaughter would fill my heart with joy."

"I am sorry you never had children," she told him. "You'd have made a fantastic father, and I'm sure your children would have been wonderful people – just like you."

"It's okay. It was not meant to be. But now I have Emma for my wife, Clifton as my son, and you and Luke for grandchildren. I'm truly blessed."

"And we're blessed to have you as part of the family."

The sun had already started to rise, and Leah had not been able to get back to sleep. She got up and quietly went downstairs. She had the bacon fried and the first of the pancakes going before anyone else got up.

"You're up early," Granny Em said.

"Is Hawk still sleeping?"

"He is. He woke up when I did but turned over and went back to sleep."

"Did you know he was up again with me this morning?"

"No, I didn't. Another bad dream?"

"Yes, but I didn't yell out this time. I just woke up drenched in sweat. Somehow, he still knew to come. Your husband is the most amazing man I've ever met."

Granny Em's face turned radiant. "Don't I know it, and you don't know the half of how amazing he really is."

"I smell breakfast." Hawk came out of the bedroom still buttoning his shirt. He paused and looked at them. "Okay, what's going on? I can tell by the looks on your faces you were talking about me."

"You know very well it would be nothing but good things," Leah said. "We're your most fervent admirers." She turned to Granny Em. "The only thing wrong with being Hawk's wife is that you could never keep a secret from him."

"And who would want to keep a secret from me? Certainly not Emma. She's the one who believes in complete openness and honesty. She's already stripped me of every secret I've ever had."

"I don't know what you're talking about. Name one."

"How many women I've been with."

"Granny Em! You didn't?"

"Well, I thought, as his wife, I had a right to know."

"Hmm . . . I never thought to ask Luke that one, but then I don't need to. I know what kind of man he's always been."

"What's going on here?" Dr. Moretz came down.

"Your mother probably needs to learn to curb her tongue," Granny Em told him.

"Well, we all know that already."

CHAPTER FIVE

Confederates

THEY'D JUST EATEN BREAKFAST, CLEANED up the kitchen, and done the outside morning chores when about eight Confederate soldiers rode up. Hawk started to pick up his rifle.

Leah knew she needed to do what Luke had told her and pretend she supported the South. Could she do it? She hated pretense and lies, and she knew God did too. She looked at those around her. She would do what she had to in order to keep them safe.

"No, this is my turn," Leah said. She turned to Patsy. "Play the slave again, Patsy. Use your slave dialect if you can remember it."

Leah walked out to the porch hoping the nervousness she felt didn't show. She smiled welcomingly at the men.

"Well, hello there, gentlemen," she said in a thicker Southern drawl than usual. "What are y'all doing out so early?"

"I'm Captain Moore, madam. We've come to conscript Luke Moretz into the Confederate army."

She smiled sweetly. "Well, I declare, Captain Moore, my husband already joined up . . . just last week."

"Really?"

"Yes, indeed. He surely did. He said, even though he'd miss me something terrible, he just couldn't stay out of it any longer. I'm sorry you nice gentlemen had to ride all the way up here for nothing. Could I offer you some refreshment?"

"Some water would be appreciated, madam."

"Why certainly. Patsy, come here right away!"

Patsy appeared. She kept her eyes lowered and didn't look directly at Leah or the soldiers.

"Yes, Missus Moretz."

"This is my slave girl, Patsy. Patsy, take these nice Southern gentlemen down to the springhouse and fetch them some good, cold water." She looked back to the soldiers. "I declare, this is the best water you ever did taste. You tell me if it's not."

"Thank you, madam," the captain said. "It's a real pleasure to meet a fine Southern lady like you, but you don't sound like you're from these parts."

"How perceptive of you, sir. No, I grew up on a plantation in Anson County. Gold Leaf. Perhaps you've heard of it."

"Is that the Morgan place?"

"It is. Paul's my brother, half brother really. He's off fighting the Northern aggressors too."

"You have your slave well trained. It's good to see. Too many of the darkies have gotten right uppity since the war."

"Yes, I think proper training is the key. They've got to be taught what's expected of them. We had a couple more slaves, but they ran off. Patsy's a good girl. She's as faithful as they come."

"Well, you have a nice day, madam." He tipped his hat and went to join his men.

Leah went inside. *That went well.*

"Now, you're amazing, Leah," Dr. Moretz said. "I would never have believed you had a deceptive bone in your body, but you put on quite a performance."

"Ivy could have done a much better job. She's the real actress in the family, but this role wasn't hard for me. I grew up seeing all around me."

"Whatever gave you the idea to even do this?" Granny Em asked.

"Luke. He told me in this dangerous war to lie, pretend, or do anything I needed in order to be safe and God would understand. Do you think so? Do you think this is acceptable?"

"Under the circumstances, yes," Dr. Moretz said. "After all, you didn't hurt anyone in your pretense. Just like Hawk did on Monday, you kept everyone safe."

"If they'd found out Luke has been fighting for the other side, things could have been bad," Granny Em said.

Leah looked at Hawk. For some reason she needed his affirmation too.

"I agree with Clifton, in that no one harm came to anyone, and your actions kept the peace. Normally, I would never agree to pretense, but this seems different." He suddenly smiled. "And, I think you gave an outstanding performance."

"That was almost fun." Patsy came in laughing. "I don't mean the pretending to be a slave again, but that we pulled the wool over the eyes of those Confederate soldiers."

"You were great, Patsy," Leah said.

"Well, I didn't have to do that much, just lower my gaze and not speak unless spoken to."

"Did they ask you any questions?" Granny Em asked.

"Just how long I'd been with my missus."

"What did you tell them?" Dr. Moretz asked.

"I's guess it mus' be 'bout twenty years now. I come to da missus when I's 'bout twelve."

They all laughed, and Leah hugged Patsy. Patsy smiled and seemed very pleased with herself.

Granny Em cooked venison for all of them for dinner. She said she'd fixed it like she had for Edgar, when he'd come to visit at her family's cabin before he and she were married. She soaked it in some apple cider vinegar and water to get the gamey taste out, beat it to tenderize it, simmered it tender, and smothered it in gravy.

"Emma, I didn't know you could cook like this," Hawk said. "I've never tasted such delicious venison, and I've had it every way imaginable."

"This is good, Mama," Dr. Moretz said. "I remember you used to make it like this occasionally, but it's been years since I've had it."

"Could you show me how to make it?" Leah asked. "I know Luke loves this."

"He does, and yes, I'll show you."

Hawk and Dr. Moretz went to do some work in the barn, and the women prepared supper. Granny Em had thought she'd fixed enough venison at dinner to have some for supper, but they'd eaten most of it.

"Let's just cook some kraut and sausages," Granny Em said. "That's fairly fast and easy, and, Leah, you can make some cornbread and your potatoes in that white sauce to go with it."

"I'm not familiar with any of this food, except the cornbread and sausages," Hawk said later, when they all sat around the table.

"This is sauerkraut," Granny Em told him. "It's sort of like pickled cabbage. I guess you've never eaten with any Germans before."

"No, just Cherokee and Irish." He grinned. "Are you German?"

"No, I think the Cagles are mainly of French decent, but the Moretzes are German. I don't know much about my mama's people."

"I've never had potatoes fixed like this, either," Dr. Moretz said.

"They're Leah's recipe. Luke loves them."

"I'm not sure he's a fair judge," Dr. Moretz said. "Luke loves everything about Leah." He tasted his potatoes. "I take that back. These are good."

Hawk liked it all too. He ate some of everything.

"Luke left a week ago tomorrow," Leah said. "A lot has happened in this week. It's been a long one."

"Yes," Dr. Moretz said, "we've been visited by deserters and Confederate soldiers. Perhaps we should expect some Union soldiers next."

"I don't think I'd joke about it, Clifton," Granny Em told him. "They might just show up."

"Then it'll be time to switch sides." Leah laughed.

"It sounds as you have already made plans," Dr. Moretz said.

"Actually, they're more Luke's plans. He tried to think of everything, and he gave me suggestions on what to do before he left."

"Luke's a good man," Patsy said.

"Would you like to go out to milk with me, Leah?" Hawk asked.

She knew he thought she might need to talk. They'd had another situation with the Confederate soldiers earlier, and tomorrow would mark a week since Luke left. She didn't think she needed to talk, but she wouldn't have thought that about the deer dream either. She enjoyed talking with Hawk anyway, so she decided to join him.

"I know you miss Luke," Hawk told her, "but you seem to be handling it pretty well."

"Besides having nightmares, you mean."

He laughed. "At least, you haven't been sobbing in your pillow every night."

She started to ask him how he knew that, but she decided not to. He seemed to read way too many of her thoughts and dreams, and she didn't know how she felt about that. "I took it very hard until I read the letter Luke left for me. It made me feel much better. I know there's nothing I can do to alter the situation, and worrying isn't going to help a thing. Praying and giving it to God seems to be the best thing I can do."

"Is tomorrow going to be more difficult for you?"

"It could be, especially around the time Luke left, but I have a plan. This week has been so busy, I haven't written him, not since last Friday. I want to sit down tomorrow morning and write him a good long letter."

"Are you going to tell him about our two sets of visitors?"

"I don't know. I want to tell him every important thing, but I don't want to worry him. What do you think?"

"I would think it might make him feel better to know we've handled the situations well, but you know him better than I do."

"I think you're right. If I tell Luke only the mundane or good things, he'll know I'm hiding some things. By telling him everything, it will put his mind to rest. At least he'll know we're fine and taking care of things as they come."

"You were remarkable today, Leah. I'm very proud of you."

"Thank you. That means a lot coming from you."

"Do you think you'll dream of what happened today?"

"I have no idea. I wouldn't have thought I'd dream the other ones either. I've never had a problem with bad dreams before, not even when Papa died. If I dreamed, they were always good ones. These new dreams concern me, but there's one good thing. Each one has gotten milder and less traumatic. Maybe if I dream tonight, it won't be a bad one."

"You call me if you need me. I mean it, Leah. Just call out my name, and I'll hear you. Even if the dream isn't bad, but you want to talk, call me." He looked at her carefully. Leah wondered if he were reading her mind. "Is something else bothering you?"

"Not really."

"You can tell me."

"I'm not sure. It's about you."

He looked surprised. "Have I offended you in some way?"

"Oh no, Hawk. You are the most special person I've ever met outside of Luke. I guess that's part of it. I don't understand this special connection we seem to have. Dr. Moretz and I became good friends the first time we met. He said he wanted to become like a father to me, but even our relationship is nothing like what you and I seem to have. I've known you for such a short time. How can I feel like this? How can you know when I need you without me saying anything?"

"I don't know if I understand it either. As I told you, Emma is the only other person I've ever experienced this with. When I came here, I fully expected to see Emma. I would have known if something had happened to her. I would've known through the years if she'd needed me. When her sons died, I knew something was wrong, but I didn't know what. I became despondent myself, although I didn't feel that I could help, even if I came. Much later, I learned from Sheila and Connell what had happened. At another time, I felt she might be very sick and in need of me, but the feeling left suddenly as if someone else had come to help her."

Leah couldn't believe this. "When Luke and I had gone to take care of Ivy after she ran away, we came back to find Granny Em seriously sick with a fever. Dr. Moretz had come back with us, so he'd be here for Luke's and my wedding. Between us, we managed to pull her through."

Hawk just nodded. He didn't seem surprised.

"I can see all this better with Emma, since you've loved her for so long, but why me?"

"I've thought about that too. Like I told you, I think you're much like Emma would have been at your age. On top of that, I wonder if God didn't send me here for the three of us—for you, Emma, and me. I think we all need each other right now. I know Emma would've been even more devastated over Luke going to war if I hadn't come."

"You're right about that. In fact, even before he decided to join, she seemed almost on her deathbed. She'd seemed to lose her will to live. You came and changed all that."

"She's done so much for me too. God has been good to me and my dreams have come true. In another way you've helped me too, Leah. It's gratifying to be needed and useful."

"And why were you sent for me?"

"I think I've been sent to help you cope. I am so attuned to you, so I can help you in your time of being separated from Luke."

They'd finished milking several minutes ago. Leah stood, walked to Hawk, and kissed him on the cheek. "Thank you." She picked up her milk bucket, and Hawk did the same. Leah felt at peace as she walked back to the house.

"Well, I wondered if something had happened to you," Granny Em said. "I thought Hawk had run off or something."

"You know I wouldn't leave you." Hawk smiled. "My heart is right here." He kissed her forehead.

"Well, if she's joking about it," Dr. Moretz said, "you can bet she's not too upset."

"Hawk told me she was too sure of him to ever worry," Leah said.

"That's the honest truth." Granny Em nodded. "We're both very sure of each other. What we've found is too special to abandon."

They held their family devotion and went to bed. Leah planned to start her letter to Luke as soon as she got up.

What was Leah doing at a ball? She wasn't supposed to be here. She should be at the farm in the mountains. She didn't even like these affairs. Ivy should be here instead of her.

"Miss Morgan, how nice to see you, dear. I'm so glad you could join us."

Miss Morgan? What about Luke? They should be calling her Mrs. Moretz now.

"The pleasure is all mine, madam," Leah told her hostess, afraid to say too much until she found out what was going on.

"The general hoped you'd come. Oh, here he comes now."

"Miss Morgan, I'm delighted you've joined us. Now, the night will be enchanted."

The general looked fairly young, probably in his late thirties, and had an attractive moustache, but he appeared slightly overweight although he carried his extra weight well. She didn't want him flirting with her though. How did these people know her, and she didn't know them?

"Miss Morgan, you're here in time for that first dance you promised me." This young man looked nearer her own age and had a startling resemblance to Luke.

"Miss Morgan, surely you're not going to leave a general for a captain," the general said.

"Let's see, one dance to the captain for every two the general gets. How's that? I'll expect to dance with you next, General."

"Of course, my dear. I'll be waiting."

"You're doing great, Leah," the captain said as he led her onto the dance floor. "You have all the Southern officers in Richmond eating out of your hands. The general there is a real conquest. We've been trying to get to him for ages."

"Exactly what should I do?"

"Why, get as much information as you can from him about the Confederacy's plans, of course. The same as always. You know what to do. You have an amazing talent, and you're the best spy we have. I'll meet you tomorrow morning in the park to see what you've learned. Our country is depending on you, Leah."

"I'll do my best."

"Your best will do fine. It always does."

They finished the dance in silence. The captain had turned out to be a very good dancer, and if he pulled her a little too close, no one seemed to notice. She hoped the general would dance as well.

The general stood waiting for her. He smiled in appreciation as she approached, and the captain reluctantly handed her over.

The general didn't dance as well, but, at least he didn't step on her feet. He stood both taller and heavier than the captain. "Well now, Miss Morgan, I expect you to give me two dances in a row. I might never see you again, once the other officers find you're here. Besides, I'll need to call it an early night. I'm leaving Richmond in the morning."

"That's disheartening news, General. I'll miss your company. Whatever can be so important to take you out of Richmond?"

"There is a war going on."

"Well, I know that, but it seems to me a man like you would be of more use here planning strategies. Let someone like the captain lead the men in the field. He's more dispensable."

The general's expansive chest expanded a little more. He looked at her adoringly. "I'd much rather stay here and spend all my time with you, but this is an unusual operation, which requires a sharp mind and perfect timing." He moved closer to whisper in her ear. "We're marching to take Washington. This will probably end the war."

"Oh, that's such good news, but you must be careful. I couldn't stand the thought of losing you."

"I promise I shall, and when I end this war you will be waiting for me, won't you, Miss Morgan?"

"Oh, I'll be waiting. You can count on that."

"Could I escort you to the balcony? It seems to be as hot as blazes in here."

"I'm not hot, but if you need some air, I'll accompany you, and we'll just count it as one of your dances."

"You're so kind. Oh no, here comes my aide."

"Your presence is required immediately, General," the aide said. "Your troops are moving out tonight."

"In the dark?"

"There's a full moon and clear sky, sir."

"Of course there is. Please excuse me, my dear. I hope I can call you that, because it's how I think of you. I'll see you soon." He bowed.

Leah looked intently across the dance floor. Where was that captain? She needed to get him this information now. Tomorrow might be too late.

She couldn't find him anywhere. She checked the refreshment table, the smoking room, and the balcony, and still no captain. She started to panic.

"Looking for someone?" He stood so close behind her, if she turned around, she would be in his arms.

She took a step before she turned to face him.

"I'm outmaneuvered again." He might be teasing, but she couldn't tell by his serious expression.

"Captain, I need to talk to you in private."

"I have a carriage. I'll see you home if you aren't feeling well."

She understood he meant his last comment for the ears of others. She played along. "Thank you, sir. You are most kind."

"The perfect gentleman for the perfect lady," he whispered in her ear. "Send a slave to fetch your girl from the servant's hall," he said aloud.

Patsy came quickly. A tiny smile curled up her lips, but she kept her eyes lowered.

The captain whisked Leah out in a hurry and had her seated in his carriage before she had a chance to think. She hoped he would prove to be a true gentleman. The driver helped Patsy into the seat next to him on top.

Leah turned to the captain. "I didn't say my good-byes to the hostess. What will she think of me?"

"She won't. Tell me what's so important, Leah."

"The general left the ball to lead an army toward Washington. He said they would take it and win the war."

"That is important information. You've done it again, darling. I'm so proud of you."

Who was this? Could it really be Luke? He did resemble and sound like her husband, but she couldn't be sure. His eyes were the same color, but she hadn't seen them sparkle when he teased her, nor had she seen his mischievous grin.

His lips were moving toward hers. Did she let him kiss her? She could surely tell if this was Luke then, but what if it wasn't? She didn't want to kiss anyone but Luke. His lips were almost upon hers when she jerked back. "No!"

Leah woke with a jerk. Had she said something?

She heard Hawk's soft tap on the door. She didn't need to talk tonight—didn't want to talk. She hadn't lit the lamp, so she lay still and pretended to sleep. Hawk must have left.

What a weird dream! Apparently, she'd been a successful spy for the North. That wasn't the disturbing part, however. It seemed she couldn't recognize her own husband, and she'd awakened before she found out if it had been Luke.

The darkness of the room surrounded her, and she wondered at the time. She got up and lit the lamp. The clock said four o'clock.

Before she could get back to sleep, it would be almost time to get up. The room seemed more isolated and lonely than usual. She picked up the photograph and stared at it for a long time. Luke had always been so handsome, even in the posed photograph. She needed the living, breathing Luke beside her though. She'd tried to stay strong, but she missed him so much that the loss seemed like a sickness.

The bedroom had suddenly grown oppressive, so she got dressed, collected her writing material, picked up the lamp, and quietly moved downstairs. She stirred the fireplace, added kindling, and put in some wood when the flames started. She decided to make some coffee, went to the larder, and ground the beans. While the coffee made she started her letter.

She told Luke about the deserters and how Hawk had talked so bravely he'd scared them away. She told him of her portrayal of the Southern sympathizer and Patsy's part as the slave. She wrote of Hawk's hunt and the deer he'd killed.

By that time the coffee was ready, and she poured herself a cup. She sat back down and continued writing.

> I've been having some strange dreams. I've never had this problem before. Hawk thinks it's due to the abrupt changes, especially being separated from you.

> Last night I dreamed I attended a ball in Richmond, as a spy for the North. The person who helped me, a man pretending to be a captain in the Confederate army, looked very much like you. As I said, it's all very strange.

> I've read the letter you left in the desk drawer over and over again. It has lifted my spirits and made me feel better each time. I think you were right about the things you said, and I've been trying to follow your advice. It's helped.

> I know it's too soon to hear from you, but I want to so badly. I want to know how you are and what's happening to you. I miss you so much! I'm very aware you rode away a week ago today. It's been a dreadfully long week.

> Because I have Hawk, your father, Granny Em, and Patsy with me, I'm not as despondent as I would be otherwise. I'm keeping as busy as I can, too. I guess half your father's time here is up, and I'll be sad to see him leave in two weeks.

> I hope you remember how much I love you. I'm looking forward to the day you will come home. Can you imagine

the celebration we'll have? I'll be whole again then, for I can never be whole without you.

All my love,

Leah

CHAPTER SIX

The Runaway

"GOOD MORNING." HAWK CAME INTO the kitchen. "Do I smell coffee?"

"Yes, come and join me for a cup. I've just finished my letter to Luke." Leah got up and poured him a cup. She looked up to see him staring at her.

"I thought you were having another dream last night. I heard you cry, 'No!' I came up and tapped on your door, but you seemed to be asleep."

"I did have a dream, a strange one but not frightening. I heard your soft tap, but I didn't feel like talking then."

"I see. Was the dream disturbing?"

"I guess, in a way. I feel like talking now, if you'd like to hear it."

She told him her dream. He listened intently.

"It bothered me that I couldn't tell if the captain was Luke or not. I should know my own husband."

"It's just a dream, Leah. For some reason, you're being extra sensitive now. You're taking elements of whatever happens during the day and forming dreams around them. As you said, however, they're getting less terrifying."

"Good morning." Dr. Moretz came up.

Leah got up and started breakfast. Dr. Moretz had a lonely look as he sat down. Perhaps she'd been neglecting him in her new dependence on Hawk. She vowed to make some special time for the doctor today.

"I think I'll ride into Boone tomorrow, pick up a few items I need, and check the mail," Dr. Moretz announced. "Would anyone like to go with me?"

"Do you think it's safe?" Granny Em asked.

"I think so. We'll be careful, of course."

"I'd better stay here," Hawk said. "It's always been better for me to stay secluded as much as possible, and I need to be here for Emma and Patsy too."

"I'd like to go," Leah said. "Luke bought me another side saddle a few years ago."

"Good," Dr. Moretz said. "I'll be glad for your company."

Friday morning Leah slept later than usual. She awoke to sounds coming from the kitchen.

Granny Em had started breakfast. "You must have slept better last night."

"I did, and with no dreams. Is Hawk still asleep?"

"No, he's in the barn milking."

Hawk came from the barn and Dr. Moretz and Patsy came down at the same time. They ate breakfast, and Leah and Dr. Moretz made preparations to leave.

"Does anyone need anything?" the doctor asked.

"Get some Irish oats, if you can," Granny Em said. "Hawk likes them, and I'm kind of partial to them myself, especially when the cooler weather gets here."

It surprised Leah to find some empty store shelves. The war must be causing shortages already.

"Are you new here?" Leah asked the clerk. She'd never seen him before.

"Yes, ma'am. I'm Layton Parsons. I'm working here part time."

"Things are getting harder and harder to get," Mr. Parsons told her. "If you see something you're going to need, you'd better get it now, for I might not have it later. I just got in a shipment of salt, too, but that's rare. It once sold for five or six dollars a bushel, but I'm going to have to sell this for thirty-five dollars. The next shipment I get, if I can get one, is bound to be over fifty dollars a bushel."

"We'll take at least two bushels," Dr. Moretz told him. "We use some to make leather as well as preserving meat."

"That's all I can let you have. To try to get it distributed around and be fair, I'm limiting it to two bushels a family. Even at that, it'll probably be gone by tomorrow evening."

Dr. Moretz got the Irish oats, some coffee and sugar at ridiculous prices, and a little sack of candy for Granny Em. "Hawk insisted on giving me the money for the candy. He wants to give it to Mama from him."

Leah got three spools of thread, a pack of needles, a bottle of ink, and some pen points. She would have bought more thread, but they were out of white, black, and natural and almost out of all other colors. Most of the textile production went into making uniforms, blankets, and supplies for the soldiers.

There was a letter from Luke! She didn't know how it had gotten to her so quickly, but she rejoiced to hold it in her hands.

She'd brought her two letters in the same envelope in case she had one from him and could get his address. She didn't really expect there to be one, however.

The letter didn't have a return address, and she panicked at first. When she opened the letter, however, she found one on the inside. She borrowed a pen and some ink from Mr. Parsons, addressed her envelope, and wondered how long it would take it to get to Luke in Tennessee.

She waited until they were back in the wagon to read her letter. There were two sets of papers. She glanced at the one. It seemed to be Luke's enlistment papers. She read the other.

My darling wife,

I miss you more than words can convey. You have been in my thoughts every spare moment, since the morning I left you. Leaving you was the hardest thing I've ever had to do. I'm just thankful Father and Hawk are there with you.

Thank you for the letter and photograph. They made that first night away from you more bearable, and they've brought some comfort ever since. I turn to them often, especially in the evenings.

I must hurry to get this to you. I've just arrived in Tennessee and enlisted. I wanted to send you a copy of my enlistment papers. You can use them if you ever need to prove I'm in the Union army. I have a copy and so does the army.

They've told us not to be too specific about our locations or where we're going until after the fact. They're afraid some helpful information might fall in the wrong hands.

I'll be training to be part of General Samuel P. Carter's brigade. He was sent to Tennessee on special duty from the War Department by request of Senator Andrew Johnson. He is to organize and train Union troops here. I haven't started any of it yet. I'm writing to you just after I enlisted. I'll write more later and tell you what things are like.

All the Watauga County men, who came with me, will be training here, as well. There were eight of us. At least you know we made it to the army with no problems. Please let the Blankenships know, if you see them. Raymond's sons don't read or write.

I can't wait to hear from you, now that you have my address. I'm sending this with a soldier who has special leave and will be going through Boone on his way home. I'm hoping this will allow you to get it sooner, because he seems to be in a hurry.

Please don't worry about me. I'll be fine, especially while we train. We'll just trust in God and pray this war is soon over. I'm thankful to have missed a year of it already.

You know I love you more than anything on earth, and that love will never change, other than to grow deeper. The love we have, along with our faith, will also enable us to make it through this. Please take care of yourself.

Your loving husband,

Luke

Leah read the letter twice. On the second time, she read Dr. Moretz the parts that weren't private.

"I'm glad we came in today," he said. "It's good to know he made it safely and has enlisted easily."

"It looks like the shortages are going to get worse, doesn't it?"

"I'm afraid so, as long as this war lasts."

She and Dr. Moretz went home and shared all the news with the others. They were glad to hear from Luke too.

"A shortage of salt is going to be a big problem," Hawk said. "We can use honey to sweeten if we have to, but there's no substitute for salt."

In the week that followed, Leah had two more dreams. In the first one, Luke was seriously wounded in a training accident. He was taken to a military doctor, but Leah couldn't get any information about him. She didn't know where he'd been taken, how he was doing, or if he'd recover. The dream left her feeling frustrated, anxious, and frightened.

In the last one, Luke was trying to get home to her, but something kept happening to hinder him. The weather turned bad, people gave him wrong directions, he ran into Confederate troops, and he fell sick.

Each time, she woke up but didn't call Hawk. She talked to him about them the next morning.

"I think Hawk is probably right," Dr. Moretz said. "I think Luke's leaving, our unexpected visitors, the stress from the war, and trying to keep things going here are all causing the dreams."

"Do you think they'll go away soon?" Leah asked him.

"I don't know. They might, but they could continue until Luke gets home."

Leah hoped not. The dreams were draining. They seemed so real that it felt as if she were actually going through those awful experiences.

Dr. Moretz had planned to return to Salisbury on the seventh of June, but he decided to stay two more weeks. June became a busy month on a farm with plenty of work to be had.

They'd gotten the garden planted, and the early peas were blooming, so they'd have peas before too much longer. However, Leah knew she couldn't bring herself to make the soup Luke liked so much. It would be salted with her tears if she did.

They picked the first strawberries and made jam. Hawk made rabbit traps, but he wouldn't set any of them until the fall. The weather would soon be too warm to trust the meat.

Luke had cut plenty of wood, but all of them spent a few days getting more. They mainly gathered the downed trees. Clifton did most of the trimming, but Hawk would do some too. Leah and Patsy helped carry it. Granny Em went, but she usually collected herbs. She stopped to rest often. Stooping over bothered her, but she was doing better than she had been in a long time.

"Would you walk with me up the mountain trail?" Dr. Moretz asked Leah one Sunday afternoon. "Sarah and I used to call it our mountain. I haven't been back since she died. I think I want to go today."

"It's where Luke took me the day before we were married. Do you remember when you and Granny Em said it would be okay for us to go off by ourselves?"

"I remember. Mama had been sick, and you and Luke hadn't had a chance to talk. Since you were getting married the next day, we thought you probably needed some private time. If it would be too hard for you, you don't have to go. I'll understand. I can go alone."

"I think maybe we need to go together. We can sympathize with each other."

────────────

They walked slowly up the mountain trail. Clifton could almost feel Sarah's hip touching his leg as they navigated the narrow path. He shook his head. No one was beside him. Leah walked ahead. They climbed to the top saying little. Then they stood quietly looking out at the spectacular view. The day had turned sunny and bright, and they could see for miles.

"Looking at this always gives me peace," Leah said.

"The first time I brought Sarah up here, we had so much fun. She'd been so shy that I tried to move slowly and let her get to know me. I told her I cared for her right over there on that rock.

I'd already fallen in love with her, but I didn't want to scare her off. When we went back down the mountain, she would gain momentum and run toward me. I'd put out my arm to stop her, and for a moment she would be in my arm. We laughed all the way down." He smiled as he thought of it. He could almost see it all again.

"Luke and I did so much talking on the way up, some of it serious and some just teasing each other and laughing. Here at the top, he kissed me to calm any fears I might have. He tried so hard to make things easy and right for me."

"This is also where I proposed to Sarah. She sat on that rock again, and I knelt in front of her. Belinda Schreiner, a girl I'd seen on two occasions before I met Sarah, had tried to stir up trouble between us and make Sarah think I had committed to her first. Sarah didn't know what to think, so she pulled back. I finally got her to talk with me and understand. Over the next week things got better, and I brought her here again. I told her I loved her and wanted to marry her. She said yes, and I later learned she'd been in love with me for a while too. I wouldn't have taken it so slowly if I'd known. She even agreed to move down the mountain after we were married so I could start my medical practice. We loved each other so much." He sighed.

"Apparently, God isn't finished with your work on earth. He must still have plans for you."

"I wish I'd done like Hawk and waited to remarry. I could have lived alone better. I don't think God wanted me to marry Frances, but I didn't think to ask Him. I still hurt too much to think."

"Do you love Maggie and Teddy?"

"Oh yes, of course I do. Frances spoils Teddy, probably much like your mother did Ivy, but I still love him. I'm worried about Maggie, though. She's such a sweet girl, but Frances doesn't give her much positive attention."

"Then you need to focus on your children. They need you. From what Luke's told me, Sarah must've been a very good mother. She would expect you to counteract Frances's effects on the children and do your best to bring them up to be well-adjusted, caring people."

"Yes, she would. I remember when I asked Sarah if she'd like for me to hire a nanny for Luke. The very idea appalled her. When I saw how she dealt with Luke, I could see why. No one else could have done as well."

"What was she like?"

"If you put Hawk's caring and efficiency into the most beautiful Cherokee woman possible and added a shy reserve until she got to know you, well, that was Sarah. She put God first, but her family came before anything else."

"I'll be praying for your situation. God can work miracles."

"Yes, He can. Thank you for listening to me. I think I needed to talk about Sarah. When Luke gets home, I need to tell him about her too. I've never been able to before."

"I hope that's soon."

"I'm afraid it won't be, but I do believe he'll come home. You need to believe that too."

Leah nodded. "I can for spells, but it's so hard not to let the fear creep back."

———————

They continued to work around the farm, and things went smoothly, for everyone worked well together. They felt comfortable with each other, and a certain peace came in the uncertain time.

On Monday Patsy came running into the house. She'd been getting water from the springhouse, but she'd left the bucket behind.

"What's wrong?" Leah asked.

"Please come with me and hurry."

When they were outside, Patsy began to explain the problem. She rushed to get it out before they got back to the springhouse.

"I came to get the water, and there's a man in there. He's an escaping slave, and he got separated from his group. He's scared to death. I told him we're Yankee supporters, and your husband was off fighting for the Union, but I don't think he believed me. I knew he'd be too frightened of one of the men, so I told him to wait while I got you. I don't know if he did or not. He might have run off."

The slave crouched in the corner, but he looked ready to flee at any moment. His eyes darted around as if he were considering his options. His dirty, ragged appearance indicated he'd had it rough, and some of his wounds looked raw.

"Hello there, I'm Leah Moretz. What's your name?"

"I be Thomas, Missus Moretz."

"Where were you headed, Thomas?"

He looked afraid to tell her, but the soft tone of her voice seemed to be calming him. He needed a good meal, a bath, and some better clothes.

"Never mind. I'm guessing you are headed over to the Union lines to safety."

He nodded.

"You look like you could use some rest and food."

He nodded again.

"If you'll come in the house, I'll get you what you need."

"No, missus. I wouldn't feels right in yo' house."

"How about the barn then?"

He nodded.

"Patsy, there's some ham and biscuits left over from breakfast. Bring those and a glass of milk. They'll do him for now, and we'll bring him some dinner later on."

Patsy went to the house to get the food while Leah showed Thomas to the barn. She took him to a clean stall. "Stay down here for now. If someone comes for you tonight, you can go to the loft. There's plenty of hay there you can sleep on or hide under, if need be. We're pretty isolated here, though, so I don't expect anyone will come."

Patsy came with the food, and he began to eat like an animal who hadn't had anything to eat for days. Leah noticed his legs and wrists were very raw where shackles had been. Someone must have cut them away.

"Stay here with Thomas until I get back," Leah told Patsy.

Leah went to Luke's wardrobe. She pulled out his oldest set of work clothes. They were clean and much stronger and better than what Thomas wore, and he looked to be close to the same size as Luke. She also got some ointment, bandages, soap, and a towel.

"I need to doctor your wrists and ankles," Leah told him when she returned, "but I need you to wash up first. There's a small creek on the far side of the pasture there. The bushes grow close and keep it out of sight. I want you to go wash and put on these clean clothes. I'll be waiting here with the salve and bandages."

He started to protest.

"I mean it," she said. "I can't doctor you until we get you cleaned up. I don't know how far you have to go, but this will help some."

He looked at her a moment then nodded again. He took the items and headed toward the creek. She sat down with the bandages and ointment to wait. He came back looking much better. He seemed to feel better too.

"Do you have a family, Thomas?" Leah asked to make conversation.

"Yes, missus, but I's don't know where dey be. I's a wife and three chilluns."

"There are five of us in the house. Besides Patsy and me, there's Granny Em; her husband, Hawk, who's a Cherokee; and Dr. Moretz, my father-in-law. All of them support the Union and are against slavery. I need to tell them you are here, so if any trouble comes, they'll know what to do."

"De Cherokee is fightin' for the Rebs, ain't dey?"

"Not this one. Hawk is one of the best people I've ever known. He'll be coming out to milk later on. Of course, I can come with him, if you'd like that better."

He nodded.

"I'll have Patsy bring you some dinner and supper. You eat it all now."

He nodded.

"Don't you leave tomorrow until I pack you a bag to take and put some more medicine on your wounds."

He nodded. "Tank ya, missus. Tank ya kinely."

Leah smiled and nodded.

"That man sure can eat," Patsy said when she brought back the plate and glass. "He's not bad looking either, since he's all cleaned up."

"He told me he's married," Leah told her.

"I figured as much."

When Leah told the others about Thomas, Dr. Moretz wanted to go immediately to help him. Leah and Patsy convinced him Thomas would be nervous about his company.

"Leah already took care of him," Patsy said. "She's fed him, got him to wash up, gave him clean clothes, and bandaged the sores on his wrists and ankles."

"Well, I guess I'm not needed then." Dr. Moretz smiled at Leah.

Leah went to milk with Hawk. Thomas apparently hid.

"How do you feel about slavery, Hawk?" Leah asked.

"I think it's always been on earth as long as there's been re-cords kept. It's certainly in the Bible, but I still think it's wrong. I'm not sure I felt that way until Emma came into my life. I could not see her as Sliced Arm's slave or anyone else's for that matter. When I took her from Sliced Arm, I never treated her like a slave."

"Would you help Thomas escape even from your own people?" Leah asked, because she wanted Thomas to hear what she knew the answer would be.

"Yes, I would. I'm Emma's husband first and foremost. My worldly allegiance is to her and this family. All of you are my people now."

She saw Thomas peering down from the loft, trying to get a good look at Hawk.

"Come on down, Thomas. It's all right."

"I's never seed a Injun."

Hawk looked up and smiled. Thomas came to the edge of the loft. He crouched in plain sight, but he didn't descend the ladder.

"It's a pleasure to meet you, Thomas. You're welcome to stay with us as long as you'd like."

Thomas nodded.

"Thomas says if it's okay, he believes he'll stay one more night," Patsy announced at breakfast that morning.

"See if you can convince him to come to the table for dinner," Granny Em told Patsy.

"I doubt if he'll do that, but he'll listen to Leah better than anyone else. He's used to obeying white folks, and he thinks she's an angel because of how she's helped him."

"I'll see if I can get him to come when it gets close to dinner-time," Leah said.

When Patsy and Granny Em began setting the food on the table, Leah walked to the barn. Thomas sat in a stall and looked at her as if he'd expected his meal.

"Patsy's busy in the kitchen. I came to see if you'd come eat at the table with us to help us out, so we won't have to carry yours out and then collect the dishes to wash."

He looked uncertain but shook his head.

"All right then, I suppose I'll need to be the one to wait on you today."

"Dat ain't right." He shook his head again. "I's guess I can come." He began to follow her to the house.

"Patsy has eaten at the table with us since she and I came here. It's how we do things in this family."

Everyone smiled at him when he walked into the room. Leah seated Dr. Moretz where she usually sat, so Thomas would be straight across from her and beside Hawk. Thomas took his place where she indicated, and Hawk said grace.

Thomas answered all their questions with a nod or the shake of his head if he could. It seemed to be his favorite form of communication. He watched Dr. Moretz more suspiciously than anyone.

"I'm a doctor in Salisbury. My wife has gone to visit her sister, because our views about the war are so different. I've always hated slavery. It's just wrong according to Christ's teachings."

Thomas nodded. He seemed to relax a little.

When they'd finished, Patsy began cleaning off the table, and Thomas started helping her with the dishes. He washed while she dried and put them up.

"You don't need to do that, Thomas," Leah told him. "I didn't bring you into the house to put you to work."

"I's want to be a hep. Yous sho' hepped me."

"You're welcome to stay here with us."

He shook his head.

"Well, I'll send Patsy to get you for supper."

He looked uncertain again. When he started to refuse, Leah added, "It'll help us out."

He nodded.

They'd just finished eating supper when a small band of Confederate soldiers rode up. Thomas started to run, but Leah stopped him.

"It's too late for that. Dr. Moretz, quickly pull those bandages off him. Thomas, you and Patsy just act like our slaves. It's time for my lady of the South act again." Leah walked out on the porch.

"Well, I declare, what brings you fine gentlemen out this late?"

"Evening, ma'am. We got word an escaped slave's been seen heading in this direction. Have you seen him?"

"The only two slaves I've seen are Patsy and Thomas. I've got them working in the house. Is this escaped one dangerous?"

"I don't think so, but he may be desperate. Could I come in and look around?"

"Well, of course, Lieutenant. I declare, where're my manners? We've just finished supper. There's not enough for all of you, but you're certainly welcome to what's left."

"No, thank you. We're in a hurry, but I'll just see inside."

"My family will be glad to meet you."

Leah took him inside and introduced everyone. "I didn't catch your name, Lieutenant."

"I'm sorry. I'm Lieutenant Conners. Do you have papers for your slaves?"

"Well, of course we do. Shall I get them?"

He looked at Thomas without answering. "Why's there manacle marks on this one's arms and legs?"

"He tends to be on the lazy side. Why, sometimes he hides, so he won't be called to do as much work. My father-in-law showed him what could happen when he acts like that. He chained him to the barn wall for one whole night. You have to keep them in line, you know."

"I don't think we'll have any more problems with him," Dr. Moretz added. "He seems to have learned his lesson."

"Is that true, Thomas?" the Lieutenant asked.

"Yessuh. Sho' 'nough."

Lieutenant Conners looked at Hawk. "And this Indian is part of the family?"

"Yes, sir," Leah said. "He's a Cherokee who'd been living with an Irish settler for years. I'm sure you're aware most of the Cherokee are siding with the South as we speak."

"That's true. Well, we need to ride on, if we're going to capture that slave."

"Yes, sir. You be careful going down the mountain. It can be treacherous in the dark."

"Yes, ma'am. It's been a pleasure."

He put on his hat and left. Thomas immediately decided to leave the next morning.

"It might be better to stay a while," Leah told him. "You wouldn't want to run up with those soldiers again."

Thomas remained adamant about leaving, however. Hawk drew him a map, which mainly took him off the main roads, to get him to the Union forces in Tennessee. Leah and Patsy packed him a large bag of food. Dr. Moretz said a prayer to ask for Thomas's safe journey, and Thomas thanked everyone again before going to the barn. He would be gone by the time they got up in the morning.

CHAPTER SEVEN

Getting the Mail

LEAH RAN AS FAST AS she could, but the sounds of the hounds were getting closer. She ran so fast, she didn't have time to look for the markings on the trees to tell her which way to go. Well, she wasn't going to go anywhere but the grave if she didn't get away from these patrollers.

She tried running through the shallow creek, but that didn't seem to throw them off. Hopefully, it would slow them down for a minute. Surely the dogs would need to sniff around before they could pick up the trail again.

Leah hurried to a fallen log and sat down. She quickly pulled out a small container of black pepper from her sack. She rubbed the pepper into the worn soles of her ragged shoes and hoped what she'd heard proved correct, and it would throw the dogs off her scent.

She stood and listened. The hounds were braying again, and she took off. She ran to the top of a hill and looked back. She saw a mountain lion, but it headed toward the dogs and not up the hill toward her. She turned and went down the other side of the hill.

She tried to find a sign, so she'd know how to find the next stop on the Underground Railroad. There had to be a station close, because she'd been traveling most of the day before the dogs had found her trail.

She rounded a tall clump of briars and realized she must be coming to a clearing when she almost ran into someone. She should have been more cautious and looked around before she moved into view.

The man put out his hands to steady her as she tried to avoid colliding into him. He was an Indian! Hawk? Was it Hawk?

"Come with me," he said. "I can take you to safety."

Leah slowly opened her eyes. The soft light of morning had already filtered into her bedroom. She guessed the situation with Thomas had triggered this dream. It hadn't been as bad as the others, though. Hawk had been going to keep her safe. She got up, dressed, and hurried downstairs to begin her day.

Dr. Moretz planned to leave on June twentieth. They all hated to see the day come. "Would one of you like to ride down to Boone with me to check the mail?" he asked.

"I'm afraid some of the men around might try to harass me," Hawk said. "Besides, I'd hate to leave the women here alone now."

"I'll go," Leah said.

"It would be too dangerous for you coming back alone," Dr. Moretz said. "There are Confederate soldiers and marauders to worry about as well as some undesirable civilians."

"I can dress as a young man," she said. "I did it to get home to Luke once before. I can hide just outside of town and let you collect the mail. You can get it, meet me, and head down the mountain while I come back here. There won't be as many people about on a Friday as there'd be on a Saturday."

"I don't know, Leah. That could be too dangerous."

"Please. It's been a month since we checked the mail. I know I must have another letter from Luke, because he said he would write again soon. I'd like to mail my other ones to him too."

"It's not winter, Leah," Granny Em said. "You won't be able to cover yourself as completely as you did that first time."

"I'll put a handkerchief under the back of my hat, as if I'm covering my neck from the sun. It'll hide the hair I can't conceal in my hat. I'll dirty my feet and go barefooted. You've all said I'm a good actress. I can do this."

They hesitantly agreed.

Leah hurriedly wrote Luke another letter. She told him all about Thomas and how busy she'd been. She included the part where the Confederate soldiers came looking for Thomas and how they'd all pretended again. She wrote:

> I promise you a stack of letters soon. Your father is starting home now, but I've spent some time enjoying his company. I'm sure when the weather turns cooler, all I'll want to do with any spare time is write to you.

She ended by telling him she would put this letter in the mail as his father left. She told him how much she loved and missed him and for him to take care of himself.

"I hate to go," Dr. Moretz told them before he mounted his horse, "but I really need to get back to my patients before the summer fevers hit harder. It's been a pleasure, Hawk. I know you'll take good care of the women." They shook hands and gave each other a quick hug.

Granny Em hugged him tightly. "Please come again soon," she told him. "I don't get to see you nearly enough, and I love to have you with me."

Leah had dressed in her boy's clothes. She got on the horse, and waved good-bye. It felt good to be in a regular saddle again.

They met no one going down the mountain. They passed a few people as they got closer to Boone. Leah hid in a big grove of trees and bushes just to the south of the town.

She dismounted, tied the horse, and sat on a log to wait. Dr. Moretz came back in about thirty minutes. He tied his horse and sat down beside her.

"You have one from Luke and one from Ivy." He handed them to her and waited for her to read the one from Luke.

My darling Leah,

I've received your two letters with great joy. I had been anxious to hear from you. I'm particularly glad to hear of your attempt to stay positive. I am, too, and I keep praying for you. That the letter I left in the desk drawer has helped you makes me feel especially good. I want to help you as much as possible, although I can't be there.

I can see you staying in our room the day after I left. That day was hard for me, too. It felt as if my heart and life source had been ripped from me. I'm glad to hear Hawk is taking such good care of you.

No friend I could ever make will come close to being the support you are to me, but I can deal with everything if I know you are well and doing okay. You are right in saying the Lord is our best support and provider.

I'm impressed with how Hawk stood up to the band of deserters, and, because of what he said, they rode away. I'm so glad he's there with you and Granny. I think he'll manage to take care of you, regardless of what comes. He seems to be so capable, even at his age. He must have been really something when he was young.

I smiled when I read your account of the visit by the Confederate soldiers. I can see you playing the role of the refined, prejudiced, Southern lady. I know it's not how you really feel, but you grew up hearing and seeing all of that. I can also see Patsy backing you up and acting your slave. I bet Father got quite a surprise, however. He's always seen you so differently. I'm just glad you decided to pretend, because it's what you needed to do at the time.

That a man Hawk's age is able to do so much work and even track down a deer is amazing, too. If I'd have known he'd be so efficient, I wouldn't have worried so about leaving enough meat to see you through the winter. I'm assuming no one has bothered your supplies, since you mentioned both the deserters and the Confederates left without causing any harm.

I'm sorry to hear you're having worrisome dreams. Are they still occurring? I'm glad you're talking about them. Maybe that'll help. I have that teasing look you love when I say, I can see you as a Northern spy in Richmond, but I'm happy you'd want no part of that kind of life. I'm seeing you in my dreams, too, but in mine, I have you in my arms.

I'm guessing you received my first letter, or you wouldn't have had my address to send yours. Put those enlistment papers in a safe place that wouldn't be easily found if Confederate soldiers decide to search the house. They may very well do so, if someone notices you are getting mail from or sending letters to your husband in the Union army. I tried to think of another way for us to correspond but couldn't come up with anything. At least I won't put my return address on the outside of the envelope. Otherwise, we'll just have to take the risk, since I don't think either one of us could tolerate not hearing from the other. I'm hoping things won't be too difficult for you, since there are many Union sympathizers in Watauga County.

All we recruits have done so far is drill, drill, and drill some more. It gets monotonous and tiring. The other soldiers complain about it more than I do. I understand they want us to be able to act upon orders without thought and know what to do in the field. Besides, if I could choose to drill for the rest of the war, I would, except I do want to help end this mess. The other men around me are itching to get in the fight as soon as possible, but I can imagine the horrors, and I can wait just fine.

I'll be looking forward to getting that stack of letters you mentioned. If I can stand to wait, I'll do as you suggested and open one each day.

I've found there are sutlers, who follow the armies and sell supplies. This is good to know. I should be able to get more paper, ink, or whatever else I might need that the army doesn't provide.

Instead of a stack of letters, it seems I'm writing long ones. I do need to end this now and get it in the mail.

I love you so much. Never a spare moment goes by that I don't think of you, and I dream of you every night. I'm glad things have gone well for you, even amid possible dangers. It eases my mind that you're all coping.

Your loving husband,

Luke

As she read to herself, Leah summarized aloud the parts Dr. Moretz would want to know. He sat quietly and listened. "I'm so glad to hear things are well with Luke," the doctor said when she'd finished. "Now, I'd better head down the mountain."

Leah stood with him and hugged him tightly. "I'm so glad you came." She felt tears forming in her eyes. "Thank you for all your help, and please come again soon. I'll miss you."

"I'll come when I can," he told her as his eyes grew watery, "but I'm afraid, as the war goes on, travel is going to get more difficult. You take care of yourself now and be careful going home. I'll be praying for you."

She nodded, afraid she would start crying more if she spoke. She kissed him on the cheek. "I love you," she whispered.

He untied her horse and helped her mount. "I love you like my own daughter. In fact, I wish you'd consider calling me Father like Luke does."

"I'd like that. I used to call my own father Papa, so it would be easy to call you Father."

He smiled, took her hand, squeezed it, and mounted his horse. He looked back at her before they parted.

"You take care of yourself, Daughter."

They left in opposite directions. Leah would save the letter from Ivy to read when she got home. She'd read Luke's again, too, and share parts of it with the others. She tucked them both inside a saddlebag.

There were more people out than when she'd impersonated a boy before. Then it had been cold and getting late. Now, the middle of the day had turned warm.

She tipped the brim of her hat and nodded to several men who spoke, but she didn't slow long enough for them to ask questions. She could tell many of them were curious by the look on their faces.

When she started up the mountain, she didn't see anyone else for a while. She rounded a curve, however, to see three men riding down. As she got closer, she realized they were members of the gang of deserters who'd come to the farm and feared they'd recognize her.

"Where're you goin', kid?" the leader asked.

Leah thought fast. "To the Blankenships' cabin."

"You don't look like one of their young'uns."

"No sir, just a friend of theirs."

"That so? I might jus' demand a fee to let ya pass."

"I don't have any money."

"What's ya carryin'?" He looked at the saddlebags.

"Just some letters for the Blankenships."

"Lemme have a look."

Leah's heart fell. They were bound to see the addresses on the letters. "If I show you the letters, will you let me pass? I need to hurry."

"Maybe."

She said a quick, silent prayer and with her heart nearly beating out of her chest, she opened the saddlebag and extracted the two letters.

He took them and looked at them. "Who's writin' to the Blankenships? They can't read, can they?"

Apparently, neither could these men. Leah realized they weren't able to read the envelopes, and she said a quick thank-you to God. "Some of their sons are off in the war. They have someone write their letters for them, and I read them to Raymond and Polly."

"Whar'd ya say ya lived?"

"On the other side of the Blankenships."

"I didn't know thar wuz inny folks further up the mountain. We'll have to check that out, boys." He handed the letters back.

Leah put them in the saddlebag and started up the mountain again. As the men continued on the way down, Leah breathed a huge sigh of relief. What if they'd decided to search her to see if she did have some money? What if they'd discovered she was a woman? She definitely needed to figure out another way of getting the mail, one that didn't involve so many risks.

When she got back, Hawk took one look at her face and asked, "What happened?"

"I'm fine."

"Now, that's not what Hawk asked you," Granny Em said. She had followed Hawk out to meet Leah.

"I'll put the horse up, and you can tell me all about it when I get in," Hawk said.

"Come on," Granny Em said, "Patsy's fixing supper."

Leah told them about the three deserters when Hawk returned. Worry and concern covered their faces. "I'm so thankful the men couldn't read," she said. "I admit, they scared me for a while."

"We'll need to figure out another way to get the mail," Granny Em said. "Maybe we can pay someone in Boone to bring it out to us."

"That's a good idea." Leah wondered why she hadn't thought of it.

"I'm going into town with you the next time to see about it," Hawk said. "I think you and I together can probably handle any problems for one time. Emma and Patsy can come, too, if they feel like it. If not, maybe we can drop them off for a visit at the Blankenship cabin."

"I guess Clifton left without problems," Granny Em said.

"He did. He asked me to call him Father instead of Dr. Moretz, so that's what I'm going to do." Leah shared portions of Luke's letter with them. Then she sat and read it completely through one more time to herself. By then, the women had the meal ready. She planned to save Ivy's letter until after supper to read. But as it turned out, she didn't have a chance to get to Ivy's letter until after they'd had their devotion and sat and talked for a while. When the others started to bed, she opened the envelope.

Dear Sister,

Things are even more worrisome here. There's much talk about changing the conscription law. The poorer farmers see it as unfair that they have to go off and serve in the army, while men like Lawrence don't. I'm sure I'd agree with them if Lawrence and I were poorer, and he couldn't buy his way out. However, as things stand now, I'm hoping they won't change the law. I can't bear the thoughts of Lawrence having to go to war. So many of the men never come home again. I see their names published, and the lists grow longer all the time.

I'm sorry, Leah. You said in your last letter that Luke has joined the Union. I wish him well, although I can't say the same for the Yankees in general. The South just has to win. I'm sure Lawrence and I will lose everything if they don't.

Half our slaves have already run off, but we're still better off than most of the other plantations. With Paul not there to see to things, all but the old faithful slaves have left Gold Leaf. Of course, Jasper and Bertha are still there. I know they were two of your favorites. Hester Sue is still with relatives, and we never see her.

Bertha is doing fine, but Jasper's health seems to be failing some. I don't know how old he is, but he's bound to be getting on in years. You'll probably want to remember him in your prayers.

Remember us all in your prayers. This war's just got to be over soon. We should've won it a year ago. Lawrence says he can't understand why the Confederacy didn't take Washington right after Manassas, when we had the upper hand.

I hope this finds you well. Please write me often. I know you're probably writing to Luke and Dr. Moretz, but I need to hear from you, too.

Love,

Ivy

Leah went up and got ready for bed. She read Luke's letter one more time before she turned out the light. She planned to find time to write to Ivy tomorrow. Then on Sunday she'd have time to write Luke a long letter.

That night she dreamed she was a soldier drilling. All day long she drilled in the hot sun. She carried the rifle until she thought her arms were going to fall off. She drilled through all the different field maneuvers until her legs began to buckle under her, and still she drilled.

July turned hotter than usual, and plenty of work needed to be done on the farm. They ate from the garden, dried some beans, and tended the root crops and corn to harvest later.

The crops this year were not what they'd been in past years. There'd been less rain and more heat. In addition, the Confederacy now required all farmers to give a tenth of their yield to help support the troops. The requirement would cause additional hardships, especially for those families who barely raised enough to feed their families in the good years.

Still, the women at the Moretz farm made what jams, preserves, pickles, and kraut they could. Whenever they worked away from the farm, they all went. Hawk was always a great help despite his age. Granny Em often sat and watched, but she still moved around well on her own.

CHAPTER EIGHT

Expecting

LEAH BEGAN TO SUSPECT SHE might be pregnant. She hadn't thought much of it when she'd skipped her first monthly after Luke left. She knew it had been an emotional time for her. When she began to feel too nauseated to eat much in the mornings, and she missed her next monthly, she felt fairly certain.

In one sense, it thrilled her, because she'd wanted a child for so long. She and Luke had prayed for one and talked about having another, but it also worried her. The twins had died. What if something happened to this one? In addition, she doubted Luke would be here during this labor, and there was no telling when he might get to see the baby. She refused to consider the possibility he might never see it.

"When were you going to tell us?" Hawk asked one evening after their devotion. "Emma and I have known for a while."

Leah knew immediately what he referred to. "Which of you suspected first?"

"Hawk told me," Granny Em said. Her eyes softened as they always did when they fell upon her husband.

"Told you what?" Patsy asked.

"I'm in a family way."

"Oh, I'm so happy for you!" Patsy exclaimed as she got up and hugged Leah.

"Are you worried?" Hawk asked.

"Some. The twins died before they were a week old, and I'm afraid something might happen now. I also wish Luke could be here."

"I know he'll hate he's not," Granny Em said. "I couldn't run him away when you were in labor before. He had to be right there."

"He gave me a lot of help and support," Leah said. "I'm glad he came."

"Maybe a grandfather could help this time." Hawk smiled.

"When are you going to write Luke?" Granny Em asked.

"I don't know. I can't decide if it would make him worry more and want to be home even worse or if it would give him an additional reason to survive. I want to be completely honest with him, however. What do you think, Hawk?"

"I think he's yearning to be home right now whether he knows about the baby or not. Knowing about it will probably cause him to worry more, but it might also give him an additional incentive to get through some hard times to get home."

"I also think he'd be hurt if you don't tell him," Granny Em added.

"I'll write him and tell him Sunday then. Can we go into Boone the first of next week, Hawk? I'm going to have several letters I need to mail, and I'm sure there's one from Luke waiting. It's been a month since Father and I went to get the mail."

"Have you figured up your dates?" Granny Em asked. "How far along are you?"

"I'm guessing about two and a half months. Near as I can tell, the baby should be born along the middle of February. Are you going to feel like delivering it, Granny Em?"

"The good Lord willing, I'd like to see anyone try to stop me. But I'm not sure you should be riding a horse into Boone. What do you think, Hawk?"

"I think riding the horse will be easier on me than taking the wagon," Leah interjected.

"Leah has a point, but the problem could come if you fell off the horse," Hawk said.

"I could fall out of the wagon, too, especially if something broke."

"That's probably true," Granny Em agreed. "It happened to my sisters and me once."

"I'm willing to let you choose," Hawk said, "but I want this to be the last time you go into Boone until after the baby is born. Let's pray we'll be able to get someone to bring the mail out every time you get one from Luke."

Leah wrote Ivy first. Hers would be the shortest and easiest to write. They would all be mailed at the same time anyway. She wrote the doctor next.

> Dear Father,
>
> I have some good news. Luke and I will be adding to our family in February. I'm very excited. It's been a long time since the twins died, and we've longed for a child.
>
> I must confess, however, I'm also worried. I'm afraid something may happen to this one, too. I wish you could come to be with me, but in the cold of winter and in a war, I'm sure that's impossible.
>
> I haven't been to the post office since you left, but Hawk and I plan to go soon. Granny Em suggested we try to find someone in Boone we could pay to bring our mail up to us. That's an excellent idea. I don't know why I hadn't thought of it before.

I expect to have another letter from Luke, when we go. I'll try to write soon and let you know what he says. I wanted to get my news to you now. Are you ready to be a grandfather?

Take care and write soon. I miss you.

Your loving daughter,

Leah

She had a harder time starting the one to Luke, but she had no trouble writing once she began. She decided to wait and tell him about the baby near the end.

Dearest Luke,

I'll be sending you five letters in this package, however, I'm going to label for you to read this one first. I have something to share with you. I've answered most of your last letter in the others. I expect there'll be at least one more waiting for me, when I get to the post office.

Hawk and I are going to Boone in a few days. We feel sure we can hire someone to bring the mail out to us. That way, I can get your letters quicker, and not have to travel down the mountain. Hawk says this will be the last time I go, in any case, until later. Read on to know why.

Your father asked me to also call him "Father," which I've gladly agreed to do. He's about as dear to me as my own papa.

I hope things are going well for you. I understand that all the drilling can be boring and tiring, but I agree with you. It would be fine with me if that's all you did until the end of the war.

How long do you expect to train? Do you think you'll stay in Tennessee or be assigned elsewhere?

I've not had a strange dream for several weeks. I'm hoping they're over, although the telling of them has given some entertainment. Father thinks I should make short stories of them. Can you see me as a female Edgar Alan Poe or Nathaniel Hawthorne? I can't.

Now for my news. Are you sitting down, Luke? If not, please do so. I'm expecting our child. I know this is not the ideal time, with you away and a war raging. However, we've wanted a child for so long that I'll take it with joy anytime the good Lord sends it.

I'm doing fine. I've had some morning sickness, but it hasn't been too bad, and it's almost gone now. The best I can figure, it must have happened sometime during the last week we were together. That would mean it would likely be born around the middle of February. I can feel my waist thickening, but I'm not showing yet.

Please don't let this add to your worries. I promise to take good care of the little one and me. I also have Granny Em, Hawk, and Patsy, and God will take care of us. You must help me decide on names, however.

I pray the war will be over by February, but I think that's unlikely. I do wish you could be here, as I know you do, but I'll be fine. Instead of a wife waiting for you when you get home, you'll have a wife and child. Come home to us, Luke. We both need you.

With your child growing within me, I somehow feel even closer to you than I did. I can almost feel you beside me. Perhaps you are here in spirit, if not in flesh.

I'm so excited about this baby. I just know everything will be fine this time. I think this is an answer to our many prayers.

I love you more than anything or anyone on earth. I miss you and can't wait until you are beside me again. Please be extra careful.

Your adoring wife,

Leah

Leah read back over the letter. Right now, she did believe everything would be all right. The doubts and worries would try to sneak back in, though. They seemed worse at night. Alone in the dark, her memories crowded on top of each other, piling, pushing, and tumbling. Sometimes they weighed her down so much, she couldn't get to sleep.

Monday she and Hawk left early to go to Boone. Hawk gently helped her into the sidesaddle. At least the trip wouldn't take so long on horseback.

Granny Em had refused to leave the cabin. "There's very little chance that someone will come while you're gone," she'd said. "Since you're taking the horses and don't have many errands, you should be able to go there and back without it taking all day. Patsy and I will be waiting for you."

"Don't you want to go visit Polly Blankenship?" Hawk had asked. "I can tie my horse to the wagon and leave the wagon at their place."

"I really don't. Now, if Oralee were alive, it'd be different, but Polly's so much younger than me, I wouldn't feel right."

"We'll hurry," Hawk said as he kissed her good-bye. "Do you need anything?"

"Just you."

The fog hung heavy as they left, but Leah expected it would burn off before the morning passed. Hawk held a lead to her horse as they went slowly down the mountain, although she still controlled the reins. Part of her rebelled that he might think she couldn't take care of herself, but the other part appreciated his concern and care.

They made it down the mountain without incident. As they neared Boone, Leah could feel the stares, but they rode straight to the store, which looked even barer than before. Mr. Parsons stood behind the counter, but Leah wondered how busy he stayed with so little merchandise. "Mr. Parsons, I'd like for you to meet Granny Em's new husband, Hawk O'Leary. Hawk, this is Layton Parsons."

"Pleased to meet you," the shopkeeper said, and Hawk gave a surprised smile. Mr. Parsons handed her a letter from Luke and one from Dr. Moretz.

Leah asked, "Do you know anyone who'd be willing to ride up to our place with the mail as soon as they're able, after I get a letter from Luke? We're willing to pay them."

"Well now, we should be able to find someone. Money's getting hard to come by for many. I had three men come by this week asking about a job, and we didn't have anything for them."

"Could you handle it for me, Mr. Parsons? I trust you to hire someone dependable, and it would be doing me a great favor."

"I'd be happy to, Mrs. Moretz. I'm sure I won't have much trouble, since you'll be paying in cash."

"I figure it will take at least half a day for them to get there and back."

"True, but it won't be hard work, just riding a horse. They'll be some who'd jump at a job like that."

They took the letters and left. Hawk reached out to help Leah on her horse when two dirty-looking men came up.

"Weel, what we got here? I do believe I see me a Injun."

"You recollect when Grandpa wuz keeled in that Injun raid?"

"I shore do."

"What ye doin' here with this Injun, woman?"

"He's a longtime friend of our family. I'm Leah Moretz, Luke Moretz's wife."

"You inny relation to Edgar Moretz?"

"He was my grandfather-in-law."

"He wuz a right good man. I liked Edgar."

"I'd like to stay and talk, but we told Granny Em we'd be home for dinner."

"You bothering these people, Henry?" Mr. Parsons came from the store.

"No, I hain't botherin' nobody. We's jist jawin' a spell."

"Thank you, Mr. Parsons." Hawk tipped his hat and they rode off.

They heard some shouts and comments on the way out of town, but they rode on and turned to head home. Leah gave a silent prayer.

"Now if we can get home without anyone following us," Hawk said.

"Do you think someone will?"

"It wouldn't surprise me."

Sure enough, a group of men came toward them riding hard. There looked to be five or six riders.

"It's too dangerous to try to outrun them with you riding side-saddle and in your condition. I want you to ride on, Leah. I'll catch up to you in a little while. You have the baby to think of."

"Hawk, don't make me leave you. If something happens to you, they'd catch me in no time."

"It's me they want."

Hawk didn't have time to argue with her, because the riders were getting close. He took out his rifle, and Leah did the same.

"Don't you fire your gun sitting on that horse like you are," Hawk told her, "and hold on good if there's any shooting. At least get a little ways behind me."

Leah moved up the trail like he asked. She wrapped the reins around her left hand, and the horse seemed to sense her wariness. She hoped it would be ready to move quickly if she signaled. "God please help us and keep us safe," she whispered softly.

With cold eyes and tense postures, the men slowed to confront them. They looked like they'd ridden hard for a fight.

"Hold it right there," Hawk pointed his rifle at what looked like the leader.

"What you goin' to do with that rifle? You shoot and you're a dead Injun."

"That may be true, but I figure I can take some of you with me, and you'll be the first. We aren't looking for any trouble. We just want to head home."

"You live in these parts?"

"I'm staying at the Moretz farm. I escorted Mrs. Moretz into town, and we're going back now."

"We don't cotton to no Injuns comin' 'round ar families."

"I don't plan to come back down the mountain."

Another rider came riding up in a hurry. When he neared, Leah saw he wore a sheriff's badge. "What's going on here?" he asked.

"We're just escortin' this Injun out of town, Sheriff."

"I don't think that's your job, Crayton."

"We just didn't want no harm to come to him or nothin'."

"Why don't you ride on back to town and see if you can stay out of trouble."

The men looked like they disagreed, but they did as they were told. Leah rode back down to be beside Hawk.

"Thank you, Sheriff," Hawk said.

"You're welcome. Mr. Parsons sent me word there might be trouble. I thought I would just see if I could prevent that. I believe I'd stay out of town, though, if I were you. There's still those who remember the Indians as the enemy."

"I plan to do that. Thanks again." Hawk tipped his hat and they left.

"I was so afraid things were going to get out of hand," Leah said.

"I felt the same, and I'm not happy you didn't do as I asked, Leah. I can't protect you if you're going to be headlong and stubborn." Hawk's eyes held a look of hurt before they turned serious and hard.

"I'm sorry, but I couldn't bear to leave you here alone. I really think if something happened to you, they'd have come after me. I think we were better together."

"Do you see yourself as the head of this family?" His tone cut.

"No, not when you put it like that."

"Luke asked me to take care of you. I can't do that if you won't listen to me."

"You're right. I trust you and your abilities, and I should've done what you asked. I promise I will next time."

"I hope there won't be a next time."

When they returned to the farm, Granny Em and Patsy were waiting for them. "What happened in Boone?" Granny Em asked.

"Mr. Parsons is going to get someone to bring us the mail, and I'll pay him when he comes," Leah said.

"Did anyone cause any trouble?"

"A couple tried," Hawk said, "but nothing came of it."

Granny Em looked from one to the other. "Let's hear it."

Leah left Hawk telling Granny Em what'd happened. She went into the sitting room to read her letters. She read the one from Luke first.

My dear Leah,

I found your account of Thomas very interesting. I guess if the same soldiers ever came back, you can always say he ran away, which is true. As I read your accounts of your acting, I see you haven't blatantly lied. For the most part, you've just let them make some wrong assumptions. I feel you've done what's required, and I hope you think so, too.

It certainly reassures me you've been able to handle all the situations so well. I've always seen how capable you are. You're like Granny Em in that way. She's always relied on God, done her best, and things have turned out well for her in the end. I think this was true when the Cherokee captured her and after Grandfather died. When Hawk came, her grief had subsided, and she turned to him. I'm happy for her.

The officers here seem impressed by the skills of us mountain men. From what I've seen, many of the Northerners come from towns and cities these days. The fact that we can already shoot and do many of the tasks required of a soldier puts us at an advantage.

I've taken a lesson from your portrayal of the Southern lady and have pretended I'm not a very good shot when we have target practice. You see, I heard two officers talking about making me a sharpshooter, and it suddenly became hard for me to shoot straight.

I would hate it if I had to sit in a tree and shoot whichever Rebel came into sight. Sometimes, I would even be ordered the exact person to hit. I know this is war, but I prefer to meet my enemy on the field where we both have a chance. I don't want to become an assassin from afar.

The sharpshooters are no safer than anyone else, either. The enemy tries to pick them off and end their rain of bullets.

I hope telling you all this doesn't make you worry more. It helps me to be able to tell you everything, as we always have. I certainly couldn't explain to anyone here why I didn't want to be a sharpshooter.

I pray you're telling me everything, too. I think you have, for the most part. I feel you've held back a little, especially in reference to your dreams. I sense you've had other, more disturbing ones than you've told me about. I'm guessing they may have been about me getting hurt or killed in this war.

It actually makes me feel better when you confide in me. I don't feel as isolated from you, and I still feel I can be a help and support to you. We've always been those for each other.

The training period is over now, and we've already marched out. I expect some engagement soon. There's too much going on to be able to avoid the conflict. After all, that's why we're here.

We hear some of the current news, especially those which speak of Union victories. In April we took control of the Mississippi River all the way to Memphis, and New Orleans fell. These are going to be important in the Western campaign. I guess I'm in the eastern part of that front now. In May, Natchez, Mississippi also fell to Farragut. In June, our men were able to take Memphis. Rumor has it we were unable to take Richmond, but our efforts may have kept Lee from launching a northern offensive.

A soldier's life is like camping out all the time. One of the problems, however, is I don't have a pretty, dark-haired woman with green eyes to cook me delicious meals. It hasn't been too bad yet, because the weather has been good. It's been hot marching and drilling, but not as hot as it would be on the coast or in the east. I expect things will be much more difficult through the cold winter and the spring rains.

I'm still waiting on a packet of letters from you. Each one you've sent is about torn apart from the many times I've unfolded and refolded them to read. Sometimes I go to sleep at night with your photograph in my hand. The men who've asked to see it are very envious of me.

Darling, I love you and long for you with a desire that permeates my very being. I've been gone a little over two months, but it seems like more than two years. I'm wondering how I'm going to make it for many more months. I pray this war will be over soon.

Tell everyone I love them and miss them. Of course, this is true for you most of all. I know it's difficult for you to get to the post office to mail them, but please write me as often as possible. Your letters are my lifeline.

Your devoted husband,

Luke

Leah regretted the gap in Luke's and her correspondence. They seemed to always get a letter from the other before they received the answer from the last one.

She stopped and prayed a special prayer for Luke. She hoped he still marched around without being engaged but realized he would soon be sent into action. Maybe he was already fighting. She prayed for his safety and for their baby before she fell asleep.

July passed, and August followed. They continued to harvest the garden and put away what would keep in the root cellar and cave. They had sown the turnip and mustard seeds, and they were growing.

Hawk tried to keep an eye out for bummers. With the shortages growing, he said he feared there'd be more raids. Things like flour, sugar, and coffee were now impossible to get in the mountains, and if they could, they probably couldn't have afforded them.

Hawk built a hidden door behind the wardrobe in the guest bedroom. They hid what salt they had left there. They would need it if Hawk managed to kill another deer this year.

A few weeks after Leah and Hawk had gone to Boone, a man rode up. He looked to be in his late fifties.

"Hello," he said. "I'm Josiah Hendrix. Mr. Parsons said you needed somebody to brang you the mail. My sons have done gone off to fight, and me and the missus could use a little cash along. Seems no one wants to hire a sixty-year-old man. 'Course there's not much work to be had here abouts anyway. You'd have to go down the mountain for that." He handed Leah a letter from Luke.

She ran inside to get the coin she'd promised, the envelope with her two letters to Luke, and the money to mail it. "I appreciate you doing this," she told him. "I'm unable to make the trip anymore."

He nodded as he hurriedly glanced at her small protruding belly. She had begun to show now. "I understand you jist want me to come when you have a letter from your husband, and I should brang any others then, too, but I'm not to come more often than once a week."

"That's right."

"You don't know of anyone else in this dye-rection that might need the same service, do you?"

"No, I don't. The Blankenships don't read nor write. You might check with the Hunts out toward the Linville River. They bought Granny Em's old place years ago. We used to see them at the circuit rider's services some, but I don't know if they'd be interested or not."

"Thank you, Mrs. Moretz. I'll see you again when you git another letter from Mr. Moretz."

She hurried inside to read her letter. In her eagerness, she ripped it open on the way.

My dear, wonderful wife,

I was indeed very surprised by your news. We've been trying for a child for so long that I hadn't even considered the possibility you might be expecting with me gone. I'm glad you're feeling well and are so excited. I'll be praying for you both now.

Of course, I'm very pleased and excited, too. I only wish I could be there with you. I don't want you going through this without me. I know Granny Em and Hawk will take good care of you, but I want to be by your side as before. I felt so much a part of you, then. I felt I was being the husband you needed, and I think it pulled us even closer. I hate I'll be missing such an important event in our family.

We've been involved in some successful raids around eastern Tennessee. These are more like skirmishes than battles, and some not even that. I think the purpose is twofold—to destroy some structures important to the Confederacy and to tie up some of the Rebels, so they won't be available to help in other battles.

Although we didn't lose as many men, as we would have in a larger battle, it was still hard to see young soldiers ripped apart. There were casualties on both sides. If the raids we went on are any indication, I think the killing is going to be hard to get off my mind. A man can be alive and yelling one minute, and lying in a river of his own blood the next. It's hard to hear bullets all around you and see someone beside you hit the ground to grow cold. Even with the enemy, I can't help but think they too have families, hopes, and dreams. Many of us serve the same God. How can we be killing each other like this? I guess I think too much sometimes.

I just don't like this. I don't like seeing the dying, and I don't like to kill. My own dying is not so scary, other than I can't stand the thoughts of leaving you and our little one. It's seeing others die that bothers me and knowing I'm killing, too.

Forgive me, darling. I shouldn't be telling you the gloomy details. It would trouble me greatly if I caused you to have nightmares again. No bullet came close enough to me to even break the skin.

You asked me to be thinking of some names. I've tried. I would like "Sarah" for a girl, but I'm afraid Father might not be ready for that, even now. He seems to still be grieving over Mother. Perhaps "Rachel" would work. I've always found the story of Leah and Rachel in the Bible interesting, and I like the name "Rachel." I still haven't come up with a boy's name, but I'll continue to think. Perhaps you'd like to name him Benjamin after your own father. I like the name fine, and we could call him "Ben."

I haven't seen the Blankenship brothers since we finished training. I guess they're in a different company.

Thank you so much for your letter and for sharing the news about our baby right away. It relieves my mind that you're being honest and forthright with me. We've always shared everything and been so close that I don't want that to change.

Be extra careful and don't take any risks. I love you more than life itself. I always will.

With all my love,

Luke

CHAPTER NINE

Antietam

SEPTEMBER BROUGHT SOME COOLER WEATHER, especially at night. Leah welcomed the change and liked to sit alone on the porch before bedtime. She sat wrapped in a blanket and thought of Luke as she watched the night sky and wondered if he rested somewhere gazing upon the same moon and stars. As she absently worked her fingers around the folds in the blanket, she tried to will him some peace and comfort over the miles. She knew by his letters he needed them. *Lord, keep him safe and give him Your peace which passeth all understanding.*

They continued to harvest and store vegetables from the garden. The women baked apples, made some apple butter to use right away, and dried apples. Hawk made apple cider. The sugar supply dwindled fast, but they'd have enough for this year. They all prayed the war would be over before another harvest season came.

One day Patsy went to the springhouse but didn't come directly back as she usually did. Leah went to see if something was wrong and found her crying. "What's wrong, Patsy?" Leah put her arm around her shoulders, hoping to comfort her.

"Oh, I'm just being silly." Patsy sniffed and wiped her eyes.

"Are you unhappy here?"

"No, it's just that. I'd like to have a family of my own, but I don't see much hope of meeting anyone right now. You're married and expecting a baby and even Hawk and Granny Em have each other, but there's no one for me."

Leah gave her friend a hug. "You may have to wait until this war is over, but I'm sure you'll find someone. You're too special not to."

Leah hadn't gotten a letter from Luke in over a month, and she worried about what might have happened. She did get one from Dr. Moretz. Mr. Hendrix brought the news as well.

The armies fought a Second Manassas at the end of August, he said. *It ended about the same as the first one, with the Rebs winning. The papers are reporting Lincoln has replaced Pope with McClellan.*

Leah felt fear creep over her. She hoped this battle hadn't been the reason she'd not heard from Luke. Surely he hadn't been sent to Virginia to fight.

She gave Mr. Hendrix the letters she'd written to mail. Then she read her letter from Dr. Moretz. Mr. Hendrix should have waited until a letter from Luke came before he brought this one, but as she scanned the letter she realized she needed to get this news.

Dear Leah,

I write to you, but I know you'll tell the others my bad news. Frances and Teddy are dead. They died in Charlotte of scarlet fever. I wasn't even informed until it was too late, and they were already gone.

Frances's sister insisted they be buried there. I was too upset to argue. We buried them, and I brought Maggie home. Her aunt tried to get me to leave Maggie with her, but I refused. I'm sure Maggie needs me more now, and I need her, too.

The poor girl is heartbroken. I've hired Mrs. Price to stay with her while I'm working, but I'm spending as much time with her as possible. I also help her in her studies. She's smart and catches on quickly. It's hard for me to believe she's fifteen now.

I'm glad things continue to go well with you. I'm still looking forward to being a grandfather.

Being pregnant might have contributed to the nightmares you were having, because your body had been going through many changes. I've known several women who've had strange behavior during such a time.

I hope you're not still worrying the same thing might happen this time as before. Twins are usually small and have a harder time of surviving. I'm sure things will be just fine, although I know Luke will hate not being there with you. I feel the same and would be there, if I could. Wars sure do make life hard.

You take care, daughter, and write me soon. Maggie sends her best, too.

Love,

Father

Leah shared the letter with the others. They were all concerned.

"Poor Clifton," Granny Em said. "He's now had to bury two wives. Even if Frances hasn't been the best wife, no one wanted this. I sure wish we lived closer."

"Let's pray for him and Maggie," Hawk suggested, and he led them in prayer.

The baby moved and kicked regularly now. Leah rejoiced with each one, because it signified the little one was alive, and she hoped well.

Luke had been marching on and off for weeks. The days had all run together with marching. He hadn't had a chance to write Leah. He knew she probably worried about him, but there was little else he could do but march on.

A platoon of about fifty men from Tennessee had been sent to join General Burnside's troops. Burnside had been responsible for taking much of the coast of North Carolina. In July he had gone to the coast of Virginia, and now they were to meet him as he headed northwest.

They were able to take some trains, but it became a complicated and sometimes dangerous affair. They'd spent much more time on marches than riding the trains, although they'd covered more distance on the rails.

After meeting up with the Ninth Corps, they marched into Maryland. Luke's boots were falling apart. Neither the boots nor his feet were made for so much walking. They usually marched until it grew too dark to see.

"What do you think we're here for?" Richard Crowder asked. He came from the Knoxville area and looked a little older than Luke.

"I'd guess there's about to be a battle," Luke told him. "I can't see us marching this long and hard otherwise."

"Most of the men who've been with Burnside say they like him," Tommy, the youngest in their group, said. "He's a jovial guy who's pretty easygoing."

"I don't see why they march a few of us all the way here to join with all these men," Ronald complained. "It don't make a lick o' sense to me."

"We still have to follow orders, whether they make sense or not," someone else said. "The military don't have to make no sense, nohow. There's a lot of thangs in this war that makes no sense to me."

"We'd better get some sleep," Luke said. "We'll probably have a long day of marching tomorrow."

On the morning of September the seventeenth, Luke and the soldiers with him began to hear heavy firing all around at different times. Some of it seemed to be coming from the direction of Sharpsburg. They received orders they were to take a bridge over the lower part of Antietam Creek. Confederates almost surrounded it.

They had four divisions of about 11,000 infantrymen, so they shouldn't have had much trouble. From the start, however, things didn't go well.

For one thing, the usually jovial General Burnside's mood turned foul. Rumor had it that McClellan chided him for moving too slowly when given orders, and McClellan had taken Hooker's corps away from his command. In addition, General Cox seemed to also be in charge, which meant they had two commanders over their corps—an unusual situation.

Luke soon realized getting the troops across that fifty-foot bridge would not be as easy as it appeared. The nearby bluff hid Confederate troops, who were ready to fire down on the enemy. In addition, the Southern soldiers had about a dozen artillery pieces with them on the higher ground. Luke could hear intense firing from other locations and knew a major battle had begun.

"Men," an officer announced, "you will have plenty of reinforcements once we take that bridge."

Yet, the men didn't move right away. Luke didn't know what caused the delays. Finally, late in the morning, orders came to charge the bridge.

Some of the officers took their men downstream and tried to ford the creek. The swift water made it difficult, and everyone who tried to cross met with gunfire. They were easily picked off in a slaughter. When the artillery shells hit the soldiers, everything exploded, and body parts flew in all directions. It seemed more like a bad dream. Nothing felt real, but that almost made it easier to bear.

Tommy was one of the first ones hit. He took a direct hit from a shell and fell to pieces before Luke's eyes. Luke didn't let it register in his mind. He didn't have time, because he had to shoot and stay alive himself.

Most of the men Luke knew from Tennessee ended up fighting with a group of soldiers from Pennsylvania. Luke helped tear down a rail fence to use for cover. After a while, he also used the stone wall, which ran near the creek. The bullets rained down all around. Luke had never encountered anything like it.

Ronald Crowder fought beside Luke and took a bullet in the forehead. Luke saw it and noted how strange the perfectly round hole looked between the man's eyes before it started gushing blood, but he kept fighting. He would grieve later.

Together with the Fifty-First New York, Luke and the Pennsylvanians began to make headway. They eventually found themselves only twenty-five yards from the enemy.

Their officer, Colonel Hartranft, yelled commands until he lost his voice. Around one o'clock, the Confederate fire lessened. A few men ran ahead and found the enemy had indeed retreated.

They'd lost over five hundred men trying to take that bridge. There were bodies all around, and many more lay wounded. Still, they weren't finished fighting.

It took about two hours to get all the men across the bridge. All the blood made it so slick that it became almost impossible to walk across it without sliding down. Luke tried not to think about it or look down as he almost skated across.

They were told they needed to advance, and their orders said to converge on Sharpsburg. Other divisions joined them, as the long lines of soldiers marched toward the town from the south.

Luke thought of Shakespeare's comment that the greater the danger, the greater the courage. That might not be true. He didn't feel at all courageous right now. He felt sick and depressed. He rubbed the back of his neck as he marched, but the tension didn't leave.

Suddenly the Ninth Corps experienced the heaviest fighting yet, much worse than the bridge. Men were falling everywhere. Luke shot, reloaded, and shot some more. His rifle became hot from the firing. He grew numb, but he continued to fight without thinking. Over and over again, he did what he'd drilled to do, what he had to do. The smoke from all the guns became so thick no one could see, and Luke's eyes burned as if they were on fire too. Would this nightmare never end?

When they'd lost about a fifth of their men, Burnside pulled them back. As he turned to leave, a bullet caught Luke in his upper left arm. He picked himself up and ran to catch up. The blood gushed out of his arm, but he couldn't stop now. They retreated back to the bridge, but this time they took to the heights on the west bank.

Luke sat down, too weak to do much more. Another soldier took a large handkerchief and tied it tightly around his arm to curb the bleeding.

About twelve hours from when it had begun, the battle ended, although random shots still fired now and then. The moans of the dying filled the dusk. There'd been too many wounded and dead men to collect them before dark.

Night fell and the only men helped off the field were those who could get themselves up. In the morning, the removal of so many bodies would be a daunting task.

The next morning, the two armies awoke across from each other. Between them lay an unimaginable number of bodies. No matter how Luke turned, he saw the same sickening scene. Some cadavers were already beginning to turn dark and smell.

Smashed caissons, broken wheels, fallen cannons, and items from the soldiers were strewn everywhere. It looked like a mighty storm had hit. Luke later learned there'd been almost 23,000 Federal casualties and 12,000 Confederate ones. The Union had had nine generals killed. His mind couldn't conceive it all. One in every four men in the battle had fallen.

The battle had ended in a draw with neither side winning. Yet, as the gruesome details sank in, neither side wanted to resume the fighting. What a waste!

Luke waited to have his arm tended. At least the bullet had passed through it. He knew the doctors had lines of more severe patients to see first. When he did manage to go to the doctors, he saw wagons still carrying off amputated limbs and more of the dead.

While waiting to see a doctor, Luke learned the soldiers holding the bridge had been Georgia boys under the command of Brigadier General Robert Toombs, who'd declared he intended to distinguish himself. He had only about 550 men. Their position and artillery had given them such an advantage that there'd seemed to be many more.

"We'll need to amputate this arm," the surgeon told him. "At least it's your left one."

"No!" Luke held up his good hand. "It's not that bad."

"It will be when the infection sets in."

"I've been hit in the arm once before, and it healed fine."

"Well, you were lucky. Almost every wound gets infected, and once it does, there's little we can do but watch you die. There's no guarantee gangrene won't set in even if we do take the arm off, but your chances are much better. I can get some men to hold you down."

Luke felt a panic rising within him. He shouldn't have come here. He clutched his wounded arm as if holding it would keep it on. "You said my chances are only some better with amputation, so why not let me decide. I'm sure you have more serious cases to see to. Let me wait and see what happens. After all, it's my life I'm gambling with."

"You'd be sent home," the doctor told him. "A one-armed soldier won't be much good. I've had men shoot themselves, just so they'd be sent home."

Luke wavered for the first time. *Home.* He would love to go home and be with Leah when the baby was born. Then he thought of all the farm tasks he needed two arms to do. He didn't want to be a burden on Leah. "I'm a farmer. I need both my arms."

"Suit yourself." The man shrugged. "But you may live to regret it. I don't expect you'll be much use on that farm dead."

When he got back to camp, Luke removed the blood-soaked rag himself, but he had to wet it with water to get it off, because the blood had already dried to the wound. He washed around the wound, but he left the open area alone. He feared the bleeding would start again if he messed with it. The outside flesh on his arm looked pretty mangled. The shot had torn away more flesh than the one he'd taken near Wilkesboro. His father and Leah had taken care of him then. How he wished Leah could be available to nurse him now! Luke's arm ached so badly he couldn't get much sleep. If he'd been in Tennessee, he'd have asked for a furlough, but he didn't think he could make it back now as weak as he felt.

The Ninth Corps would be moving again soon, but Luke hoped this march would be at a slower pace. Before then, he'd write Leah.

At least he could use his right arm. So far, the Union had done a good job of getting his mail to him. Other soldiers often seemed jealous when he got a packet of letters from home. He sure hoped they kept coming. They raised his spirits more than anything and helped get him through all the difficulties.

When Luke became tired enough that he slept some in spite of his arm, he had nightmares. He could see the battle over and over again. He watched the mutilated bodies pile up and saw body parts rain from the sky. Tommy would be running up to the bridge one minute and the next he had died, his red blood splattered all about. Luke watched as the bullet made a large round hole in Ronald Crowder's forehead, and he died with his face crunched in pain and disbelief. Scenes he hadn't taken time to consider during the battle came crashing down on him now and buried him in horror and grief.

The soldier he now shared the tent with had been drinking to mask the memories. There always seemed to be some liquor to be had. Arnold would be turning into a drunk if he didn't slow down.

Luke wondered how much the war would change him. He might not be the same man when he got home, but he would get home. He felt more determined than ever to make it through the war. He figured if he could survive Antietam, he could survive anything.

Luke wrote to Leah and told her all about Antietam. He explained the march to Maryland accounted for why he hadn't been able to write sooner. He told her about the battle but just said it was a bloody one with fierce fighting. He didn't go into the gory details. He wanted to spare her, but he also wanted to spare himself from reliving it.

He told her he'd been grazed in the upper arm again, but it was a flesh wound, and no bone had been hit. He wrote that he sure wished she could take care of him again. He signed off by writing, *You know I love you and our baby. My love is so intense, you must feel it, even all those miles away. I miss you more than words can tell.* What an understatement!

They were marching again, but no one had told them where. It had been cloudy, so Luke didn't even know for sure in which direction they were headed. Even though the pace moved slower, Luke felt weaker, and his arm wouldn't stop aching.

That night, when Luke went to replace the soiled bandage on his arm, his fear became a reality. Pus oozed from the red wound. Perhaps, since the infection hadn't spread yet, they could still amputate. He would go to the medical wagon in the morning and see. He tried to look on the bright side and remember he'd now get to go home.

Arnold staggered into the tent, still carrying his booze. He tripped and fell, splashing the whiskey all over Luke's wounded arm. It burned so badly, Luke clenched his fists, stiffened his body, and gritted his teeth, but he still had to yell out. Arnold passed out half on his bedroll, and Luke just left him there. He didn't feel like trying to drag him up.

The next day, Luke's arm seemed some better. He remembered his arm had been drenched in whiskey and wondered if that had anything to do with it. He vaguely remembered his father mentioning something about a study done by Oliver Wendell Holmes Sr., and a report in England from a nurse, Florence Nightingale. Both had talked about the benefits of keeping wounds clean, and Holmes had advocated the use of an acid. Maybe the whiskey would serve as an acid. It probably wouldn't hurt anything, except sting worse than a roomful of hornets. If it saved his arm though, he would endure it.

Arnold seemed surprised when Luke gave him some money and asked him to buy him some whiskey, but he did it. He brought back a bottle for each of them.

Luke's arm continued to improve after he kept pouring whiskey on it. Luke knew Leah made her tinctures with liquor as a preservative. Perhaps that's what had kept his first gunshot wound from becoming infected. He also recalled she insisted upon changing his bed to clean sheets, and he'd laughed at her. He should've known her instincts were good. When it came to healing, she and Granny Em seemed to have a sixth sense.

———————————————

October had turned cold, as it usually did in the mountains. Hawk set his rabbit traps again. If he caught enough at one time, they sometimes skewered them in the fireplace. If not, they made rabbit stew.

They had harvested all the vegetables except some of the turnips and greens. They would be good for a little longer. Hawk would pull the rest of the turnips and put them in the root cellar before the ground became frozen for an extended period of time.

Leah's middle continued to grow, but she wasn't as large as she'd been with the twins at five months. Granny Em thought it would be one baby this time, but no one knew for sure.

CHAPTER TEN

Christmas

TOWARD THE END OF OCTOBER, Leah heard a wagon pull up. She looked out to see Lawrence help Ivy and Patrick out of a wagon. A large male slave also hopped out of the back. Something must be wrong, because Ivy had vowed never to set foot in the highlands again. Leah hurried to find out.

Ivy hugged her and laughed. "I bet you never expected to see me up here again."

"Not after what you've told me. Come inside out of the cold wind and tell me what's wrong."

Introductions were made. The slave's name was Moses, and he was Jasper's son. Leah had to tell the slave to sit down twice before he did.

"Moses can't talk," Ivy informed them, tears filling her eyes.

When Ivy could no longer speak, Lawrence explained why they were there. "The Confederate Conscription Act has been changed, and all those who originally paid not to go are eligible again. I've been called up, and I'm to report in a week."

By now, huge tears were rolling down Ivy's face. "It's just wrong," she sputtered.

Lawrence put his arm around her. "Now, crying isn't going to help, dear," he said softly and kissed her forehead.

Patrick had scooted closer to Lawrence on the sofa with a worried look on his small face. Lawrence was the only father Patrick knew.

"You'll stay with us then," Leah said to her sister as she realized the intent of this visit.

Ivy nodded and looked at Granny Em. She and Granny Em had been at odds the last time Ivy had been here, but Ivy had changed a lot since then. She'd accepted Christ as her Savior, she'd fallen in love with her husband, and they both doted on Patrick.

"Of course you'll stay with us," Granny Em told her. "Where else would you go?"

"Gold Leaf is pretty deserted," Lawrence explained. "Hester Sue has moved in with some relative out of state, and most of the slaves have run off. A few of the older ones, like Bertha and Jasper, are left."

"My mother has died," Lawrence said. "I guess Ivy wrote you about that. We discussed it, and bringing her and Patrick here seemed like the best option. I didn't want to leave them at Fair Oaks alone."

"Come," Leah said to Ivy, "we'll rearrange some things while the men bring in your things."

"We brought some flour, sugar, and salt," Ivy said. "There wasn't much to be had, but Lawrence managed to use his influence and get a large sack of each."

"That will be a big help," Leah said. "We're running really low on sugar and salt, and we're completely out of flour. There's none to be bought here. I'll put you and Patrick in the room with the trundle bed. Moses can have the back guest room, and Patsy can stay with me."

"I don't mind if Patsy rooms with me." Ivy turned to Patsy. "I won't treat you as my slave this time."

"I think this will work better for us all," Leah said. "With Luke gone, our bedroom seems awfully big. It's more like a suite, really."

"When the baby comes, I'll be there to help tend it too," Patsy said with a smile.

Leah noticed Ivy came with just two trunks this time, one for Patrick and one for her. Moses had his things in a half-full gunny sack. When he and Lawrence set the last trunk in Ivy's bedroom, Moses handed Leah a letter from his pocket. It read:

> My dear chile,
>
> I'm sendin you my son, Moses. I'm gettin old and week, and I don't think I'll last the winner. Don't greeve for me. I've had a good life and I'm reddy to meet my Maker.
>
> You knows I've always loved you. Moses be needin a good place to stay till this awfull war be over. I think he mite be a help to you to, if your husband has to go off to fite.
>
> Moses was sold and lived away from me for years. He had his tonuge cut out for talkin back to his marster, but he can rite. He's reel smart and picks up things fast. He's riting this letter as I tale it to him.
>
> He be none to sure bout comin there, but I told him to give it a try. I be sure you'd treat him good.
>
> Agin, no that I love you sweet Leah. I'd come too if my helth was better. I'd love to see you one more time but we might have to save that for Paradise. You take care now.
>
> Love,
>
> Jasper

Leah felt tears slide down her face. She looked up to see Moses watching her, and she smiled at him through her tears. He nodded slightly and went downstairs to help Lawrence get the rest of the things from the wagon.

Lawrence ate supper with them and stayed the night. He would leave right after breakfast in the morning. He planned to leave the wagon and three of the horses. He'd ride his fourth horse home.

"Do whatever you want with any of it," he told them. "If the horses get too much to feed this winter, sell them, give them away, or whatever."

The next morning, Ivy and Patrick walked out to tell Lawrence good-bye privately. The others had already said theirs. Her sister and nephew both came back in crying. Leah knew how they felt. War separations were about the worst kind. She missed Luke more every day.

Leah could tell Moses felt very uncomfortable at first. He sat with them when they told him to, but he watched everyone cautiously. After Hawk encouraged him, he followed Hawk and helped with everything from milking to checking the traps. Eventually he began to smile when someone teased or something funny happened.

Patrick behaved well for a boy of seven. He had bright blue eyes and blond hair. He loved to follow Hawk and Moses around when his mother let him. They took him to help check the traps if the weather allowed, and he came back telling Ivy all about what he'd learned. Hawk made a good teacher.

Moses seemed especially careful around Patsy, but he watched her often, especially when she wasn't looking. Leah thought he might be interested, but he probably didn't know how to begin to show her.

Leah went out of her way to be kind to Moses and make him feel welcome. She'd loved Jasper as her second father on the plantation, and her heart went out to Moses. That someone had cut out his tongue made her shudder. It reconfirmed Luke had chosen the right side.

When she looked at Ivy, however, she remembered what a good man Lawrence had always been, and he would be fighting for the Confederacy, the same as her half brother, Paul. They'd be fighting to kill Luke. What a miserable thought.

"I still don't know how to cook or do many household tasks," Ivy said, "but I'd like to learn."

"You sure have changed," Granny Em told her. "I wouldn't have thought you're the same girl."

"I'm not. Jesus changed me."

"Hallelujah!" Granny Em exclaimed.

Leah began making Luke's Christmas presents. She wanted to have them made and get them in the mail in plenty of time to reach him for Christmas.

She'd knitted him four pairs of socks and a navy-blue wool scarf. She knew by some of the things he'd said that keeping dry socks without holes could be a problem.

Hawk and Granny Em had also helped her make a pair of leather gloves. Hawk took rabbit pelts, tanned the hide, cut out the gloves, and trimmed the hair, especially in the finger parts. Leah and Granny Em sewed them to make a warm pair of gloves. The leather felt soft and supple, and the rabbit fur on the inside made them silky and warm. Leah felt pleased with how they looked. She mailed the package off in November.

November brought their first snow, a pretty, fluffy one. It left the farm whitewashed and full of wonder. Ivy went out with Patrick and let him play.

Moses didn't have a coat. He'd been wearing two or three shirts, but he owned only three. The women set about to make him a winter coat.

Leah and Granny Em measured him. He appeared extremely nervous if Patsy touched him, and she seemed hurt by this.

One of them worked on it for the most part of four days. They'd padded and lined it to make it warmer. Hawk had fashioned some oblong wooden buttons from tree twigs and meticulously worked holes in them.

Moses smiled from ear to ear and mouthed *thank you* to each one, even Patsy. It did Leah's heart good to see his happiness.

The next morning, Moses sat at the kitchen table waiting for Leah to come down. Leah or Hawk usually got up first, and the others would come by breakfast time. Moses handed Leah a note that read:

I's likes to step out with Patsy. How does I go bout it?

Leah sat down at the table too. She looked at Moses, and he watched her every move. "It'll be harder since it's wintertime, and you can't comfortably walk around the farm. Why don't you ask her to come with you to check for eggs and feed the chickens or to go to the springhouse to get some things we need. When you get outside, hold her hand to let her know you like her. You can write her some notes too. Patsy can read."

Moses nodded. He wrote something down on his paper with his small pencil, which he always carried in his pocket. He handed it to her.

Does you think she like me?

"Yes, I do, but I think she'll be very surprised that you like her. You need to smile at her more and not act so afraid of her."

Moses started his courtship at breakfast. He smiled at Patsy a great deal and would meet her gaze without turning away. Granny Em noticed it too.

"Is there something up between Patsy and Moses?" she asked Leah as they did the dishes.

"Not yet, but there may very well be something starting."

Leah still got some letters from Luke, but they came less often. She knew he stayed busy soldiering, and she tried to keep the worry at bay, but it became harder when she didn't hear from him. When he'd told her about Antietam, she also became worried. She feared infection would set up in his arm, but apparently it had begun to heal.

She followed the accounts of the battles and skirmishes he sent. He seemed to tell her the facts, but she knew he left out many of the details. He might as well go ahead and tell her, because her imagination would likely paint them far worse than they actually were, and she told him as much.

Moses took Leah's advice. At first, he'd watch for Patsy to come outside for a task, and he'd join her. Then, he began holding her hand when he thought no one else saw. Finally, he started sitting beside her whenever he could.

Patsy appeared pleased. She smiled and laughed easily and seemed content with the situation.

They would need to make all their Christmas presents this year, and with seven in the house, the adults decided to just make gifts for Patrick. Patsy would make him some handkerchiefs with his initial embroidered on them. With a little help, Ivy planned to make him two shirts out of homespun cloth the other three women had woven. Leah wanted to make him a stick horse using one of Luke's old socks for the head. Moses started carving him a wooden gun, and Hawk made him some leather moccasins.

"I'll make him a leather jacket to match," Granny Em said. "I made Edgar a leather jacket the Christmas before I was captured. This one will be even easier, since it's smaller."

They all worked hard on their presents. Since they had to conceal them from Patrick, they worked on them in turns. It wouldn't have worked if they'd all been sequestered at the same time.

As Christmas neared, Emma sent the men to the woods to cut a Christmas tree. Patrick went with them, hardly able to contain his excitement.

"I hope he's not disappointed by the homemade presents," Leah told Ivy. "I know you and Lawrence well enough that I'm sure he's had some lavish toys on other Christmases."

"He's still young," Ivy said. "He doesn't look at the price of the gift but at how much he likes it. Trust me, he'll love these gifts."

"Well, I'm so glad you're here this year," Leah said. "Having a child in the house makes Christmas so much more special."

"It sure does," Granny Em agreed.

"Next year, you'll have your own baby to celebrate with," Ivy said.

The men came back with a pretty tree that made the house smell wonderful. They decorated it by adding holly with red berries; strings of popcorn; bright red hand-tied bows; and a few candles. Patrick chattered the whole time.

Christmas Eve came on Wednesday, and the women baked. They used more of the precious sugar than they had in a long time, but this was Christmas. Special treats would be a Christmas present for them all.

Mr. Hendrix came riding up, leading a mule with a rocking chair tied on it. "This is a Christmas present for the mama-to-be," he said, "from her husband."

He gave a pleased smile. The gorgeous chair had been handcrafted in beautiful detail with oak leaves and acorns carved into the back.

"How did Luke manage this?" Leah asked.

"He sent Mr. Parsons some money and told him to get someone good to make it, and for me to bring it up for Christmas. I've got a bunch of letters for you too."

"I've got some for you to mail. Let me get them. Won't you come in and have a Christmas cookie and some hot spiced cider."

"Well now, I don't mind if I do."

Leah read her letter from Luke first. It came tucked inside a beautiful Christmas card.

> My dearest Leah,
>
> The sutler had some Christmas cards, so I'm sending one to you, Ivy and Patrick, Granny and Hawk, Patsy, Moses, and Father and Maggie. I'm including letters in yours, Granny's, and Father's.
>
> I got my Christmas package from you and opened it with great enthusiasm. I love it all. The socks and scarf were sorely needed, and that's the most wonderful pair of gloves I've ever seen. They're so warm and comfortable. Thank you so much.
>
> I hope you received your present from me the same time this letter was delivered. I knew we still had a cradle there at the farm, but I also knew we didn't have a rocking chair. If I can't be there to hold our baby, at least you can rock it in the chair I provided. Merry Christmas, darling.
>
> Thank you for all your letters. You've been consistent in sending me a packet every time one of mine is delivered to you. They do me more good than you'll ever know.
>
> Along the first week in November, the President relieved McClellan of his command and gave it to General Burnside.

He wants to launch a new campaign to take Richmond, and I imagine that will entail some fierce fighting.

I think the horrors of war are worse than any of us thought they would be. Camp life also leaves much to be desired, and it's going to get even harder as winter becomes rougher.

I've been involved in another large battle. I didn't receive a gunshot wound in this one, but it turned out to be a disaster. General Burnside had planned to race to Richmond before Lee's army could stop him, but we didn't receive the pontoon bridges we needed to cross the Rappahannock River. We ended up having to build the bridges ourselves. By the time we did all this and started to cross, the enemy had set up and began to fire. We also had to fight in the city, and none of us had trained for that.

The Confederates were entrenched on the high ground again. They held their positions, both south of Fredericksburg and on a strongly fortified ridge, known as Marye's Heights, just west of the city. We were told to charge the ridge.

The whole hill seemed to be on fire. Flames from the heavy fighting and artillery were everywhere, and the Rebels kept firing. Bullets fell from the sky like hail, or you could spell it another way. I fell down by a body thrown into me from the blast of a shell, and I lay stunned for a while. When I gathered my wits and got up, we were in retreat. I only had some minor scratches.

Our men tried to take that hill at least two more times. They fell in masses, the carnage unreal. When the battle ended, and we left in defeat, there were so many bodies covering the area up to the ridge that I couldn't see any ground. Before me lay a carpet of dead men.

It appeared almost as bad in Fredericksburg itself. Layers of corpses lay around, often several men thick. Some even dangled from balconies. A surgeon had commandeered a house, and the legs and arms piled up higher and higher in the corner.

The battle lasted for almost five days, and, it seemed to me to be the worst defeat we've had. The total casualties have been reported at 18,000, with two-thirds of those Union. I'm praying each battle isn't as bad as Antietam and Fredericksburg—all these dead and wounded, and nothing to show for it. We tied at Antietam and have been defeated mercilessly at Fredericksburg.

About now, you must be wishing you hadn't asked me to give you details. I apologize for the appalling descriptions. After all, this is Christmas. I'm fine, so we can be thankful for that. After this battle, it's quite a miracle.

When you go to bed on Christmas Eve, know I'm imagining myself beside you. When you get up on Christmas morning, I'll be pretending I'm holding you in my arms and kissing you. Know that my thoughts are always with you. I adore you.

All my love,

Luke

Each one in the house got mail that day. How like Luke to be thoughtful enough to send Moses a card, although they'd never met. Moses held it for the longest time and looked at it. Leah felt sure he'd never gotten any mail before.

Ivy got three pieces of mail. Besides the card from Luke, she and Patrick got a package from Lawrence, and she also had a letter from him.

When Ivy gave him permission, Patrick tore into his package right away. He had a game of quoits, where rings were tossed at a stick.

Ivy had a beautiful royal-blue lined wool cloak and a cameo brooch. The cloak would be good for the cold winter. She seemed even more interested in the letter, however, and she gave bits of information as she read. "He says he hasn't been given much training, but he's been promoted. He's been in some skirmishes, but nothing major. They're now headed west toward Tennessee but they'll be quite a bit south of here. He says to tell everyone Merry Christmas for him and to tell Patrick he loves him, misses him, and thinks of him often."

They sang some Christmas songs, and Leah wished Luke could be there to play his fiddle. She sighed. She just wanted Luke home. When she went to bed, she thought of Luke somewhere in the cold and tried to imagine him here beside her instead.

The next morning Leah heard Patrick trying to get his mother up to open presents before daylight. She smiled to herself. Her baby gave a hefty kick.

"Are you wanting to get up, too, little one?" she whispered.

She again thought of Luke pretending he was holding and kissing her. She touched her lips. How she wished it could be true. She closed her eyes and said a prayer for him. Her own thoughts fluttered around his memory like a moth to a candle.

They ate a breakfast of eggs, sausage, grits, biscuits, and pre-serves. It'd been a long time since they'd had this much, because they'd been trying to conserve. Then they opened presents.

The tree couldn't contain all the presents, and they stacked out into the room. Someone hadn't remembered the adults weren't giving each other presents. Leah was one of them, but she'd just knitted socks for all the men and wool stockings for the women. There were more packages than that.

Many of the presents were wrapped in homespun and tied with yarn. The homespun had been folded and not cut, so it could still be used later. Some of the items were in cloth bags tied at the top.

They all watched Patrick open his presents first. Leah hadn't tried to wrap her stick horse but just placed it under the tree. She'd embroidered eyes and a nose on the sock, used scraps for the ears, and added threads for the mane. She'd stuffed the sock and tied it onto the large end of the stick Hawk had cut for her.

Patrick seemed thrilled. He came and hugged her neck, and then he tried it out. He looked adorable galloping around on it. "Thank you, Aunt Leah."

He opened his wooden gun from Moses. He loved it, too, and hugged Moses and thanked him. Moses looked very pleased.

Patrick had to put on the moccasins from Hawk right away. He walked around enjoying the feel of them with a proud grin on his face. He treated the leather coat from Granny Em the same way.

Patsy had embroidered a P on his three handkerchiefs. She'd made one with white, one with light blue, and one with black thread.

Ivy had made him a white shirt and a light-blue one, but she'd also brought a new picture book for him when she came. He hugged her neck and thanked her, like he had everyone else.

Leah gave hers out to the adults next. They started protesting. "You weren't supposed to do anything for us," Granny Em said.

"It's not much, just something I made."

"How did you manage all these?" Hawk asked. "How many pairs of socks or stockings did you make?"

"A dozen pair. I mailed Father and Maggie a pair too. All of you thought I've been working on Luke's, but they weren't all for him."

"I thought you were knitting slower than usual." Patsy laughed.

"There are many more presents under the tree," Hawk said with a knowing smile.

"Hawk, what are you up to?" Leah asked.

He handed out the presents, and they all had a beautiful pair of moccasins. Moses also had a pair of leather gloves. Hawk had been busy too.

They sat and talked while Patrick played. They cooked and ate a special Christmas dinner of wild turkey Hawk had killed. Hawk and Moses did the chores, but otherwise everyone stayed together all day.

Leah felt sure Hawk and Granny Em had given each other something special in private. Since they didn't volunteer the information, however, she didn't ask. She also wondered if Moses and Patsy had done the same. They were both giving the other special looks.

They ate leftovers and baked goods for supper. Hawk read the Christmas story from the Bible that night, and his rich voice filled with intensity.

Emotion washed over Leah. "I'm so glad you're all with me this Christmas. You've made it very special."

CHAPTER ELEVEN

Birth and Death

THE ONLY GOOD THING ABOUT Luke being gone now was he couldn't see her bulging, cumbersome stomach. As the new year progressed, Leah grew more and more uncomfortable. She felt stretched and bloated, and she had a hard time stooping, sitting, or lying down.

When a fierce snowstorm hit, only Hawk and Moses braved the cold. The blizzard piled the snow in drifts, and the wind continued to whip it around, even after it stopped snowing.

Moses would come in from the barn and shake his head to say he didn't like this weather. Leah understood. She hadn't been accustomed to the mountain winters when she first came here either.

Leah started giving Patrick some of his lessons. Once she got down into a chair, she could sit and do that while the others did the other chores. Getting up could be a struggle, though.

Leah had started knitting and sewing clothes for her baby. She'd spent the months before Christmas knitting Christmas presents, but she knew she had time to get things ready. Besides, she still had most of the things she'd made before the twins were born, and Granny Em and Patsy liked to help too.

The weather had been so bad most of January that Mr. Hendrix didn't make it up the mountain. Then the snow melted, and the roads turned into a slick, muddy mess, which would freeze again. He finally came near the end of February. He told them President Lincoln had formally signed the Emancipation Proclamation on January the first.

"Does that mean Moses is free now?" Patsy asked.

"As far as we're concerned, he's been free," Leah said, "but he won't be free if the South wins the war."

Leah had letters from Luke and Father, and Ivy had one from someone she didn't recognize. Leah tore into her letter, but she noticed Ivy opened hers reluctantly.

Leah had started reading her letter when she heard Ivy scream and start sobbing. Leah knew what must've happened—the same thing she'd tried to keep pushed from her thoughts. Leah went to her sister and held her the best she could with her protruding stomach. It took several minutes before Ivy stopped wailing, but silent tears replaced it.

"It's Lawrence?" Leah asked.

Ivy nodded and handed her the letter. It was a short one. Lawrence had been killed in Tennessee at the Battle of Stones River near Murfreesboro. Twenty-five thousand had been killed or wounded that day.

The Union forces had held higher ground, and their artillery had cut the Confederates to pieces. After three days, General Bragg realized Union reinforcements were coming, and he withdrew his Confederate troops.

Ivy took to her bed, and Hawk led Patrick to the barn. When they came back, Patrick had been crying, but he seemed better than Leah expected.

Leah left Ivy alone the rest of the day. Her sister stayed in her room and didn't come down for supper. Moses took Patrick to sleep with him for the night.

Leah read her letters. The one from Father just thanked her for the presents. He said Christmas had been hard for Maggie and him, but having each other had made it bearable. They were growing close, and he was grateful for that.

Luke's letter spoke mainly of the difficulties of camping in the cold. He also kept thinking of Leah as her time grew nearer, and he hated he couldn't be with her. Then he began to describe another offensive. According to the dates in the letter, this one had gotten to her quickly.

General Burnside is determined to restore his reputation and the morale of his Army of the Potomac. To accomplish this, he planned a surprise crossing of the Rappahannock River south of Fredericksburg. This would allow us to flank Lee's troops. At the same time the cavalry would cross the river at Kelly's Ford, about 20 miles to the north and strike Lee's rear, as well as destroy his supply lines. Some officers complained to President Lincoln that the plan involved too much risk, and the President stopped the assault. Therefore, Burnside revised his plan but reversed the original sequence. Instead of crossing the Rappahannock south of Fredericksburg, he planned to move upstream and cross at Banks Ford. We began marching on January twentieth in unseasonably mild weather. That evening a steady rain began, and it persisted for two days. Everything became saturated, including us. The roads were knee-deep in mud and almost impassable. After struggling for two days to move troops, wagons, and artillery pieces, Burnside yielded to complaints from his subordinates and reluctantly ordered his army back to camp near Fredericksburg. This time the weather defeated us. The Mud March became Burnside's last chance to command the Army of the Potomac. Lincoln replaced him with General

Joseph Hooker on January 26, 1863. I'm now under Hooker's command . . . .

Well, at least Luke had been in Virginia when Lawrence had been killed in Tennessee. Now if Luke would just stay safe. But how could a soldier be safe in war?

When breakfast was ready the next morning, Leah went to get Ivy. Her sister looked horrible. Her eyes were red and swollen, and her eyes had a distant, forlorn look.

"Now, this won't do, Ivy. You can't pull within yourself like you did when Mama died." Leah thought Ivy wasn't going to answer, and she didn't even know if her sister heard her. She seemed to be lost in her own nightmare.

"I had Lawrence to see me through then," Ivy finally said and started crying again.

Ivy had turned away from Leah, so she put her hand on Ivy's shoulder for comfort. Leah tried hard not to imagine what she would do in the same situation. She knew Ivy needed to grieve and the hurt must be almost unbearable, but she couldn't allow her to give up and waste away. "You know Lawrence wouldn't want this. Get up and come down to breakfast for him. Do it for Patrick. Patrick needs you now more than ever, and you need him too."

"Patrick?" It sounded as if Ivy thought of her son for the first time. "I haven't even told Patrick." Tears were still streaming down Ivy's face, but she'd come back to the present, and her eyes looked clearer.

Leah felt relieved. She could help this Ivy. "Hawk took him to the barn and told him yesterday. I don't know what he said, but Patrick seems to be doing fairly well. He'll be doing better when he sees you're okay."

Ivy thought a minute and nodded. Leah left so Ivy could get dressed. She met Patsy at the door.

"I came to help you dress this morning," Patsy said to Ivy. "It'll be like old times."

"Thank you," Ivy said.

Leah went downstairs marveling at how Ivy had changed over the years. She knew it, but she'd never been around Ivy in recent years to actually see it. At one time, Ivy wouldn't have dreamed of thanking a slave or former slave.

Ivy immediately went to Patrick and hugged him as tears wet her cheeks again. Patrick held on to her too. "I love you, son," she told him, and he said the same to her.

Ivy ate some toast and drank some of Leah's herbal tea. Regular tea and coffee couldn't be had at any price.

They went about their daily tasks, but the day hung heavy around them. Ivy and Patrick took a nap together in the afternoon, although Leah doubted Ivy slept much.

That night Hawk read Bible verses that told of God's promise of eternal life. He looked directly at Ivy. "You can take comfort in knowing for sure Lawrence is with God now, and your salvation gives you the assurance of meeting him there someday."

"But, I'm not even going to get his body to bury."

"He's not in that body now anyway, Ivy," Granny Em said tenderly, "and besides, the ground here is frozen too hard right now to bury anyone."

Ivy only nodded. At least she no longer shut out everything around her.

"Would it help if we held a memorial service of our own?" Hawk asked.

"I think you just did," Ivy answered. "Lawrence would've liked this. He was such a good man. I grew to love him so much."

Leah could tell Ivy tried hard to hold back the tears, but they came anyway. Patrick looked at her and teared up too.

"It's all right to cry," Hawk said. "You need to let your grief out."

"I know you're not ready for this now," Granny Em said, "but God might just have a lot more happiness in store for you down the road. I loved Edgar as much as you do Lawrence. I was devastated when he died, but I went on for Luke, just like you're doing for Patrick. Then, God sent Hawk to me, and now I love him just as much as I ever loved Edgar. At this moment, I love him more, because Edgar was the love of my life in the past, but Hawk is the love of my life now. God may have someone else for you too."

"I don't think so," Ivy said. "I could never love anyone else as I do Lawrence."

Granny Em smiled and looked at Hawk. Leah knew she thought she'd once felt the same way.

Leah wanted to get her delivery over with. She felt uncomfortable and hideous. She still had some uneasiness, but delaying things wouldn't change the outcome.

Her labor started very early in the morning on February the nineteenth. She lay in the dark and didn't move. The first pains were light, and she knew she didn't need to disturb anyone for several more hours. At least she'd experienced the process before and knew what to expect.

Hawk cracked the door but didn't come in. He must have sensed what was happening.

"Are you okay, Leah?" he whispered.

"Yes," she whispered back. "Go back to bed. I won't need anyone until much later."

Later, Granny Em came up to check on her, but Leah sent her down to breakfast. The pains were getting closer together, but she felt they still had time before anything happened. Granny Em had just come back upstairs carrying some of the things she'd need when Leah's water broke.

"This one is a considerate little thing," Granny Em teased. "It let me eat my breakfast first."

The pains became more intense and closer together, but nothing else seemed to be happening. Leah didn't remember the ache being this severe. She felt as if her insides were being ripped apart. Granny Em wiped her forehead with a damp cloth, and Leah realized she'd become drenched in sweat.

"You're doing fine," Granny Em told her. "Just relax between the pains and try to push down when they come."

During one episode so acute Leah had to yell out, Luke took her hand. He took the cloth from Granny Em and wiped her forehead. She tried to turn to see her husband, but everything had turned blurry. The pains were too intense now, and she had no time to ponder anything.

The agony went on and on. Without Luke, Leah didn't think she would have been able to endure it. With a scream she couldn't stop, she felt the baby leave her body. She gave herself a few minutes to partially recover, and then she turned toward her husband. Hawk held her hand. She gave his hand a squeeze and closed her eyes.

"You got you a big, healthy baby girl," Granny Em said, "and she's going to be a beauty."

Leah opened her eyes. The baby lay beside her on the bed, and Ivy sat in a chair by her side.

"I must have slept."

"You slept for about three hours. It's about three o'clock in the afternoon now."

"So, Rachel was born about noon, I guess."

"Yes, just before then. Granny Em stayed with you for about six hours. I'm sorry I didn't come to help, but Patrick seemed upset, and I stayed with him."

"That's fine. I had plenty of help."

"Yes. When you started yelling out, Hawk went to you. He said he couldn't stay down here when you needed him."

"He was a big help."

Leah didn't know if she wanted to tell them she thought Hawk was Luke at the time. Perhaps Luke had been there, too, at least in spirit. If he'd known what was happening, she felt sure he would have been.

Granny Em came in. "I thought I heard voices. Do you feel like company, Leah? Everyone's dying to see the baby."

Leah pulled herself up in bed a little, and Ivy put another pillow behind her. She picked up her daughter and stared at the little bundle. She weighed almost three times as much as Emmie, the biggest of the twins. She unwrapped her. What a beautiful baby! She had black hair long enough to hang down on her neck. Rachel opened her eyes and looked at Leah. She had dark-blue eyes, but Leah guessed they would darken to brown later.

Patsy, Moses, and Patrick came in. Moses smiled at Leah and Rachel and reached for Patsy's hand. Patrick seemed enthralled with his tiny half-cousin. He began to ask question after question, so Ivy took him downstairs, where they could have a long talk.

Hawk and Granny Em came in last. Hawk looked at her tenderly.

"Thank you," she told him, and their eyes spoke to each other.

He must have known. Hawk must have known she'd seen him as Luke, and he probably understood that's what she needed at the time.

"He's just like Luke," Granny Em said. "I tried to tell him we didn't need him, but he wouldn't listen. I've never seen such men who want to be present at a birthing. It's just not proper, especially when the man's not even your husband."

"It's all right," Leah told her. "I did need Hawk. He gave me the strength to get through the pain."

"Rachel's a big baby." Granny looked at the newborn. "I bet she weighs over nine pounds, but she looks healthy as they come."

"Thank you, Granny Em."

"Pshaw, you did all the work. Now, we're going to move you downstairs until spring. This room's just too cold for the baby. When we just had the downstairs part, we kept a bed set up to the back of the sitting room. We're going to set your bed up in that back corner, and we can hang quilts as a partition if you want."

Amid Leah's protests that she could walk, Moses picked her up as if she weighed no more than Patrick and carried her downstairs. He carefully deposited her on the sofa, then, he, Hawk, and Patsy moved the bed downstairs. When they had it set up in the corner, where the spinning wheel had been, they brought down her bedside table and Rachel's cradle.

"Do you need anything else now?" Hawk asked.

"I'd like to have the desk."

He nodded, and they moved it too. Ivy and Patsy helped her back to bed.

Being at one end of the sitting room meant she heard all the kitchen noises and couldn't easily nap. That didn't seem to bother Rachel, though.

Ivy put Patrick down for a nap, because he seemed more tired than usual. Then, she came downstairs.

"Pull a chair over and talk to me for a while," Leah requested. "Couldn't you nap with Patrick?"

Ivy shook her head. "I feel so jittery inside. I can't sleep, even though I'm not sleeping much at night."

"Is there anything particularly wrong?"

"I'm having nightmares about Lawrence getting blown to pieces."

"I'm sorry." Leah put her hand over Ivy's. "I had nightmares after Luke left, but they left once I found I was expecting."

"Well, that's not a possible cure for me. I know I'm not pregnant. Lawrence and I had been hoping for another child, but it never happened. Lawrence assured me, Patrick was enough for him. He couldn't have loved the boy any more if he'd been born his son. I miss Lawrence so much. Do you think it'll get any better, or will it just get worse?"

"I'm not going to pretend to know exactly how you feel. I know I'd be devastated if Luke died, but I don't think we ever know the full extent of something like that until it happens. I would think it would get easier after some time, but it may get harder before it gets easier."

"I have all the important papers from the plantation. Lawrence wanted me to bring them in case marauders destroyed the house or something. I don't think I'll want to go back there, though, not even after the war."

"Ivy, I love having you and Patrick here. It's been a great treat for me. You're welcome to stay here as long as you need. I would be happy if you stayed forever, but you don't need to make the decision now. Take your time and see what God has planned for you."

"Thank you."

They sat in silence, each with their own thoughts. Suddenly Sam Whitley came to Leah's mind. "I don't think I've told you that we've seen Sam Whitley twice. Once was under bad circumstances, but the other seemed much better."

"Really? I haven't given him much thought in the last years."

Leah proceeded to tell Ivy that Sam was one of the bandits who'd robbed them when she, Luke, and Dr. Moretz were coming back from Ivy's wedding in Salisbury. "He was arrested and served time in prison. Then, he came here to see Luke and me before Luke went in the army. He said he'd felt badly about how he'd treated you and wanted to make sure you were okay."

"He's a little too late with those sentiments, don't you think?"

Leah took a moment to consider her answer. "He really seemed repentant and changed. I don't guess it's ever too late for those feelings, especially with God."

"You're right. I shouldn't hold a grudge against Sam. What happened was as much my fault as his, and I did end up very happy with Lawrence and Patrick. You didn't tell him about Patrick being his son did you?"

"I just told him you were happily married and had a son. He didn't ask any more questions, and I didn't volunteer any more information. Luke and I didn't want him making trouble for your family."

"Good. You did the right thing."

"You haven't told Patrick about his real father then?"

"No. Lawrence became his real father. Sam was just the man who caused me to get pregnant and then abandoned me. He has no claim on Patrick."

"Do you really think that's true? If Sam has changed and is as responsible now as he seems, he might be a help to Patrick as he grows to manhood. Do you have the right to keep them apart, especially now that Lawrence is gone? I don't know the answer, Ivy, but I think you should give it some thought and not make a hasty decision."

"I see your point. Okay, I'll think about it, but neither Patrick nor I are ready to meet Sam now. Did he even tell you how to get in touch with him?"

"No. After we told him you were happily married, he left, saying now maybe he could forgive himself. We might be able to track him down through his father. Mr. Whitley left this area, but he's probably still preaching somewhere in North Carolina."

"No. It's better to leave things as they are. I'll consider what you've said, though, for Patrick's sake."

Despite Granny Em's protest, Leah got up that afternoon and sat at her desk to write Luke. She wanted to tell him about Rachel right away. Hopefully, it wouldn't be too much longer before Mr. Hendrix would come by.

My dear husband,

You are a father! I couldn't wait to tell you the news. I gave birth to Rachel a little before noon today. She's a beautiful girl with jet-black hair and dark blue eyes, which will probably turn brown like yours. The labor took about eight hours in all, and Granny Em thinks she weighs over nine pounds. Rachel and I are just fine. Granny Em suggested to name her Rachel Leigh Moretz.

I saw you beside me during the labor, and that made things easier for me. It turned out to be Hawk holding my hand, but I saw you sitting there, like you did the first time. Perhaps it's because I wanted you here so much and knew you wanted that, too.

As I've told you already, I love the rocking chair. I plan to feed her sitting in it as soon as some of my soreness is gone.

I'm not going to write a long letter this time. I still need to stay in bed. I just wanted to make sure you knew as soon as possible. I love you so much. I can't wait until you're home and can hold us both.

Your loving wife,

Leah

She wrote an even shorter note to Dr. Moretz, and Granny Em added her letters to each of the envelopes. Leah went back to bed, fed Rachel, and they both fell asleep.

Mr. Hendrix came the next day with a small parcel for Leah from Luke. Ivy handed him the two letters Leah had prepared, and Leah opened her package. She pulled out a beautiful silver baby rattle. "How did he know?"

My darling wife,

Are we parents yet? I'm thinking we probably are. I've counted from the last week I was home, and I'm guessing our baby will be born the third week in February. I started to have "Rachel Moretz" engraved on the rattler, but I was afraid to trust my gut feeling that much, in case it turned out to be a boy. We can have it engraved later, for a keepsake, if you wish.

My main problem, as far as the soldiering goes, is surviving the cold and bad weather. Many of the men have been sick from such extreme conditions. We sent two soldiers I knew to the field hospital yesterday.

Some of us have devised a way to have a fire in our tents. I think we would've frozen stiff these cold nights without one. We dig a small area four feet long and two feet wide, half in and half out of our tent, put a flat stone over the ditch, and have wooden barrels stacked outside for chimneys. The chimney draws most of the smoke out. The biggest problem is keeping wood for it. The forest is often quite a walk from our encampment.

When we're in camp for several days, we drill again. At least it keeps us warmer than sitting around, but we're all tired of drilling.

There've been so many desertions that they're now checking our knapsacks to make sure we have no civilian clothes, which would make it easier to leave. The gruesome battles, severe weather, and thoughts of home add to the reasons to desert. Some of the men, especially the few from the South, have gotten letters telling of shortages and deprivation. Some families seem to be starving. I hope nothing like this is happening with you. You would tell me, if it were, wouldn't you? Remember, no secrets.

We've had some shortages of fresh supplies, such as eggs, but the army provides us with enough to keep us from starving. It's not always what we'd like, though, and the sameness of it gets monotonous. With your ingenuity at cooking, however, it wouldn't be a problem. I wish you could cook for me. You'd devise some delicious dishes from these mundane supplies.

If we're in camp, we have services every Sunday. I always go, although many of the men don't. I can't understand this. Of all times in their lives, you'd think they'd need God even more now. I know I do. I read my Bible every day, if I have a chance, and I pray so much it's become a habit to talk to God about everything.

I look at the picture of you, too. I can tell the others, who've seen it, are envious. I not only have a gorgeous wife, but I also get more mail than anyone else. You are such a blessing to me, Leah. I thank God for such a wife.

May my love surround you and build a hedge about you. May God keep you in the palms of His hands, and may we soon be reunited. I'm living for that day.

All my love,

Luke

The whole household changed to revolve around the baby. At first Patsy got up at night and handed Rachel to Leah for feeding. She also took care of diaper changes.

After the first week, Patsy had offered to sleep on a pallet on the floor of the upstairs bedroom, but Leah told her she wanted her to stay downstairs with her. Patsy seemed happy to comply.

Patrick would often play beside the cradle, and sometimes he would just sit and watch Rachel. She fascinated him. When she began to latch onto his extended finger, he became her champion. "Is Rachel hungry?" he would ask. "Does her diaper need changing? May I hold her?" He didn't want her unhappy and crying for one second. In his opinion, whatever Rachel wanted, she should have. He would crawl up on the bed beside Leah and hold Rachel with a contented look on his face. No big brother could have been more devoted.

Rachel soon had the other two men in the family wrapped around her little finger too. Moses's face would light up every time he looked at her, and Hawk was just as devoted to her as Patrick.

"If she's this much of a charmer now," Granny Em teased, "you'd better watch out when she gets a little older."

Granny Em was one to talk. She did everything she could to make things easier for Leah and Rachel. She set up small washtubs in the larder and strung a clothesline around two of the walls. If Patsy or Ivy didn't wash the diapers and baby clothes before they began to pile up, Granny Em did them. She also instructed Leah on foods she should avoid while she was nursing.

CHAPTER TWELVE

Unexpected Visitor

LEAH STAYED IN BED A few days, and then she resumed some of her usual tasks. The days passed more quickly when she stayed busy, and Rachel sure helped with that.

The last days of February turned fairly mild, but March became even rawer than January had been. The wind howled and blew so hard, even the men had a hard time battling against it on their way to the barn. It cut through every inch of exposed skin and sliced into clothing.

Mr. Hendrix came on one of the better days and told them the president had signed a Conscription Act for the Union on March the third. Now, both armies were forcing men to join.

Luke had written a letter full of excitement over his daughter. He sounded elated that Leah and Rachel were doing well.

> I woke up early in the morning on February the nineteenth and I couldn't shake the feeling you needed me. I almost felt you beside me. The feeling lasted for a couple of hours, and I couldn't get back to sleep. Then, it felt as if you had someone to help you, and I relaxed some. I'm glad Hawk came to hold your hand and help you through it. It also comforts me to know you thought I was there. In that way, perhaps I managed to help again. I can't wait to see Rachel . . . .

March went out raging when a blizzard hit the last week. The wind blew so hard, Leah feared the windows might break. Only Moses went out to the barn, because only he had the strength to get through. The snow drifted into piles over a man's head in places.

They were beginning to run short on feed for the animals, but they had enough potatoes to get them by if they had to resort to them. Granny Em said many of the early farmers fed their livestock potatoes over the winter, and the early grass should start coming in before long.

At the end of April, they started losing some of their animals. Someone stole one of the milk cows first. With seven people in the family, not counting Rachel, it would be hard for them to make it with just one cow. They did have a third one with calf, and Hawk put her in the cave, along with two of the horses. If the animals had to stay confined there for an extended period of time, they'd have to muck out the cave, but they couldn't afford to lose all their animals to thieves sneaking around in the night.

Next, they lost one of the horses Lawrence had given them. When three of the six spring pigs were taken, Moses took a rifle and started sleeping in the barn.

The thieves broke into the root cellar and took about half of their food. Moses hadn't heard anything, but a week later they tried to take some chickens, which put up a huge squawk. Moses ran from the barn with his gun, and Hawk and Leah came from the house.

Moses shot first, and the robbers ran. There appeared to be three of them, perhaps a father and two almost-grown sons.

Hawk shot next and knocked the hat off the father's head. "I just wanted to scare him enough, he wouldn't be back. I'm guessing the family must be starving, and they've resorted to stealing."

It must have worked, because they had no more night thieves, and Moses moved back to the house. After a couple weeks with no problems, they also brought the animals from the cave.

Spring came, and the romance between Moses and Patsy had grown stronger. Moses had been paying Patsy special attention all through the winter, but now they were together often. If Moses plowed, Patsy would take him water or drop the seeds behind him.

"What do I do if Moses asks me to marry him?" Patsy asked Leah one night.

"If you love him, and it's what you want, say yes," Leah told her. "I like Moses, and I think he's a good man. Jasper's one of the most special slaves I've ever known and like a second father to me."

"I'm surprised Moses isn't bitter about what happened to him. I think he might have been at first, but I think you've shown him all white folk aren't the same."

They worked hard to get the garden and fields planted. Moses was indispensable. They could never have done all the work without him. Granny Em stayed inside, took care of Rachel, and cooked their dinner, but everyone else, even Patrick and Ivy, helped.

They had to plant more than before. They still had to give a tenth of what they had to the Confederate army, and there were more mouths here now.

Thanks to Hawk's hunting, trapping, and fishing, they'd kept plenty of meat, but they'd run short on vegetables. In addition, they were almost out of flour and sugar, despite how sparingly they'd used it. As an alternative, they wanted to plant more corn for corn-meal, and Hawk hoped to harvest some honey for sweetener.

Another letter came from Luke. He sounded the most despondent of any time yet, and Leah worried about him.

My dearest wife,

I'm doing my share of fighting, and every battle ends in defeat. Are we never going to have success and win this war?

The last battle took place over several days along the first week in May. Our army under Hooker was pitted against Lee's army with about half our numbers. I regret to say that man has an uncanny ability in warfare. I must reluctantly respect him and his men. Lee did the unthinkable and divided his small army to face our much larger force, but he must have known what he was doing because to them went the victory.

Hooker had planned to attack Lee from both his front and rear, but when Lee split his army, that tied up part of our troops. In addition, Lee sent Stonewall Jackson's corps to flank the Union XI Corps. Jackson was wounded by his own man, who mistook him for a Union soldier, and J.E.B. Stuart replaced him. That will be a blow to Lee, for the commander relied heavily on Jackson.

The bloodiest part of the battle came on May the third when Lee launched multiple attacks on our positions at Chancellorsville. The fierce fighting raged on, and the casualties became so heavy, I thought none of us would make it through. At the same time there were other battles taking place nearby.

I received a small graze on the right side of my head. It parted my hair in a strange place, and I had a horrible headache for a couple of days, but it could have been much worse. I'm fine now.

After some other action, Hooker withdrew our army the night of May fifth into the morning of the sixth. It all ended on May the seventh when Stoneman's cavalry reached Union lines east of Richmond. He'd not been the problem to Lee's army Hooker had hoped.

You asked me how I knew so many details about the leaders and battles. Of course, being here gives me some first-hand knowledge, but they tell us little about motives or the Confederates. Someone usually gets a newspaper, and we read about everything. The reporters are thorough in their coverage of all aspects of the war.

I'm glad to hear you're not suffering too greatly in shortages and have enough to eat. It's good Lawrence could bring some staples with him. Lawrence was a good friend, and I'll miss him greatly. I'm keeping Ivy and Patrick in my prayers.

I think of you and Rachel all the time. Please send me reports on how she's growing and what she's doing. I promise you, you won't bore me with those details. Tell me everything that happens with both of you. I need to be able to be back there, if only in my mind. Know that I love you both immeasurably.

Your devoted husband,

Luke

With warmer weather, Leah moved back into her upstairs bedroom. Of course, Rachel and Patsy moved too.

Hawk made three bee gums. He took a section of a hollow tree and added a makeshift roof to house the bees and their honey. He went to the forest, smoked the bees, captured enough of the honeycomb to get some eggs and the queen, and moved her and others to his bee gums. "The other bees will find her, and this will make it easier for us to collect the honey."

"What about the other boxes?" Patsy asked. "Are you going to fill them up too?"

"If I find another hive, I will, but if I don't, we can divide this one later."

"May I help with the bees?" Patrick asked.

"You'd better wait until you're a little older," Hawk told him. "I think you should be around twelve first, but I will need someone to learn how to handle the bees."

Leah looked at Moses, but he shook his head. If Moses didn't want to help, she knew neither Patsy nor Ivy would.

"I will," Leah said, "but you'll have to teach me everything. I know very little."

Hawk smiled at her. "It's not complicated. I think you'll be good at it."

So, Leah's instruction began. Whenever Hawk worked in the bees, she went too. He was a good teacher and explained everything thoroughly.

"Why don't you take that old lace tablecloth that's getting threadbare, attach it to a hat, and it'll keep the bees out of your face," Granny Em suggested.

Leah liked that idea. She also wore gloves, so with long sleeves and skirts, she felt pretty well protected.

She discovered the honeybees weren't as aggressive as she'd thought. Unless they felt threatened, they wouldn't sting. With Hawk's help, she and the bees grew to understand one another, and Leah found she enjoyed beekeeping.

Moses and Patsy came to Leah at the first of June. They both smiled so brightly, Leah guessed what they wanted.

"Moses has asked me to marry him," Patsy said, "and I agreed. What do we need to do?"

"That's a good question. Luke and I and Granny Em and Hawk were married by an itinerate preacher, but I haven't heard of one in this area since the war heated up. Let me talk with Granny Em, and we'll see what we can come up with."

Granny Em didn't have any ideas either. In these uncertain times, no one wanted to leave the farm, and there didn't seem to be much else to do. Leah prayed for a solution.

Leah heard two riders come up, and she looked out. Mr. Hendrix was one, but she didn't recognize the other one at first. She ran out to get her mail and stopped short. Sam Whitley!

Mr. Hendrix gave her the letter, collected his money, and left.

Sam stood waiting. "I hope it's all right for me to come by," he said. "I was in the area, and I wanted to ask about Ivy. I know many of the families in the South are having hard times. Have you heard from her?"

"You might say that. She's here. She came to stay with me when the Confederate army conscripted her husband. He was killed the last of January."

"Is she okay?"

"She's taking it hard, but she's making it by focusing on her son."

"May I see her? I'd like to apologize to her for the way I treated her."

Leah didn't know what to do. It wasn't her place to tell Sam about Patrick. Neither did she know if Ivy would ever want to see him again.

Patrick ran from the barn where he'd been playing with some new kittens. When he saw Leah and the stranger, he slowed down and walked up.

"Sam, this is Patrick Nance," Leah said. "Patrick, this is Samuel Whitley."

"How do you do, Mr. Whitley?" Patrick put out his little hand.

Sam stood rigid, as if frozen in place, and he stared at Patrick. He had turned pale, almost white. "I'm fine, thank you." He finally took Patrick's hand. "How old are you, Patrick?"

"I just turned eight in April. We had a birthday dinner, but I didn't have presents this year. I had lots of Christmas presents, though."

Leah could tell Sam did some quick counting in his head. Because Ivy had married so quickly, however, it would be hard for him to be sure. Yet, he must be thinking about the possibility that Patrick could be his son.

Ivy came out the larder door. "Patrick, it's time for you to come in and wash your hands for dinner." She smiled at the stranger until she recognized him. Then she stopped, gasped, and looked sick.

Leah rushed to Ivy's side, afraid that her sister might faint. "Patrick, would you please show our guest in while I help your mother," Leah called over her shoulder as she led Ivy inside. "She doesn't seem to be feeling well."

Leah helped Ivy to the sofa and turned to Sam, who hadn't taken his eyes off Ivy. "Please have a seat, Mr. Whitley."

"Call me Sam." He sat down on the sofa beside Ivy, who tried to move as far away from him as she could. "Ivy, I'm so sorry to hear about your husband. My prayers will be with you."

She looked at him in surprise. It was the first time she'd really looked into his face since she'd realized it was him.

"I've asked the Lord to forgive me for my irresponsible, thoughtless behavior in the past," he continued. "I'd also like to ask your forgiveness. Do you think you could ever do that, Ivy?"

"You're serious?"

"I'm very serious."

Ivy took in a deep breath. Leah could tell she struggled to do the right thing. "I forgive you. Besides it being my Christian duty, I found a man who loved me deeply, and we were very happy together. So, you see, things turned out okay until he was killed in this awful war." Tears pooled in her eyes.

"The boy . . . " Sam hesitated. "Patrick said he was eight in April."

"Patrick," Ivy said, "go tell Hawk and Moses dinner is almost ready and wash your hands on the way back through the larder."

"Yes, Mama." Patrick left.

Sam turned to Ivy. "Is Patrick mine? He looks an awfully lot like me. Dad has a small portrait of me at ten, and we would pass for twins."

Ivy looked at the man beside her carefully. She looked unsure. "Yes," she finally said. "You left me pregnant, alone, and in sad shape until Luke and Leah came for me, and Luke arranged for me to marry Lawrence. He'd been in love with me and agreed to marry me and raise the baby as his. He was a wonderful husband and father."

"I can believe that. Patrick is one of the most well-mannered and well-behaved boys of eight I've ever met. Does he know?"

"No. Lawrence is the only father he's ever known."

"I think he should be told. It'll be easier for him the younger he is."

"What are you doing now, Sam?"

"I was conscripted into the Confederate army, but right now, I'm on an eight-week medical furlough. I was wounded in an accident, but it's healed now. I report back July fifteenth."

"I'm not sure that I want Patrick to know another father and have him killed in the war too. I think that's too much to ask."

"If I come back at the end of the war, will you tell him and let me see him?"

"Yes. I know Leah thinks Patrick might need a father as he grows up. If you come back, I'll tell him."

"Thank you, Ivy. I think you've done some changing over the years too."

"I have. Christ and Lawrence have helped me change. I think I needed it." She smiled slightly.

"Not as much as I did. Prison gave me plenty of time to think. I saw my mistakes and turned back to God."

Leah heard the men come in. "Would you like to stay for dinner, Sam?"

"If you're sure it's okay." He said it to Leah, but he looked at Ivy.

"It's okay," Ivy said.

Introductions were made. Granny Em and Patsy were the only others who knew who Sam was. Granny Em watched him closely.

Dinner turned out to be more relaxed than Leah had anticipated. Sam seemed charming, and he paid a lot of attention to Patrick.

"Why are you in this area, Sam?" Granny Em asked.

"My father is back in Boone for a while, and I came to stay with him."

"He's still preaching?" Leah asked.

"Yes, he is."

"Do you think he would come here and marry Moses and Patsy? I haven't seen any circuit riders here in over a year."

Sam smiled. "I think I can talk him into that. How soon do you want the wedding?"

"It'll just be us. Give us a week, but any time after that."

"I'll talk with Father and come back and let you know. Thank you for dinner. This is the best meal I've had in a while. Most people are getting very short of supplies."

"We are, too, but Hawk has kept us in meat, and we've had corn for meal. We're making it."

"Would it be all right if I take Patrick for a ride on my horse?" Sam asked.

"Please, Mama," the boy said.

"I guess." Ivy looked at Sam. "I'm trusting you not to say anything inappropriate."

"You can trust me, Ivy. I won't let you down again."

They watched. First Sam put Patrick in the saddle and led the horse around the area between the house and barn. Then he mounted behind the boy and they rode out to the road. They didn't go far, because they were soon back. Sam jumped off and lifted his son down. Ivy and Leah walked out.

"Don't leave me alone with him," Ivy whispered to Leah.

"Thank you, Mr. Whitley," Patrick said. "I had fun."

"I enjoyed it too. We'll have to do it again sometime."

"Yes, sir!"

"Go tell Granny Em about the horse," Ivy told her son.

"Bye now," he shouted back to Sam.

"He's wonderful," Sam said. "I'm overwhelmed with the emotions I'm feeling. Thank you for telling me the truth, Ivy, and for letting me spend a little time with my son. I'll see you again in a few days with information about the wedding."

Ivy nodded and turned to go inside. She looked back as Sam rode away. He turned to wave, and she waved back. "I see what you meant about him seeming responsible now," she told Leah.

Leah had a letter from Luke to read. This was the first time she'd had to wait to tear into one.

> My dearest Leah,
>
> It's hard to believe Rachel is almost four months old. Are her eyes turning brown? I'd prefer that she have emerald eyes, like her mother. I love everything about her mother.
>
> It sounds as if Patrick is doing a good job of acting the big brother for Rachel. He must be a fine young man. I hope we can have more children, when I get home. Do you think you'd like that? I remember you once told me you'd take as many as the Lord and I saw fit to give you.

Oh, darling, I miss our teasing. I've been gone a little over a year, but it seems like an eternity. Will this awful war ever be over? I'm ready to come home.

The U.S. Department of War has authorized the recruitment of colored troops. It makes sense to me that some of them might want to fight for their freedom. It seems the government plans to keep them in separate units, though. That doesn't seem right to me. I hope they're not discriminated against there too.

We got news Grant is attacking Vicksburg, Mississippi. He had heavy losses at first, but he now has the city under siege. I'm not sure how long they can hold out, or what may happen.

The Army of the Potomac seems to be getting ready to move again, but I have no idea where we'll be headed this time. Drill, march, and fight seems to be the extent of what's expected of me, and I'm tired of it. I received another promotion, but what I need, if this war can't be over, is a furlough. I need to come home. The problem is, if I came home now, I don't know if I could make myself come back to fight. Maybe something will happen soon to change the tide of things, and we'll win the war. Wouldn't that be wonderful!

I love you with every inch of life that's in me. Thoughts of you and Rachel make me able to endure all this. Take care of yourselves for me.

With undying love,

Luke

Leah felt his depression and desperation. This war was wearing him down. She bowed her head and prayed for him.

Sam came back in three days. His father could conduct the wedding ceremony on Friday, July the third. They planned it for eleven o'clock, and this pleased Patsy and Moses.

Patrick took Sam to see the kittens. Leah noticed they chatted together like best friends as they walked toward the barn.

"I believe Sam will be a great father," Leah told Ivy.

"Yes, it looks like it," Ivy said.

Leah couldn't tell what Ivy really thought. She sounded noncommittal, but at least she no longer seemed to have any negative emotions.

When they came from the barn, Sam took Patrick on another ride. This time they were gone a little longer, but Ivy didn't seem as worried.

"I'll see all of you for the wedding," Sam told them as he left.

The women took another of Ivy's old dresses and reworked it for Patsy. The powder-blue color looked so pale that it could have been mistaken for white.

Leah had also made Moses a new white shirt. He didn't have a suit, but she washed and ironed his best pair of pants. They were dark brown and should do fine.

Patsy had wanted to get married across the road in the meadow where Luke and Leah had married. When they got up on the third, however, heavy clouds lined the sky, and by ten o'clock a light drizzle fell.

"I believe we'd better make plans to hold the wedding in the sitting room," Granny Em said.

"You don't think it'll clear off?" Patsy asked.

"It doesn't look like it."

Reverend Whitley and Sam came a little early, and it was a good thing they did. The sky opened up just after they arrived, and it poured.

Hawk gave the bride away, but they didn't have attendants. Patrick sat enthralled with the ceremony. He sat between Ivy and Sam and watched closely.

Rachel decided to be fussy. After Hawk's part in the ceremony, he took her and kept her quietly entertained.

Afterwards, they all sat down to dinner. Granny Em and Ivy had cooked a venison stew, which could stay warming and not have to be watched while they conducted the wedding. Leah had used the last of the flour and sugar to make a cherry cake for dessert.

Sam and his father joined them. Rev. Whitley kept watching Patrick. Leah didn't know what Sam had told him, but she felt sure the grandfather recognized Patrick's resemblance to his son.

Patrick seemed excited about both the wedding and seeing Sam again, but his manners were still excellent. Sam beamed with pride as Rev. Whitley watched the boy.

"What do you plan to do after the war, Sam?" Ivy asked.

"I'm undecided right now. My uncle has offered me a place on his farm in Stanly County. Their three sons have already been killed in the war, so I'd probably inherit their farm if I went. I just don't know if that would be best. I'll keep praying about it. What about you? Will you stay here?"

"I'm unsure of that too. We own a plantation in Anson County, but I don't know what shape it'll be in when the war's over, and I don't think I want to run it. Of course, if we don't win the war, who knows what will happen?"

"You're supporting the South, then?" Rev. Whitley asked Ivy.

"Yes, we owned slaves, although my husband wasn't as fanatical a supporter of slavery as many of his neighbors. He didn't want to join the war, but he was conscripted."

"Like Sam," Rev. Whitley said. "We've tried to stay neutral, but the governments won't let us. I don't have strong political views, but if I'd had to make a choice, I'd side with the United States. Sam feels much the same way, but he waited as long as he could, and he ended up being conscripted by the Confederacy."

"It seems many of the soldiers are deserting," Leah said.

"I won't," Sam told them. "I'll do my duty from the perspective of fighting for North Carolina. I like the South as a region. If the Confederacy wins, maybe we can change some of the cruel policies dealing with the slaves and eventually do away with slavery altogether. Perhaps I should have done like Mr. Moretz and volunteered for the Union, but it's too late for that now. I took an oath, and I'm not comfortable with breaking it to desert."

"Will you get killed like my father?" Patrick asked with a worried look.

"Not if I can help it," Sam said. "If I do, I'll get to go be with Jesus, as I'm sure Mr. Nance did, but I plan to stay safe and come back and see you just as soon as I can."

Patrick nodded. Sam gave him a smile and a wink, and Patrick smiled back.

Sam pulled Ivy off to the side before he left with his father. They talked in a low tone, but Leah still heard it. "Do you need anything, Ivy? My army pay isn't much, but I'd be happy to support you and Patrick. The army will take care of all my basic needs."

"No, we're fine. Lawrence was actually well-off, so we'll have enough for a while. Money doesn't help much right now, anyway. There are few necessities left to buy."

"Could I come to visit next week? I'll be leaving Sunday, and I'd like to see Patrick before I go."

"I think that'll be okay. He's going to miss you. He has so few friends, he's become quite attached."

"I'll miss him, too, but I will return from the war. I'm going to do everything within my power, and God willing, I will come back."

Patsy moved into Moses's room that night. They seemed so happy, and Leah rejoiced for them. It made her miss Luke all the more, though.

"I'm so glad Moses came here," Patsy said the next day as she and Leah cooked dinner. "Who'd have thought such a big, strong man could be so gentle? We're going to be very happy together."

"I'm glad," Leah said as she hugged her friend.

Sam came on Friday. He arrived about ten o'clock, so he must've started as early as he could. He and Patrick walked around the farm, talking and playing until dinnertime. Patrick had wanted to ride the horse, but Sam told him to wait until just before he had to leave.

When Patrick started to protest, Sam became firm with him. "If you're going to argue about it," he told his son, "we may not get to go at all."

Patrick hushed then and looked at his father with respect. The way Sam handled it impressed Leah.

"Ivy, would you come for a short walk with me alone?" Sam asked after dinner. "I'd like to ask you something."

Ivy looked as if she were about to panic. Leah hoped Sam realized Ivy was still in mourning, and this would be too early to try to become involved.

"If Leah can come too," Ivy replied.

"If that's what you want." Sam looked disappointed.

Leah followed them out, but she stayed several steps behind. She wondered if Ivy didn't trust him or didn't trust herself. Sam Whitley was a very good-looking man, and he'd handled himself well.

"I just wanted to ask if I write you, will you answer me back? I'd like to know about Patrick and how he's doing. It'll help to get some mail along too. I got very little before, and I felt even more lonely when others were reading theirs."

"Yes. I'm not sure how quickly I'll answer, but I'll write and let you know about Patrick. He can write some too. It'll be a good activity for his lessons."

Sam smiled as if he'd just won a major prize.

Ivy looked into his face but didn't smile back.

"Thank you," Sam said.

Sam left in time to get home before dark. Before he left, he took Patrick on a longer ride. When they came back, Patrick hugged him tightly around the legs.

"You promised to come back," Patrick said.

"I promise to come back if there's any way I can. I promise to do my best to get back." He picked Patrick up, and Patrick hugged his neck. Sam shut his eyes and enjoyed the moment. "I love you, Patrick," he said as he put the boy down.

"I love you too," Patrick answered without hesitation.

Leah looked at Ivy. Her sister had tears in her eyes. Leah wished she knew what Ivy thought.

"Oh, I almost forgot," Sam said after he'd already mounted his horse. "I met Mr. Hendrix, and he sent your mail." He handed down a letter from Luke.

CHAPTER THIRTEEN

Gettysburg

MY DARLING LEAH,

We're moving again. I don't know our destination, but we're headed north. Rumors have it Lee is trying to invade the North again, and we're to stop him.

President Lincoln has replaced Hooker with Meade. We've had so many commanders by now that I'm losing count of them. I hope Lincoln soon finds one that will lead us to victory and end this fighting.

My gut feeling tells me stopping Lee is going to take a major battle. We must do our best to win this one, but success really depends on our leaders. All we soldiers can do is follow orders and fight bravely. We've been doing that and have still lost. Our generals' tactics haven't been enough. It's much like a chess game, and Lee is a very good player.

How I wish you and I could be playing our own board games again! Do you miss all our times together as much as I do? My arms ache for you, and Rachel is growing up without ever seeing the father who loves her so. I want to win this war, but even if we lose, I'm ready for it to be over. I long to be back at the farm with my family.

Since we're marching, I don't have as much time to write as usual. Never forget how much I love you. It's you, Rachel, and God's presence in my life that keep me going. Whatever happens, my love for you will never die, and I remain—

Your devoted husband,

Luke

Leah prayed and prayed for Luke. A defeatist attitude clung to this letter she didn't like. This didn't sound like the strong, competent Luke she knew. Did he feel that something bad would happen soon? She prayed not!

The Army of the Potomac had moved into Pennsylvania, and scouts were reporting Lee's army had drawn close. On July the first, Confederate forces converged on the small town of Gettysburg and drove the Union army back through the streets. The fighting intensified, but at least Luke and most of the soldiers he knew had ended up on the higher ground this time. Cemetery Hill should be easier to defend from the top.

A large building stood on the east portion of the hill. Apparently, it held seminary classes for young women, but they must have evacuated the building.

During the night, reinforcements seemed to arrive on both sides, and Luke knew this would likely be an expansive battle. With so many troops involved, this engagement might very well decide the war.

The next morning, Luke heard battles raging. He could see the smoke and artillery blazes coming from the south, and he could see some of the troops, but he couldn't tell what was happening. Then, the Confederates began attacking his position and the Union troops on nearby Culp's Hill. Fighting grew fierce as the Rebel yells tore through the air, and the enemy tried to break through the Union lines. At least the Confederates were the ones trying to charge up the hill this time. That didn't mean the Federals had no casualties, however. Men fell all along the line, and shots whizzed close to Luke.

He aimed and fired over and over, and Rebel after Rebel fell. He didn't know how many men he killed. He tried not to think about it. In this war, he had to kill or be killed. He'd killed in battle before, but he knew the numbers would be larger here. The Rebs were sitting ducks trying to get up the hill.

By evening they'd expelled most of the Confederate troops around them, but the next morning, the fighting resumed on Culp's Hill. From what Luke could see, the situation there looked similar with the Confederates trying to storm up the hill.

"We're moving a few troops over to help at Culp's Hill," Luke's sergeant called out. "My platoon, follow me."

Luke questioned the move. They'd be much more exposed if they left Cemetery Hill, and Lee could very well send another charge along the position they'd left. But he also knew his opinion didn't matter right now. He reluctantly fell in with his platoon.

At least the two hills were connected, although they couldn't move directly there, because Culp's Hill had more growth and impassible areas. Most of the artillery had been set up on Cemetery Hill, because it had a clearer line of fire. Luke hoped they didn't get caught in some of the shelling.

"We'll try to join our troops on the hill," the sergeant said, "but if we meet some Rebs, we'll take care of them on the way. Moretz, you're one of the best shots. Be on your guard and get up front."

"Yes, sir."

Luke moved to the front of the platoon with a few other men the sergeant called up. His poor performance at target practice had kept him from becoming a sharpshooter, but that didn't keep the officers from noticing him during battles.

They made it about halfway to Culp's Hill, when they ran into a company of Confederates. They were outnumbered four to one. Luke fired and downed about three. The sergeant barked a command, and Luke heard the soldiers behind him retreat. He and one more soldier were left with the enemy. Luke knew they'd never have time to turn and join their platoon without being shot. It was useless to try. He threw down his rifle and raised his hands, and Inman did the same.

Several of the Confederate soldiers raised their rifles and pointed them at Inman and Luke. "We've got no time to take prisoners today," one of them said. "Let's shoot them."

"I want no part in gunning them down in cold blood," another replied, "even if they are Yanks."

"We've been killing Yanks for three days. What's the difference?"

"We're supposed to be gentlemen. That's what the difference is." A general had ridden up. "Soldier, secure the prisoners and send two men to take them to the holding area."

"Yes, sir."

They marched Luke and Inman down the hill and through an area with no fighting. The holding area turned out to be a roughly fenced area with guards. They were shoved in and left. There seemed to be about fifty prisoners there, about the same number of men as in Luke's platoon.

"What's your first name, Inman?" Luke asked.

"Billy. Billy Inman. I'm from Union, Tennessee, and you?"

"Luke Moretz from Watauga County, North Carolina."

Billy looked much younger than Luke, probably about eighteen. He must not have been in the army for long. His eyes still held a shocked look, as if he'd seen things he wished he hadn't.

"Was this your first major battle?" Luke asked.

"It was, and by the looks of things, it may've been my last."

They spent the night in the holding area. A soldier took Luke's jacket and blanket. He looked at his boots, but they were falling apart, so he let Luke keep them. Luke had put what little money he had in the top of his boots, and they didn't think to look there. The prisoners were given water but nothing to eat, and they were moved the next day.

The Confederates herded the prisoners together and transferred them to a more secure area. Here they would be held until they could be transferred to a prison. Another guard went through Luke's knapsack and took all the items he wanted. Thankfully, he left the Bible.

From the comments Luke heard, the Union had finally won this major battle, but losses had been heavy on both sides. He heard one soldier say the railroad cars with Lee's wounded stretched for fourteen miles.

Luke and his fellow prisoners spent two more weeks in the compound. They were fed one meal a day, usually about eleven o'clock in the morning. In the third week, they marched to a train yard, where they sat and waited for the train. All the time, armed guards patrolled the area. Finally, they were placed in cattle cars for transport.

One door of Luke's car had been closed, barred, and bolted. Two armed guards stood in front of the other door. Besides their readied rifles with bayonets fixed, they each had a large revolver. Luke knew these men wouldn't hesitate to shoot to kill.

In the summer sun, the heat inside the cattle car felt like an oven. Some breeze might come through the open door when the train moved, but they'd been packed so tightly with just enough room to sit that none of it reached Luke.

Luke and Billy leaned against each other to find what comfort they could as the train rattled and swayed down the tracks. They soon discovered their train had to pull over to a side rail and wait for every passing train headed north. Luke guessed those trains were carrying soldiers to the lines, but this certainly delayed the trip.

Luke grew hungry and thirsty. He hadn't had much to eat over the last weeks and no water since early morning. His mouth and lips parched from sitting in the packed cattle car in the intense heat.

As night fell, the temperature inside the car fell some, but his thirst grew. They stopped at a station, and Luke asked the guard if he could get some water. He could see a water tank not more than a hundred yards away.

"It's agin regulations," the guard said.

"Anyone know where we are?" Luke asked those around him.

"Couldn't see," someone answered, "but I'd guess we're somewhere in northern Virginia."

According to that, they were headed south, but of course, they would be. The Confederacy wouldn't have prisons in the North. Luke wondered what awaited him. Where would he be imprisoned and what would the conditions be? Something told him they wouldn't be as good as camp life had been.

The train stopped at another station after daylight. They were allowed to get off the train and get water from the water tank where the locomotives replenished. Some of the soldiers drank the water so quickly they got sick. One poor man actually died on the spot. There were three others who'd died during the night in Luke's car. He and five other men were ordered to go carry out the bodies. At least, he didn't have to help bury them.

They were corralled at the station to wait for another train. It came about three hours later, and they were loaded in another cattle car in the same manner as before. Luke must have managed to doze, because when he became aware again, he'd lost all track of time. Hunger gnawed at him until he felt sick.

Several hours later, the train pulled into a station that looked familiar to Luke. He stared to be sure. It couldn't be!

━━━━━━━━━━━━━━━━

On Friday, July the nineteenth, Dr. Moretz and Maggie came in a wagon.

"Father," Leah said as they hugged, "it's so good to see you." She turned to Maggie. She couldn't believe this was Maggie. Why, she stood as tall as Leah. She might never be called a beauty, but she had a pleasant, unassuming expression that looked very pleasing. Her sandy-brown hair and blue-gray eyes made her quite attractive. "This can't be Maggie! Look at you. You're a young lady." Leah hugged her too. "Come in. You've got to see Rachel."

"Why do you think we came?" Dr. Moretz joked.

"To see your eldest daughter, of course, as well as your granddaughter . . . and maybe your mother and stepfather too."

Dr. Moretz laughed. "You're right, as usual."

"Look at her. She's sitting up," Dr. Moretz said as he lifted Rachel from the quilt, where Patrick sat keeping her entertained.

"Father, Maggie, this is Patrick, Ivy's son. Patrick, this is Luke's father and half-sister."

"Like Mama's your half sister?"

"That's right." Leah didn't know Ivy had explained this to her son. Whatever anyone told Patrick, he tended to remember.

"I'm named after Mama's real father. His name was Patrick Ivey," the boy said.

Leah nodded to Patrick and turned to her guests. "Let's get you settled."

"I brought an extra bed, mattress, and bedding in the wagon," Dr. Moretz told her. "I thought that might help with the sleeping arrangements."

"That's perfect. Maggie can sleep with Rachel and me, and we can set up your bed at the back end of the sitting room."

"Where I used to sleep when I was a boy."

"That's right, Clifton." Granny Em came in from her bedroom. "How wonderful to see you again. How long can you stay?"

"We're thinking about two months . . . if that's okay." He held his mother in his arms for a long time.

"And this must be Maggie. How nice to finally get to meet you." Granny Em gave her a hug. "Imagine having a granddaughter I don't get to see until she's fifteen."

By this time, Ivy and Patsy had come from upstairs, and Moses and Hawk came in from outside. Introductions were made, and it almost seemed like a party. Leah took Rachel from her grandfather while the men went to unload the wagon and take care of the horses.

"May I hold her?" Maggie put out her hands.

Rachel leaned over for her. She liked to go to anyone who wanted to give her extra attention.

"Bring her into the kitchen while I help Patsy start supper," Leah told the girl.

They pulled in a small table and chair from the sitting room into the kitchen for Patrick. This allowed all the others to have plenty of room at the table.

"This reminds me of when the Moretzes and Cagles gathered here for the first time," Granny Em said. "We had to pull in an extra table then too. It's good to have the house full again."

"The place looks good, Hawk," Dr. Moretz said.

"Thank you, but Moses has helped the most. His being here has allowed us to plant big gardens too."

"That's good. I'm glad you're here to help with the place, Moses."

Moses smiled and nodded. He seemed comfortable with Dr. Moretz and Maggie here. His attitude had come a long way since his arrival at the farm.

Maggie turned out to be great with Rachel and wanted to help with any task at hand. She might not be the best cook, because she'd grown up with two servants in the house, but she liked to try. Leah enjoyed the girl's easy personality and giving spirit. *She must take more after her father than her mother.*

Moses and Dr. Moretz started cutting wood whenever they could. They had some left over, but there'd been two extremely cold months last winter, and they'd need much more for the coming winter.

Hawk rarely went. Leah knew he would have if the doctor hadn't been there, but Hawk needed to slow down some and take things easier.

Granny Em had quit doing things outside. She still cooked, sewed, spun, wove, and made medicines, but she didn't garden or even gather herbs anymore. Leah had taken over those chores.

Leah liked to watch Granny Em and Hawk together. It gave her a special, warm feeling to see their love. She'd always assumed her mother and father loved each other, but their love hadn't tangibly flowed between them as it did with Hawk and Granny Em. Their eyes always softened when they looked at each other, and their voices held a special tone for the other.

The days passed and soon the middle of August had come. It had been a month since Leah had received a letter from Luke. This had happened before only when his troop was moving into position for a large battle. She prayed nothing was wrong.

Mr. Hendrix did come at the end of August, but he had a letter for Ivy. Leah had rushed out thinking he would have a letter for her, and she couldn't hide her disappointment.

"This letter's been settin' there at the post office for more than two weeks. I was waiting for one from your husband, Mrs. Moretz, but one never came. I hope it's okay if I finally brought it on out."

"It's fine, Mr. Hendrix."

"Here, I'll pay for this one, since it's for me," Ivy said. Leah hadn't even noticed her come up. Her letter came from Sam. Ivy read it and then handed it to Leah to read. "I'm going to need your help and advice here, Leah. I feel so mixed up where Sam is concerned. Read this so we can talk about it later."

> Dear Ivy,
>
> Coming back to the army proved even harder now than it had been the first time. What I really wanted to do was stay in Watauga County, where I could see you and Patrick.
>
> Meeting Patrick and learning I have a son felt too special to put into words. I regret I missed out on his birth and the first seven years of his life, but I understand. Looking at things from a broad perspective, you probably did what was best for you and Patrick, and that's what's most important.
>
> Thank you for letting me into his life now. I'm determined to make it through this war, so I can become a real father to my son. Tell him I'm thinking of him and send him my love.
>
> I wanted to tell you how beautiful you still are when I was there, but I feared it would bother you more than please you. I'm hoping I can say that here in a letter and not make you uncomfortable.
>
> I'm going to say this one more time, and then I'll not bring it up again, unless you want to discuss it. I deplore the way I treated you before. I know I wronged you terribly. Thank you for forgiving me. Because of your forgiveness and God's, I'm

hoping, with time, I can also forgive myself. I promise you I'm not that man now. Like you, I've changed, because God has changed me for the better.

I doubt if you hear much of the news, so I'll give you a summary. The western counties of Virginia pulled out and were recognized as an independent state by the United States in June. They're calling the new state West Virginia.

A huge battle took place over the first three days of July at Gettysburg, Pennsylvania. The Union won, but there were heavy losses on both sides. Reports are saying there were 50,000 casualties. Grant also finally took Vicksburg on July fourth after a long siege.

Please write to me soon. I'll be eagerly waiting to hear from you.

Yours truly,

Sam

"He writes well," Leah said as she handed the letter back to Ivy. "When you write him back, you might want to explain the delay and tell him his letter set in the post office for two weeks. Do you want to talk now?"

"If you have time."

"Let's go to your bedroom. That way I can hear Rachel if she wakes up from her nap."

"I'm just so confused," Ivy said when they were in her room. "Lawrence has been gone only four months, and I feel as if I'm betraying him."

"Does that mean you have feelings for Sam?"

"I don't know, but I think I could have. Now, he really does seem to be the person I thought he was when we ran away together. I told myself I had feelings for him then."

"Don't restrict yourself to what you think you should feel, Ivy. I knew Lawrence, too, and he would never want you to remain tied to his memory. He would want you and Patrick to be happy. If you can be happy with Sam, then give your feelings a chance. You don't have to make a decision right away. Just wait and see what happens."

"I think I'm also afraid Sam might be killed in the war. I don't want to like him and have that happen again."

"I can understand that, but would you already be upset and hurt if Sam were killed tomorrow?"

Ivy thought a moment. "Yes . . . yes, I would, but it'd be worse if I allowed myself to care more, if I allowed my feelings to deepen."

"When we love, we always take a risk of getting hurt. But would you have refused to marry Lawrence had you known the pain you'd experience when he was killed in the war?"

"No, our love was so special. I'd have married him anyway."

"That's what I thought. Maybe Sam will become that special too. I know Granny Em loved Edgar completely, but when Hawk came to her again, she loved him. You've seen how deep their love for each other is. Having loved once doesn't mean we have no more love to give. In fact, I think a deep love enables us to love deeper."

"You think I should encourage this, then?"

"I don't think it would be wise to rush into anything, but I think you should give Sam a chance. My advice would be don't base your final decision either on Lawrence or the fact Sam is Patrick's father. Make it on whether or not you and Sam love each other enough for marriage."

"Leah, I think you're strong and independent enough to make it on your own if you had to, but I'm not. I need someone to rely on, preferably a husband. I've always depended on someone – first Mama and then Lawrence."

"I don't know why everyone always thinks I'm so strong."

"You are, Leah. You've been there for me time and time again – when I wanted to come here with Luke, after I'd run away with Sam, when Mama died, and also now. I may be the big sister, but you act more like it."

"I'm glad I've been able to help."

"Thank you. Talking to you always helps me sort things out. I know I once belittled you for being too smart, but I appreciate it now."

"I appreciate you too, Ivy." Leah hugged her sister.

Ivy answered Sam's letter after supper. She wanted Leah to read it too. Leah felt reluctant to be the mentor in Sam and Ivy's relationship. Yet if she didn't hear from Luke soon, it may be the distraction she'd need to keep from worrying herself sick.

> Dear Sam,
>
> The reason I haven't replied sooner is I just received your letter. Mr. Hendrix was waiting for one from Luke before he brought yours, because that's what Leah had originally told him to do. However, when one from Luke never came, he finally brought yours. I paid him and told him to bring yours sooner next time.
>
> Patrick was excited to hear from you, and he sends his love. He's planning to write you a letter for me to include in my next reply. His will be simple, but I think he does quite well for an eight-year-old. Leah and I are instructing him in the academics, and Hawk teaches him much about the farm and things like hunting.
>
> I know Patrick misses Lawrence, but he's adjusting better than I'd expected. The three of us were very close, but I think children are more resilient than adults. It would've been much more difficult for both of us if we were still at the plantation. Regardless of what happens in the war, I

don't think I ever want to go back there to live. It would be too hard.

I can tell you're good with Patrick, and I think you're good for him too. He needs that now. You'll never replace Lawrence, the only father he's ever known, but you can take your own place in his life.

I'll answer your remarks about the past, and then I think it's better if we don't mention it again. Although what you did wasn't right, I had some part in the wrong, too. I shouldn't have gone with you, and I should have never let you do what we did. I wanted things the way I thought they should be, and I complained when they weren't. Neither one of us were suited for the other then. Yet, how can I lament what happened when I have Patrick? Lawrence and I were never able to have another child, and we both adored Patrick. God used the bad for good. You should forgive yourself and move on. We've all sinned.

We don't hear much news anymore, just what Mr. Hendrix tells us, so I appreciate your brief accounts. I used to hate politics and current affairs, but I've come to understand how important they are. Please continue with the summaries, and let us know what's happening with you, too.

I pray that God will protect you and keep you safe. It would be hard on Patrick, even now, if something happened to you.

Sincerely,

Ivy

"I want to be neutral with my feelings now and neither encouraging nor discouraging," Ivy said after Leah read the letter. "How did I do?"

"Very well, I think. It's a good letter, but I wouldn't be surprised if Sam doesn't ask you something about how you feel in his next letter. You mentioned Patrick would care if something happened to Sam, but you didn't say anything about yourself."

"Well, if he does, I'll at least know he's interested, and I don't want to be the one who takes the lead. Besides, didn't you say not to rush things?"

"Yes, but sometimes, slowing down is almost impossible. It became like that for Luke and me."

CHAPTER FOURTEEN

Salisbury Prison

WHEN THE TRAIN STOPPED AND all prisoners unloaded, Luke recognized the town. *Salisbury!* They'd brought him to Salisbury. His heart leaped. He should be able to get in touch with his father. This was the best place they could have sent him.

Luke recognized the prison too. It had once been a cotton warehouse. The main brick structure had four stories, and it measured about forty feet wide by a hundred feet long. Six smaller buildings sat around it.

Processing took a while. They were sent through the hospital first for medical screening. The hospital had been put in one of the smaller buildings.

If things worked like they should, authorities here would turn in his name as captured to officials of the United States, and he would be listed as a prisoner instead of missing. In the meantime, he should be able to write to his family and let them know where he'd been sent.

When the soldiers searched him, they discovered the picture of Leah in his pocket, but they returned it. Luke breathed a sigh of relief. They also returned his Bible he had in his knapsack. His things had been searched several times, but he'd retained these two valuable possessions.

They said his money would be put on his prison account. If he bought anything from a sutler, it would be withdrawn from his account. He didn't have much anyway.

One of the officers at the prison read them some of the rules and regulations. He clipped them off solemnly in the tone of a barker. "You'll go to the mess hall for meals, and officers will eat before enlisted men. For you who are hoping to be released in a prisoner exchange, forget it. Most exchanges have been discontinued as of May the twenty-fifth. The armed guards have orders to shoot anyone who looks like they're trying to escape. There's a deadline dug around the inside of the stockade. If you step over that deadline, it will be assumed you are attempting to escape, and you will be shot. The prison is already getting crowded. We were first established for only Confederate deserters, traitors, and other criminals, but now they're bringing in captured Yankees, and we already have somewhere around two thousand prisoners. There're plans to extend the prison, build another stockade, and house more prisoners in the yard. Some of you may end up on the outside. Guards will escort you wherever you go, especially when you go down to Town Creek, outside the stockade, to bathe or wash your clothes. The well in the yard is only for drinking water. You will be organized into divisions of a thousand men. Each division will have ten squads of one hundred men. That's all for now. If you have questions, ask one of the prisoners who's been here a while."

"Sir, how can I get word to my father, who lives in Salisbury, that I'm here?" Luke asked.

"What's your name, prisoner?" The man sounded irritated.

"Luke Moretz."

"German, huh? Where're you from?"

"Watauga County, North Carolina."

"So you're one of those mountain turncoats who's betraying our country."

"No, sir. I was fighting for my country, the United States of America."

"Mouthing off is not going to help you here, Moretz. Men like you should be shot for treason, and getting on my wrong side will only work against you. I oversee a lot of services in this prison, including prisoner lists and incoming and outgoing mail. You keep this up and your family will never know what's happened to you."

Luke held his tongue. He realized his innocent question had just singled him out as a troublemaker, and he was nothing of the sort.

All the prisoners were marched outside. Luke looked around the compound. An eight-foot-high fence make of rough, squared poles surrounded the area. A raised platform, where guards walked, ran around the outside of the fence about seven feet up. In the northeast and northwest corners sat cannons, and they also guarded the front entrance.

About three feet from the fence he could see the deadline, a ditch about four feet deep and four feet wide cut around the entire enclosure. They called it the "deadline" for a reason, and he planned to stay away from it.

Several large oak trees gave some shade in the yard. The yard also contained a large well where the men could get drinking water. Men were milling and sitting around. Some talked, others bartered, and several were writing letters.

The prison looked like a daguerreotype—dreary and dirty in shades of gray—yet Luke felt somewhat better. This didn't look as bad as he expected, but he still felt hunger pains. "When's supper?" he asked another prisoner.

"They'll let you know. We muster before each meal, so they can make sure no one has escaped or died. Then, we'll be marched to the mess hall."

Luke remembered the spokesman at the entry telling about the mess hall, but he didn't remember anything about mustering. Maybe that's where the divisions and squads became important.

He guessed he'd have to wait a little longer to eat. He went to the well to get some water. He couldn't remember when he'd last eaten, and he couldn't remember how long the train trip had taken.

The well seemed to be going dry. "It's always like this by afternoon," a prisoner said behind him. "There's plenty of water first thing in the morning, but it dries up by afternoon. I guess there's too many of us drinking from it now."

The men were herded into the barracks of the prison, which filled up the main building of the old cotton warehouse. Luke and Billy, along with many of the men, were taken to the second floor. A huge, open area without partitions spread before Luke. It looked like some renovations had once been started, but they'd been halted.

They walked into the area, and some of the other men began to complain. They weren't going to be welcomed.

"We hardly have room to sleep like it is," someone grumbled.

Luke could see that the men here slept on the bare floor, but most of them had a blanket. Luke didn't see any for the new men.

"Captain Goodman never does seem to procure all the supplies he's supposed to," one of the guards grumbled to another. "Something's going on there, if you ask me."

"Move all the lines up, men," a guard ordered. "Clear out this back area for the new men."

With moans and grumbling, the men moved up and crowded closer together. Yet, it seemed to Luke that each man would still have room to lie down and turn over without touching anyone else.

Luke had a hard time sleeping that night. He remained hungry after his supper of a couple bites of beef in broth and a piece of bread, but he did feel a little better. He knew if he could get to sleep, the night wouldn't be so long, and breakfast would come not long after he woke up. He lay there for a long time thinking of Leah and wondering when she'd know he'd been captured. Finally he prayed himself to sleep.

Breakfast consisted of a piece of bread and a strip of bacon. Luke could have eaten much more. "Is supper last night and this breakfast typical of the food we get here?" he asked the man beside him in the mess hall.

"I guess it is. We're supposed to get more, but the longer the war goes on, the less we get. Before long, we'll be lucky to get anything. If we don't start getting a better variety than we are now, diseases like scurvy will plague us too."

"You can blame your Yankee soldiers for that," one of the Confederate prisoners said. "As the blockade on our coast gets tighter and more successful, supplies don't get in, and we get less and less. On top of that, many of our fields and crops have been ravaged by the Union armies. They can't give us what they don't have."

"Why are there Confederate prisoners here?" Luke asked when the Confederate started talking to someone else.

"They're either deserters, men who've been court-martialed, or Confederate political prisoners. There's also two kinds of us Union soldiers, those who were captured and those who defected to the South. Which are you?"

"The Rebs captured me at Gettysburg. I'm Luke Moretz." Luke put out his hand.

"Steve Talbert."

"Why would they put a soldier who'd defected to them in prison?"

"They're afraid he might've been sent to spy on them."

The summer heat felt intense to Luke in the yard, so he attached his handkerchief to the back of his hat to keep the sun from baking his neck. Someone else must have liked his idea, because his hat disappeared.

Luke looked around for two days to try to discover the thief wearing it. On the third day, he thought he saw it and started in that direction. Suddenly a shot rang out, and the suspected thief fell.

Several of the men in the yard ran to see what'd happened, and Luke went with them. The man had been shot in the chest. He lay dead.

The hat had fallen off, and Luke picked it up for a closer look. He recognized it immediately. Had the man been shot because he'd been mistaken for Luke?

Luke looked at the guard who'd fired. He stood on the elevated platform around the outside of the fence and stared at the scene.

"What will happen to that guard?" Luke asked the prisoner closest to him.

"Nothing." The man sneered. "They can shoot down anyone they want, and they won't even be removed from duty."

Luke stayed as far back from the guards at the fence as he could after that. He tried to mingle in a group too. He suspected the guard thought the man he shot was Luke. Had the official the first day been so upset with Luke that he'd ordered him shot? It seemed far-fetched, but Luke hadn't been getting any mail, and his letters probably weren't getting out either.

Luke soon fell into the pattern of prison life. It wasn't pleasant, but he could bear it. He still wrote letters to his father and Leah and eagerly waited to hear from them.

With little to do, he began to read his Bible at least twice a day. He appreciated that he still had it.

"You a preacher?" one of the prisoners asked.

"No, are there preachers here?"

"Some, especially the Quakers, who don't believe in fighting, but I don't know much about them or if they even call them preachers."

Luke kept Leah's photograph close to his heart. He looked at it often, and she renewed his resolve to get back to her.

When he hadn't heard from his father in two weeks, he began to worry. Luke had expected him to come visit him by now.

"I need to get word to my father, who lives here in Salisbury," he told Steve one day. "How can I do that?"

"Write him a letter."

"I tried that, but I got no answer."

"Maybe he's moved or gone."

"I don't think so. He's a doctor in town."

"I guess you could try to catch a civilian who volunteers to help here, but they're getting rare these days. I understand when the prison first opened up, there were plenty, and some of the ladies cooked meals and brought them in. One lady who lives close to the prison helped in the hospital and even took some of the ones who needed special care to her home to nurse them."

"I haven't seen any volunteers in the two weeks I've been here."

"I think as the prison fills up, they're not as comfortable coming. One man used to lend books from his personal library to the prisoners. They'd just send him a note listing what they wanted, and he'd send his slave carrying the books in a basket on his head. As more prisoners came, I guess it got too much to keep up with."

"I wish he'd still do that. I could use some books to read."

"The townspeople are also having a hard time getting enough food, so they aren't volunteering as much. The women certainly aren't making us meals anymore. I think when some of the prisoners started escaping, that scared the townspeople too. They now see us as a possible threat."

"Is there any other way I might get a message to my father?"

"You might see if a sutler would take a message. Of course, he'll probably charge you, and I'm not sure you'll find one who will, but you could ask."

Luke did ask the next time a sutler came.

At first the man refused. "I can't carry a letter out of the prison. The authorities might think I'm helping you escape, and I'd end up here myself."

"You can read the note."

"No, I can't be caught helping a prisoner."

"What if you just go by my father's house and tell him I'm here? That's all, and I'll pay you for your trouble."

"I guess I might could do that, but it'll cost you two dollars. With everything costing so much these days, it wouldn't be worth the trouble for any less."

Luke agreed and signed a bill for him to get the money out of Luke's prison account. Then, he waited and waited for his father to come.

When the sutler came back at his scheduled time he said, "I went to the address you gave me, but no one was there. The house looked closed up. I put a dollar back in your account. I'm sorry I couldn't contact your father for you."

Luke wondered where his father could be. Even if he'd gone to the farm for a visit, Frances should be there. She'd never go to the mountains.

The next week they were in the yard, and Luke saw a small group of Confederate prisoners surround Billy Inman. Luke didn't want to make more enemies here, but he couldn't abandon

Billy. He and Steve were the closest thing Luke had to friends in this place.

"You've been makin' lousy choices, kid," Luke heard one man say as he walked up. "Somebody needs to teach you a lesson." He gave Billy a shove, and someone else pushed him back.

There were four of them, and they looked like troublemakers. They certainly seemed intent on starting something now.

"Billy," Luke said. "I've been looking for you. Come with me."

"Billy's busy right now."

"Oh, what's going on?"

"Stay out of this, Yank."

"I've seen all the fighting I want to see, but if that's what you're trying to start, I can oblige."

"And you lost every battle, I bet."

"You'd lose that bet. You start something, and you'll see how well I fight."

Steve walked up. "You need some help here?" He had a muscular build and a self-assurance about him.

Luke saw the faces of the Confederates change. "I don't think so. Billy was just coming with me."

Billy followed Luke out of the middle of the ruffian band while Steve watched. The mischief-makers had started to walk away before Steve turned to follow Luke.

"Do things like that happen often?" Luke asked.

"They can. There's often tension between the Confederate and the Union prisoners. Even if a Reb deserts to get out of the war, we're usually not his favorite people."

"Does anyone ever escape from here?" Billy asked.

"They have, but those trying have also been caught. A group escaped once, and the townspeople helped round them up and bring them back. The luckier escapees might get some of the colored to help hide them. The best escape I ever heard of involved a ventriloquist. He and some other prisoners were on a burial detail. When they started covering the body, he had the corpse complain about them throwing dirt on him. The guards turned and ran, and the prisoners ran in the other direction."

"Where do most of the escaped men go?" Billy asked. "I imagine they might be caught if they head for home."

"That's right. From this prison, many head toward the mountains."

"How do they survive there?"

"They often join other deserters to form outlaw groups to raid the area. The deserters usually leave the army with good weapons and plenty of ammunition."

That didn't sound good to Luke. He hoped Leah and the others at the farm were okay. Since they were the only family on the mountain with a large cabin, they might be a target.

He wished he would hear from her. He'd written her again but had received no reply. He felt sure Leah would have written him if she could. Either she didn't get his letter, or something bad had happened.

As he thought about it, he knew his family didn't know where he was. If they did, someone would have contacted him by now. The official on the first day he came must have lived up to his threat by preventing his letters from going out.

A lonely feeling fell over him. What would Leah do when she never heard from him? Would she assume he'd been killed?

CHAPTER FIFTEEN

Death

LEAH HADN'T HEARD FROM LUKE since the middle of July, and now they were in September. Something must be wrong. She talked with Dr. Moretz about it, but he seemed worried, too, and didn't know how to comfort her. After a particularly hard night of crying into her pillow, she went to Hawk. "I'm so afraid something is bad wrong, otherwise I would have heard from Luke by now."

Hawk put his arm around her. "You know worrying won't help Luke, and it will harm you."

"I know, but I can't seem to help it."

"How close are you and Luke?"

"Very. You know that." She took a step back.

"Do you feel your spirit would know if he were dead?"

"I think so, but how can I be sure?"

"I know these things for the ones I love. If you will let your mind and spirit come together in meditation with God, I think you'll know too. If not, you'll still have more peace."

She paused to ponder what he'd said. "Explain what you mean."

"Remember, I told you I knew Emma needed me when she was sick. We'd been miles apart for years, but I still knew. I also knew when you were having bad dreams. Even if I'd fallen asleep, I'd wake up and know. I'm in harmony with the two of you. If you're that close to Luke, you can sense how he is."

"What do you do when you meditate?"

"I free my mind, clear all thoughts, and feel God's presence, but you may have to find what works for you."

Somehow just talking with Hawk made her feel better, but she tried what he suggested with no success. Alone, she would shut her eyes, relax, and clear her mind, but nothing happened.

Then, one night when she lay in the dark almost asleep, a knowing came over her. Luke was alive. She didn't know where he could be, but she felt sure he hadn't died.

She aroused enough to pray to God. She prayed God would be with Luke wherever he was and whatever struggles he faced. She prayed He would help her have the patience to wait and trust. Shortly afterwards, she fell asleep. That moment comforted her for days.

"I'm going to have a baby," Patsy whispered to Leah.

"That's wonderful! When do you think it's due?"

"I figure I'm about three months along now, so that would make it due in March."

"How do you feel?"

"Not that bad. I've been a little queasy early in the mornings, but it hasn't been bad."

Leah noticed how gently Moses treated Patsy, and how lovingly he smiled at her. Leah needed that. *Oh Luke, where are you!*

Dr. Moretz announced his intentions to leave on September the twenty-first.

Leah hated to see him and Maggie go. "Maggie, I'm going to miss you and Father. You've been such a help around here, and I've enjoyed getting to know you better. I love you both."

"Thank you, Leah, and I've grown very fond of you too. I know it's hard on you and Ivy to have your husbands leave for war, but at least you've known love. With all the men off fighting, I don't think I'll ever meet anyone."

Maggie hadn't talked to Leah about how she felt about anything. It surprised her the girl thought this way. "You're only fifteen, and this war won't last forever."

"It feels like it is, and Granny Em married when she was fifteen."

"Her situation was unusual, and she knew Edgar Moretz was the right man for her. Besides, people used to marry earlier then than they do today."

"She not only had one love, but two, and it's beginning to look like Ivy may have two also."

"You don't strike me as an impatient person. Wait on God's timing. Don't rush things."

"I guess I must've inherited a touch of Mother's impatience." She smiled. "Father is one of the most patient people I know. He had to be to stay with Mother."

"I'm sorry about your mother. Do you miss her terribly?"

"No, I never have. That's a dreadful thing to say, isn't it? I did love her, and I grieved over her death, but she was always so hard on me. I could never do anything to please her. After I got over the shock of her death, I don't really think I missed her presence. Father went out of his way to spend time with me, and that seemed wonderful. I think we needed each other."

"I understand, because I had a similar relationship with my mother. However, I imagine Dr. Moretz still needs you now."

"I think you may be right, but you know Mrs. Price has been staying with me while Papa goes out on calls. It's too early to tell, but I think there may be something growing between them."

This surprised Leah, but it shouldn't have. She could see the doctor and Mrs. Price together. They were two of the kindest, most pleasant people she knew.

Maggie paused a moment in thought. "Do you have anyone you can talk with about your problems? I mean, you seem to be Ivy's confidant and now mine. Do you have anyone you can confide in?"

"I do. Granny Em and Hawk, especially Hawk. I've known him for only a short time, but he seems to understand me so well. I can talk to him about anything. I can talk with your father also. Of course, Luke used to be my confidant."

"That's good. We all need someone like that."

When the doctor and Maggie left, the house seemed to be missing more than just two people. Leah, Granny Em, and Hawk probably missed them the most.

Ivy continued to get letters regularly from Sam. They seemed to be helping her outlook, and she appeared more cheerful with each one. She still shared many of them with Leah.

Dear Ivy,

Thank you for promptly replying to all my letters. Your letters have helped keep up my spirits more than anything else. It's easy to become depressed in these conditions.

Tell Patrick I enjoy his letters, too. He writes very well for a boy his age. I'm glad he's doing well in his studies and that Hawk is teaching him things around the farm. I look forward to showing him things, too, when I get back. Tell him I'm proud of him for helping with Rachel so much.

You mentioned in one of your letters you didn't think you'd ever want to go back to the plantation. What would you like to do after the war? Do you plan to stay with Leah indefinitely?

You've also talked about Patrick missing me, but what about you, Ivy? Do you miss me a little, too? Perhaps I shouldn't ask that yet, but I feel like we've gotten to know one another better through our correspondence. I hope you'll also be looking forward to my return.

You asked me about my military service. I served under General Joe Johnston until he was injured at Seven Pines, Virginia. We stopped McClellan from taking Richmond, but both sides claimed victory, and the less biased newspapers called it a "tactical tie." Robert E. Lee replaced Johnston, and after Johnston returned to active duty, he went to help Grant in the Vicksburg campaigns. This is where I received my injury that sent me home when I came by the farm. Now, I'm fighting with him again in the Western Front.

I like General Johnston. I think he's received unfair criticism, especially from Jeff Davis. Johnston was actually the senior commanding general who got the victory at the First Manassas, but he's rarely given credit for it. Beauregard, a general under Johnston, usually gets the honors.

I don't like the army, but I endure it. I think I do a good job as a soldier, because I try hard, and some of my less desirable activities in the past have actually prepared me to be a good soldier. However, I'm looking forward to all this being over, so I can come home. I'm not sure where home is for me right now, but time will tell.

Do you think all of you are ready for winter? I wish I were there to help you gather wood and prepare. My thoughts and prayers will be with you, because I know you're not used to the long, rugged winters in the mountains. I'll pray it will be mild this year for all of us. I'm concerned about you having the things you need, but there's nothing I can do but include you in all my prayers and ask God to take good care of you and Patrick. You're forever in my thoughts.

Yours truly,

Sam

All of them on the farm tried to prepare for another winter. They'd eaten the vegetables from the root cellar and cave and replaced them with fresh ones. They'd cooked most of the meat, and when they killed new, they'd bring what was left in the cave down to the smokehouse to use first and put some of the freshly cured in the cave.

They didn't have enough salt left to cure all the meat. Hawk said he and Moses would just have to hunt and trap more fresh meat during the winter. They might also need to dry some of it, but Leah hoped for a milder winter than the last one. She hated the thoughts of Hawk out hunting in the bitter cold. She also wondered if they'd have enough wood cut for the winter. They didn't have quite as much as last year.

Whenever Leah worked around the farm, she thought of Luke. He'd always been so much a part of this place. He almost felt near as she worked in the garden, gathered eggs, went to the spring-house, or milked a cow. She could feel him watching over her as she gathered berries, nuts, or persimmons. He stood by her when she helped get wood or did a hundred other chores around the farm. Yet, these memories made her miss him all the more.

September came and went quickly with all the harvesting and preparations for winter. Sam's letter told of the Battle of Chickamauga, where the Union troops had to withdraw back to Chattanooga, Tennessee.

In October, they butchered a hog on the farm and used the rest of their hoarded salt in preserving the meat. Lincoln also proclaimed the last Thursday in November a day of Thanksgiving. Leah felt thankful to God, but she would wait to hold a big Thanksgiving celebration until Luke came home.

They kept Christmas simpler than it had been last year. Leah knitted a cap, scarf, and gloves for Patrick and a cap, mittens, and stockings for Rachel. Ivy made Patrick a shirt and pants and Rachel a new dress. They both grew so fast, they needed clothing. Hawk carved Patrick a small wooden horse, and Granny Em gave all of the women homespun cloth.

Hawk carved a doll's head, arms, and legs out of wood, and Granny Em made a cloth body and clothes for Rachel. He'd drilled holds at the base of the wooden parts to allow them to be attached to the cloth body. Leah hadn't realized Hawk was such an artist, but this was lovely. Leah let Rachel see it and play with it Christmas Day, but then she put it up until she grew older. The ten-month-old treated everything much too roughly now.

Rachel could stand if she held onto something. Patrick spent hours letting her hold his hands as he led her around the house. Leah felt sure he would have her walking in a few weeks.

Right after dinner, Mr. Hendrix brought packages for Ivy and Patrick. He said Sam had sent him some extra money to bring them up on Christmas Day. Patrick had a set of glass marbles in a leather bag with instructions on how to play. Ivy opened beautiful yardage of blue silk and a letter.

> My dearest Ivy,
>
> Allowing me to call you this is my Christmas present. I managed to catch a few things that came into port through a blockade-runner. The merchant told me the glass marbles were all the rage before the war broke out. I know the silk is impractical and not heavy enough for winter, but the color reminded me of your eyes, and any manufactured cloth is

so rare these days, I had to get it for you. Besides, my choices were limited.

For me, it's another lonely Christmas in the military. Things are getting hard for us. There's not enough food or supplies, and I don't know how much longer we'll be able to fight under these conditions. I pray next Christmas will be better, and the war will be over.

Give Patrick a hug and kiss for me. I wish you both a very merry Christmas. May all your dreams for the new year come true. Dare I wish I might be in some of those dreams?

Yours faithfully,

Sam

Leah took Rachel upstairs to change her. Tears streamed down her face before she got the door to her bedroom closed. She would get no package and no letter from Luke this year. Where was her husband? What had happened to him? She couldn't even mail him anything.

She gave herself a few minutes of feeling sorry for herself. She didn't want to take away Ivy's pleasure. She just wanted to have some contact with Luke. She wiped her tears, washed her face, and went back downstairs. "I have you, don't I, Rachel?" she said softly to her daughter. "I have a piece of Luke in you."

Rachel patted her mother's cheeks and smiled sweetly.

Christmas hit Luke hard, like it did most of the prisoners. Conditions had continued to get worse as more men came. The cooks had tried to make Christmas dinner a little better than the usual fare. They had a chicken stew with milk and butter, and it tasted much better to Luke, even though he had a hard time locating a good bite of chicken in it.

The prisoners stayed cold most of the time. Few of them had coats, and only about half now had blankets. Sickness became common, but they still tried to go outside as much as possible. The walls seemed to close in when they had to stay inside all day.

Luke had enjoyed the trips outside to the creek to take a bath or wash his clothes. He liked being on the other side of the wall. He'd tried to volunteer for some of the work details, but he'd never been chosen. Too many of the other prisoners liked to get out, too, and so many men volunteered that the guards chose who could go.

Now, however, the prisoners rarely got the opportunity to go to the creek due to the cold. When he could, Luke still went. He would wash the best he could without getting in the frigid water, and he would wash an item or two of clothing.

Luke spent much of Christmas Day reading his Bible and thinking of Leah. He carried her picture in his pocket and took it out often to stare at it. He had to make a conscious effort not to lose hope in here, especially with the cold, bleak days of winter.

Billy seemed to be doing just that. After Luke had confronted the prisoners who'd been harassing him, Billy had stayed close to Luke. He almost felt like he'd had an extra shadow at times. Recently, however, the boy sat around with a vacant look on his face.

"Have you heard from your family?" Luke asked him, trying to bring him back to the present.

"I'm not sure I have any," he said without emotion. "I had two older brothers, but our folks are dead. One brother went off fighting for the South, and the other went to the North, like me. They could both be dead for all I know."

"Or they could be alive too." Luke shrugged. "Is there a lady you're interested in?"

"Not really. I liked a girl, but she seemed to prefer someone else."

"War has a way of changing things," Luke said. "Maybe you'll find her more receptive when you get home."

Then, a cold chill ran down Luke's spine. Would the war change Leah? If she thought he were dead, might she marry another, maybe someone like Sam Whitley? He shook himself. He believed in Leah and their love. He wouldn't let loneliness, hopelessness, or some unfounded fear change that. Leah would wait for him. He had to believe that.

―――――

January turned bone-chilling cold on the farm, and February felt even worse. Their biggest snowstorm hit in February, and it snowed each week for three weeks in a row. In the frigid temperatures, none of the snow melted, and Moses had a difficult time getting out to milk or do the outside chores. Mr. Hendrix didn't come at all during this time.

After the extreme cold, March didn't seem as bad. The ground thawed for a few days before it would freeze back. The cold wind howled, but didn't blow in a blizzard.

They'd used more wood than they thought, and they were trying to conserve it now. On the days above freezing, they only lit the fireplace in the kitchen, and they sat around it.

One morning toward the last of March, Granny Em and Hawk didn't come for breakfast. Leah knocked on their door, but no one answered. Perhaps they were sleeping late, but they never did that. Leah eased the door open.

Hawk knelt beside the bed holding Granny Em's hand. Silent tears were drenching his face.

Leah froze. "Granny Em?" She eased forward with her eyes on the woman on the bed. She touched her, and her body felt cool.

She put her hand in front of Granny Em's nose, and no breath fluttered over it. Leah burst into tears.

Hawk stood and held Leah to comfort her. Here he was grieving, and he wanted to comfort her. "She's gone," he whispered. "She's gone to be with our Lord."

Leah nodded. "Are you all right?"

"I'll be fine. I just needed some time with her."

"What happened?"

"I don't know. We had a good night and talked together. We reminisced about old times, told each other how much we loved the other, and went to sleep. I woke up early this morning and she was gone. She'd died peacefully in her sleep, but it'd just happened, because her body still felt warm at the time. I guess her heart must have just given out."

"I'll get her ready for burial."

"Are you up to that?"

"I want to do this for her."

He nodded. "I'll go to the barn and start the coffin. Dress her in her Cherokee dress. I know she grew to like it. She wore it after our wedding."

"Tell Moses to dig the grave. I don't think the ground will be too frozen by midday."

Hawk didn't reply, and Leah had the feeling he planned to dig the grave himself. She hoped not. It would be too hard for him.

Leah went out, told the others what had happened, and gathered the things she needed to prepare the body. She tried to scotch her tears, so she could see to her tasks, but the woman had been closer to her than a grandmother.

Leah took her time in the bedroom. Often she had to wait until the tears cleared and she could see again. She would miss Granny Em so much. The little woman had so much inner strength, and she cared so much for her family.

Luke needed to know, but Leah had no way to get him word. She would write Father, though. He would be devastated too.

Hawk wouldn't come in to eat dinner. Leah didn't feel like eating either, but she forced a few bites down and fed Rachel.

After the meal, Moses helped Hawk carry in the coffin. The beautiful wooden box had a carved cross on the lid. Hawk had beveled the edges, and it looked professionally made. Leah lined the coffin with a white quilt, and Hawk carefully placed the body inside.

Hawk's been diggin the grave all afternoon, Moses wrote on a scrap of paper. *He won't let me hep.*

"Best leave him alone," Leah said. "I don't like it, but apparently it's something he needs to do."

They buried Granny Em the next morning. Hawk read the Bible verses, gave the eulogy, and said the prayer. Leah didn't know how he managed, but God must have sent him special strength and comfort.

Hawk placed a larger matching wooden cross at the head of the grave with Granny Em's name, Emmeline Cagle Moretz O'Leary, carved into it. Hawk must've stayed up most of the night working on it.

Hawk didn't come to the house for the rest of the day, but Leah figured he needed time by himself. She thought about finding him, but he knew she'd be there for him if he needed to talk.

The following morning, Hawk didn't come out of his room. Leah's heart sank. She had a feeling something was wrong. The man had overworked trying to do so much himself yesterday. She knocked and went into the bedroom. Sure enough, Hawk lay stiffly on his back with his Cherokee clothing on. Beside his hand lay a note addressed to her.

It took Leah a long time to read the note. Her tears kept blinding her.

Dear granddaughter of my heart,

Please don't mourn for me. I've gone to be with Emma and my Savior. Be happy for me.

When we talked about my first coming to the farm, what I never told you was I thought my time to die had come then. On rare occasions, some of my people know it right before they die. I felt something might be wrong with Emma, but I also needed to see her one more time before I died.

When she was so happy to see me, and she agreed to be my wife, I found myself renewed. I'm so very thankful for the short time I've had to be Emma's husband. God has truly blessed me through this time, and you've been one of those blessings. I've had many. I got to see what a fine man Luke is. Rachel and Patrick have been my great-grandchildren, Clifton is like a son, and Moses and Patsy are my friends.

If my body were still strong, I would try to stay for you, Leah. I do regret leaving you and Rachel, but I'm worn out. I've been strong for as long as I can. It's my time. I know Moses is more able to take care of you than I.

Please don't think I'm taking my own life. I've done nothing but to prepare things for my burial and lay down to wait for my Lord. I feel that when I shut my eyes in sleep tonight, I won't open them again on earth. My coffin is ready, my grave is dug, and I've washed and put on my clothes. I'll let you and Moses handle the rest.

If I have any influence in Heaven, I will try to hurry Luke home to you. I pray now that you and Rachel will remain well and always be happy. You can find happiness in God no matter what your circumstances. My life is a testimony to that.

With deep, abiding love,

Hawk

Moses found a coffin identical to Granny Em's in the barn. Leah lined it with an ivory quilt and Moses put Hawk's body in. He and the three women carried it to the grave. Granny Em's grave now lay between Edgar's and Hawk's.

Leah read the Bible passage, gave the eulogy, and said the prayer. She managed to get through it without completely breaking down by keeping her focus on Christ. Hawk would have been proud of her. They'd also found a wooden cross with Hawk's name carved on it.

"You may want to move your things to the downstairs bedroom," Ivy told Leah. "Patsy and I can clean it for you."

"I want to wait for Luke," Leah said. "I'd like Moses and Patsy to move down here in the meantime. That way Moses will be closer to the door if anything should happen."

Luke watched the men carry Billy's body out, and he felt a deep loss. He and the boy had been captured together, and they'd become friends. He'd miss him, because Billy had made Luke feel needed and less alone.

Billy had come down with something like a cold that had grown worse and settled in his chest, but loss of will really killed him. He had almost quit eating their meager fare and often pressed his portion on Luke or Steve. He'd talked little, even when spoken to, and his eyes retained a distant, empty look.

Rumor had it the quartermaster had been working to gather supplies to put some of the prisoners in tents in the yard come spring. Something needed to be done. The main factory building now held so many prisoners that no one had enough room, and some of the little buildings were being used as barracks too. Yet, new prisoners continued to be brought in.

In the crowded prison, unsanitary conditions caused problems. The cold weather, the lack of bathing or washing clothes, and decreasing rations added to the unhealthy situation. Numbers in the hospital continuously grew.

Luke woke one morning feeling sick to his stomach. He started to get up for breakfast but ended up back on the floor. Before the end of the day, he'd become weak, feverous, and had stomach cramps. When the diarrhea started, they carried him to the hospital. He had the flux, and it soon became the bloody flux. It'd probably killed as many soldiers as the battles had and certainly plagued the prisons.

The hospital staff treated him with oil of turpentine. They also tried to get some liquids into him, mainly water and a little broth.

He became so weak, he couldn't raise his head. Sometimes he had to lie in soiled sheets, because his emergencies came so frequently. Dr. Hall saw to it the staff took care of him as soon as they could, however.

He drifted in and out of consciousness. Sometimes, he would feel Leah's touch and struggle to awareness in order to see her, only to realize an attendant stood beside his bed, and it hadn't been Leah at all.

He'd never been so miserable. Sometimes he felt it might be better to die and end this torment. Each time, however, Leah would come to him in a dream, and he would try to hang on a little longer for her.

Luke managed to endure, and by the middle of March, he could sit up and eat. The flux had left him, but he remained weak, and it seemed to be taking forever to get his strength back. But he thanked God he had survived, because most never did.

Food in the hospital consisted of soup. They had a special kitchen set up to provide their meals. The soup got monotonous, but it came regularly and provided some nourishment.

By the end of March, Luke could get up and walk short distances. When he got so he could walk to the mess house, he would be allowed to go back to the barracks. He found himself looking forward to some solid food, even if only a few bites. It would also be good to see Steve.

———————————

Rachel turned one year old on February the nineteenth. Leah fixed her favorite foods, mashed potatoes and chicken stew.

The three women had each made her a dress from homespun as birthday presents. She'd already outgrown most of her older ones. When they'd cleaned out the downstairs bedroom, Leah had found a little leather dress and moccasins for the doll. Hawk and Granny Em had made their present ahead of time. Tears pooled in her eyes. She missed them terribly. She'd relied on Granny Em for years and Hawk, since he'd come. It would be hard here without them.

Ivy got another letter from Sam in March. It told that General Grant had been named commander of all the Union armies, because of his victory at Chattanooga.

Sam said Sherman had captured Meridian, Mississippi, for the Union. The general had stated he planned to destroy the South and bring them to their knees in a policy he called "total warfare."

Sam thought this was a hideous, cruel thing to do, but the whole war sounded that way to Leah. She wished she could talk to Luke about it, but he'd probably feel the same as she. He'd hate the devastation left by Sherman's army, but he'd say the Union needed to win it and not let things drag on. The war would soon be raging for three long years.

Patsy's labor began early in the morning on March the thirteenth, a little earlier than they'd expected. Moses came and knocked on Leah's door well before daylight.

Patsy didn't want Leah out of her sight, so Ivy cooked breakfast and watched Rachel. Actually, Patrick did the most of watching Rachel. Leah tried to calm Patsy, but she remained tense and nervous.

Moses sat in the sitting room at first. When Patsy's pains intensified, and she began screaming, he went to the barn. He needed calming and reassuring, too, but Leah had her hands full with Patsy.

She heard Ivy follow Moses out and smiled. There had been a time when her sister would never have noticed the feelings of a worried slave, and if she had, she wouldn't have given the matter a second thought. Now she tried to help.

The baby made its appearance around eleven o'clock. The healthy-looking baby boy looked to be somewhere between the weights of Rachel and the twins. Leah breathed a sigh of relief. This had been the first baby she'd delivered without Granny Em.

The new parents named their son Ezra. Both of them beamed with joy.

The tiny boy fascinated Rachel. She'd go up and watch him for the longest time, although she never tried to touch or ask to hold him. Rachel still remained Patrick's favorite, however. No new baby would ever change that.

In April, about thirty Confederate soldiers came by, foraging and raiding. The dirty, hungry bunch looked as if they needed supplies.

Leah and Patsy had told Moses of their earlier pretense. He knew if the Rebels came, he and Patsy would pretend to be slaves.

They did this, but it didn't prevent the soldiers from taking what they wanted.

"I can see you poor men are hungry," Leah told the leader in her thickest Southern accent, "but we have young children in the house. Please leave us the cows and chickens. You can have anything else to feed your men. Just leave us the milk and chickens so our children won't starve."

They did. They took all the meat from the smokehouse, all the vegetables in the root cellar, all the hogs, all the horses, and the bull. They left two cows and the chickens.

I shor do hate to lose them hogs, Moses wrote.

"Well, we don't have any salt to preserve the meat with, anyway," Leah said. She became more determined than ever not to let this war defeat her. They'd come too far to give up now. They still had some meat and vegetables in the cave. Thanks to Luke's foresight, they'd be better off than most.

One of the cows would give birth soon. Moses put her in the cave. He also moved a setting hen and her eggs there, much against its angry protests. He went by to feed and check on them each day. Leah prayed no one would discover the cave.

Luke still felt weak from his illness, but he went back in the barracks and managed okay. If he could have gotten plenty to eat, he would have already regained his strength, but supplies were getting harder and harder to find.

The Confederate officer who'd seemed to hold a grudge against Luke from the first day gathered five squads from Luke's division together. Luke tried to get in the middle of the group, where he wouldn't be seen. "Who is that man?" he whispered to the prisoner beside him.

"That's Second Lieutenant Oglethorpe. He has his hand in a lot of what goes on here."

"Men, I've got some news for you," Oglethorpe told them. "Five hundred of you have been selected to be transferred to the new Confederate prison north of Americus, Georgia. It's been built near Anderson, which is a railroad station, and the prison has just been completed. The Confederacy has named it Camp Sumter. As you know, we're overcrowded here, and this should be better for you."

Luke hoped all this would be true, but he didn't trust the man. He'd certainly be much farther south and farther from home. Luke had still held some hope his father might appear to volunteer in the Salisbury prison. It sounded like something his father would try to do. Now, there'd be no chance Luke would get to see him. He'd tried without success to get another sutler to go by his father's house. It frustrated him to no end to be this close and not be able to contact his family.

"We're making the arrangements," the lieutenant continued. "You'll probably be shipped out the first of next week by rail."

Luke said good-bye to Steve, took his Bible, and stepped into the cattle car with the other men being shipped south. At least the temperature at the end of April shouldn't be as hot as it'd been in August, even if they were traveling into South Georgia.

The trip reminded him of the earlier one, however. They were given a little water, but not enough, and they didn't get anything to eat. Luke seemed to make the trip fine. Perhaps he'd recovered more than he'd realized.

When they entered the prison, Luke couldn't believe what he saw. Tiny huts, tents, blankets, and rags were scattered randomly in every direction. There were no barracks.

The overpowering stench hit him as soon as they entered. A few of the new men vomited from the smell. Never could Luke have imagined such a horrendous scene. How could anyone survive such a place? Salisbury had been luxurious next to this.

The enclosure looked like a double stockade with two rows of fifteen-foot-high logs set in the shape of a parallelogram. The logs must have been cut from the area, because not a tree could be seen anywhere within the enclosure.

Luke couldn't understand why tents and huts had not been arranged in some kind of order. Most of these were military men, so why hadn't they set up the prison camp in military style or, at least, organized rows? This haphazard array would make it more difficult for everyone.

The guards patrolled on a parapet as they had at Salisbury, and the cannon set where it could be turned to reach every section of the enclosure. Instead of this deadline being a ditch, it consisted of a series of short stakes driven into the ground with a piece of some material four inches wide nailed to them. The deadline here ran twenty feet from the fence and left a much larger forbidden area.

"Watch your possessions, or they'll be stolen," one of the guards helping with the lines told Luke as he looked at Luke's Bible. "There's no supplies to give out, and everyone's desperate. Books often become firewood."

This man seemed friendly enough, so Luke asked, "How many prisoners do you have here now?"

"I think there's about ten thousand, but as you can see, the numbers increase all the time."

"Where are you from?"

"Two regiments guard the prisoners. The Fifty-Fifth Georgia and mine, the Twenty-Sixth Alabama. You want to avoid the Georgia boys as much as possible. This war has made them bitter, and they take it out on the Yanks."

Luke knew he was holding up the line, so he moved on.

Luke walked through the conglomeration and looked for a place to settle. He chose what looked like the best spot he could find.

"Go find someplace else," a gray-haired man with a wild, scraggly beard barked. "There's too many in this area, and we don't need another crowding things more."

"I imagine everybody else feels the same, but the new arrivals have to go somewhere," Luke said.

"You'd better watch yourself. I won't put up with anybody messing with my stuff."

"I know how to keep to myself."

"Make sure you do."

"Ah, Lester, why are you trying to make it so hard?" said the redheaded man on the other side of where Luke stood. "Relax a little. Be a good neighbor. Max is gone. How about helping me carry the body out?"

"I'm not touching the corpse," Lester said, "but I need some of Max's things."

"Forget it. They're already mine." He turned to Luke. "I'm Timothy O'Neal, but everyone calls me Tippy. Would you mind helping me?"

"Sure, I'll help. I'm Luke Moretz."

They went in the tent between Tippy's and Lester's. Lester had a hut thrown together from scrap wood and brush, but the two tents looked ragged and dirty.

"This is your lucky day. You can move in here before anyone else discovers Max is dead. I could use a friendlier neighbor. Lester sure doesn't qualify as that."

"What did Max die from?"

"I think he mainly just gave up. This place does that to some. You have to have a strong will, a positive attitude, and some help from the Good Lord to survive in this rathole."

"I'd like to move in here," Luke told the little man.

"Where're you from, Luke?"

"The mountains of North Carolina, and you?"

"New York. Did you just get captured?"

"No, they transferred me from the Salisbury Prison. Have you been here long?"

"Just about three weeks. Lester there came in when the place opened in February. That's why he has a hut of wood. The first ones built them out of the scraps from where they put the stockade up. Brush piles were left inside the stockade. I got my tent the same way you did."

They carried out the body and lay it in the pathway in front of the tent. Tippy said someone would come by and collect all the bodies and put them outside until the burial detail got them for mass burial.

"Thanks for your help, Tippy." Luke forced a smile. "I'm glad to have a friend to talk with."

"Well, one thing the Irish are good at is talking." He laughed. "What ancestry do you have?"

"Moretz is German, but my mother was an O'Leary."

"I knew there'd be some Irish in there somewhere. I can always tell. Everyone who comes from Ireland has the blood of saints and martyrs in their veins. You might never guess it from the way some of us act, but it comes out now and then." He waved as he walked away to his tattered tent.

Luke got settled and read his Bible. He prayed God would be with his family, help him in this terrible place, and end this war. Then he thanked Him for the friendly presence of Tippy O'Neal and prayed Lester wouldn't be a hindrance.

The rations here came uncooked, and each prisoner had to cook his own. Yet, there didn't seem to be any fuel around for a fire.

"They're supposed to supply us with wood, but it doesn't usually happen," Tippy said. "Max had a little, so you can cook yours on my fire for now. If that's a Bible I saw you with earlier, you'd better watch it, or someone will steal it to burn. Also, I'll warn you about the cornmeal here. It has cobs, husks, and stalks ground in it to make it go farther, and it will tear your stomach up. The stuff can't be digested, so you can eat it and still starve to death."

"We probably need to sift it."

"We're lucky to have a pot, much less a sifter. By the way, I can give you an old pot, cup, and spoon Max had. I already have those. I intended to trade them, but there's not much to trade for except the rations, and no one is going to give them up."

"I appreciate that."

"You hang onto them now. Having a pot makes you one of the higher class in here."

"Is the stream down there the only water supply?"

"It is, and it ran good and clear to start with, but it's already getting nasty from all the garbage and sewage running into it, especially after a rain."

Luke decided to try to go upstream as much as possible to get his drinking water. Maybe that would help a little. He couldn't stand the thoughts of drinking water that smelled so foul.

Luke watched the compound fill up as more and more prisoners came. By May, an Alabama guard told him there were fifteen thousand. Tippy and he teamed together to watch the other's things while one went to the stream or walked around for a little exercise. Luke never walked far, because it wasn't safe. Some gangs loved to harass others. What a shame! This place would be difficult enough without the inmates making things harder on each other.

CHAPTER SIXTEEN

Long-Distance Romance

IN MAY, LEAH, MOSES, AND Patsy planted their garden and one field of corn. That's all the seed corn they'd been able to save, and they'd kept it hidden. Ivy watched Rachel and Ezra while the others worked. Patrick helped drop the seeds.

Mr. Hendrix brought Ivy a letter from Sam. "You folks be on the lookout," the mail carrier said. "A whole lot of scoundrels have banded together and are causing trouble. The home guard has a camp over at Sugar Grove, and they're trying to put a stop to the looting, but it's hard. Many of the outlaw bands are deserters, and they brought home much better weapons and ammunition than the home guard has. They like to hit remote farms like this. If they come, you'd better just let them take what they want."

Sam had news too. He'd written:

Dear Ivy,

I am so sorry to hear about Hawk and Luke's grandmother. They seemed to be such nice people, but they may have been spared the worst of the war.

Things are getting bad. We often don't have enough to eat, and we've had to resort to foraging, too. So far, I've thankfully never had to steal from people myself, but I've known men who have, and I've eaten some of the stolen food. There's often nothing else.

I'm sorry to hear the Confederates raided your farm. I hope you were left with enough to make it. With your garden and Moses hunting, I'll pray that you'll be all right. I know a lot of soldiers are deserting because their families are literally starving to death, and they've gone home to try and help. I'm afraid it will grow only worse before this war is over.

Rumor has it that Grant has taken 120,000 troops to move on Richmond. Lee has 60,000 men to try and stop him. It doesn't look good. If it were up to me, I'd surrender right now and stop this awful bloodshed.

Sherman has also begun his march toward Atlanta. He's leaving everything in his path destroyed for miles. Our men, under General Johnston, have been sent to stop him, and it's going to be a daunting task. I don't like the man, but Sherman has military savvy, and he's good at what he does.

I wish with all my heart I were there to help you and your family. I feel so helpless here in this scruffy army. You would be hard-pressed to know on which side we fight by looking at us. Our uniforms are beyond recognition, and some have even taken articles of clothing from dead Yankees.

Take care of yourself and Patrick, and give him my love. Surely this war won't last much longer.

With warm regards,

Sam

"Sam is in pursuit of Sherman's army," Ivy said. "I'm afraid he'll be in even more danger."

"Sam seems capable of taking care of himself," Leah told her, "and worrying isn't going to help either of you."

"I don't know what I'd do if something happened to Sam too."

Leah gave her sister a questioning look. Was Ivy beginning to care for Sam?

"I am beginning to care for Sam," Ivy said, as if she'd read Leah's thoughts.

"Well, tell him in your next letter. He's hinted he's been hoping for that, and I can think of nothing else that'd make him more determined to get back."

"I don't know."

"It's been a year now since you lost Lawrence. Your time of mourning should be over. Get on with living."

Ivy smiled. "You know, you have a way of bossing me around. I'm the oldest. I'm supposed to be bossing you."

"You need bossing more than I do." Leah laughed.

"So you say." Ivy laughed back.

Ivy did take Leah's advice, however. She handed Leah her reply to Sam.

Dear Sam,

I'm always so pleased to hear from you, but I was concerned to hear your troops are ordered to stop Sherman. That sounds like a daunting task, indeed. Please take care of yourself, and try to stay out of harm's way. I would be quite upset if something happened to you. I'm beginning to care for you.

Lawrence has been dead for a year this month. Leah says I should quit mourning and get on with my life. I'm going to try to do this, for I know it's what Lawrence would want. He was a wonderful man and treated me like his princess.

We are going to have a harder time at the farm this year. We have no salt to preserve our meat, and Moses won't be able to go out and hunt in the blizzards. Hopefully, the garden will produce well, and Leah says we'll gather all the nuts and berries we can. She says we can dry what we can and even dry some of the meat, like the Cherokee used to do. Leah is quite resourceful, so I think we'll be okay.

Please don't lose hope, Sam. This war can't go on forever. There's got to be an end soon. Come back safely to Patrick and me.

With warm regards,

Ivy

Sam's reply came back swiftly. Ivy had certainly raised one soldier's outlook.

Dear Ivy,

Your letter made me the happiest I've been since I got to see you and Patrick. I've read it until I've almost worn it out.

You said you'd be upset if something happened to me and that you were beginning to care for me. Those statements are music to my ears. I've cared for you for a long time. You've given me hope I have a chance with you, and I'm elated.

I'll be praying things go well for you from now through the fall, and you'll get enough food put back. I'm glad Leah is able to have a plan to sustain all of you.

Johnston's troops are still maneuvering around Sherman's. It's almost like being pieces in a chess game. I know Sherman wants to destroy us, but Johnston has kept us from his grasp by frustrating Sherman. We've entrenched our army across Sherman's path and forced his army to either a frontal assault or a flanking maneuver. So far, Sherman has tried to avoid a head-on confrontation. Our troops are prepared, and Johnston is ever alert for an opportunity to hit any of Union soldiers who break off into smaller units.

Don't worry about me. Johnston is protective of his men, and he's trying his best to keep us together as one cohesive force, while still blocking Sherman's push to Atlanta. Besides, you've given me a great reason to come back in one piece, and that's exactly what I intend to do.

Thank you for being forthright and honest with me. You'd avoided answering my hints in the past, and I was afraid to push things, until I knew you were ready. I just hoped you might welcome my suit at some point. Have I read your letter correctly? Would you allow me to call upon you, when I get back?

I pray this war ends soon. May God bless you and Patrick and keep you safely in His care.

With deep affection,

Sam

July turned as hot as February had been cold. Leah smiled to herself. When she'd first come here, she couldn't believe Granny Em got hot in what were cool summers to her then. Now she'd grown acclimated to the cooler temperatures too.

The Union soldiers rode in bent on destruction. Leah met them at the side of the house. Some soldiers had already started to uproot plants in the garden, pulling up cornstalks from horseback and trampling other plants.

"Stop that this instant!" Leah shouted at the top of her voice.

The colonel looked at her and laughed. He had a wild, reckless look about him.

"We support the Union," she told him quickly. "My husband is off fighting in your army."

"Sure he is, like every other farm in North Carolina. Most of them are Union sympathizers when we come."

"Stop them, and I can prove it."

"Hold it a minute, men. I want to see this."

The men rode their horses back to wait behind their colonel. Leah ran to get Luke's enlistment papers. When she came back out, Patsy stood behind Moses, watching.

"If you're Union, what're you doing with slaves?" the colonel asked.

"They're not slaves. Patsy's free, and here are her papers to prove it. Moses ran away from a plantation. He can't talk, because some owner cut out his tongue. Here's my husband's enlistment papers." She handed him the papers, and he looked them over.

He looked up at her with a different expression. "My apology, Mrs. Moretz. I'm Colonel George Kirk. My men were sent to North Carolina to help some mountain boys get out of the grips of the Confederacy and into Tennessee to fight for the Union. My troops have also been destroying some Confederate strongholds to aid in the war effort, but there are enough Rebel places to hit. We don't need to be making things hard for the families of our Union soldiers."

"Thank you, sir," she said as she took her papers back.

"The best to you, madam." He tipped his hat, and they rode away.

Ivy stayed in the house to keep the children. "Things sure seem to be heating up around here on both sides."

Leah breathed a sigh of relief. Damage to the garden had been minimal, but they'd intended to uproot and trample it completely. Leah knew the family couldn't afford to lose any of their food and still make it through the winter.

Leah cried that night again. She cried for Luke, Hawk, and Granny Em. She felt weighed down by the burden of being responsible for everyone. All the ones left depended on her to keep them safe and see they had the basic necessities. She was so tired of carrying the burdens. Everyone said how strong she was, but she didn't feel strong. She needed someone too.

I will never leave thee nor forsake thee.

"I'm not alone, am I, God?" she whispered. No, God would always be with her. He would see her through whatever came.

⸻

By June, an outlaw group who called themselves Mosby Raiders had taken over the prison. The name of the man who led them was really William Collins, but he went by the name of Mosby. He had been a private in Company D of the Eighty-Eighth Pennsylvania volunteer infantry.

Tippy and Luke went only to the stream. Otherwise they stayed close to their tents, so they could help each other if trouble came.

Luke got up one morning, and Tippy hadn't come from his tent. When he still hadn't come out by midmorning, Luke went to see if something had happened. Tippy lay in a pool of blood where his neck had been slit during the night. The murderers had been so quiet, Luke hadn't heard a thing. All Tippy's possessions had also been taken.

The tragedy hit Luke hard. Tippy had been a good friend who'd helped cheer Luke in this dreadful place. He would sorely miss the little Irishman, and his heart ached at finding him like this.

Another prisoner took Tippy's tent. He appeared to be a young man in his early twenties who would've probably been handsome if he'd been clean. No one looked attractive in this situation. Luke's beard had grown long and scraggly too. Layers of dirt and grime had built up on his skin, and his clothes had become threadbare and filthy. He had no way of doing any better.

Luke had seen the young man in the area. He must have been looking for a better place, and he helped Luke carry Tippy out.

Luke introduced himself and offered to help the young man. He couldn't fault the prisoner. If he hadn't moved in right away, someone else would have, and that's how Luke had gotten his own tent.

The young man answered, "I'm Aaron Carter from West Virginia. I guess we're both mountain boys."

"How long have you been here, Aaron?"

"Just a week. I've been staying out in the open, so I'm glad to have some shelter. I don't see how they keep packing guys in here. It's inhuman."

"It is, but we can't do anything right now but try to make the best of it."

"Are we going to make it?" Aaron's voice shook.

"I plan to. If we stick together, we'll have a better chance. The man you helped carry out turned out to be a good friend. I'm devastated by his needless death. He helped make this dreadful place more bearable. I'll sorely miss him, and I hated finding him like I did." Luke shook his head in disbelief.

"I could use a friend, and I agree it would make things better."

"You sound educated."

"I'd been going to the University of Virginia in Charlottesville until the war broke out. When Virginia went with the Confederacy, I went back to West Virginia and joined the Union. Of course, we weren't a separate state at that point."

They were interrupted by men gathering because they'd heard what had happened to Tippy.

"We need to do something," Luke told them.

"What can we do?" someone asked. "The authorities here ain't gonna do nothing. I doubt if they'd care if we all killed each other. It would be less work for them."

"None of us are willing to go up against Mosby and his raiders either," another said.

"Maybe we could band together and form our own group to bring some law and order to the place," Luke suggested.

"That's not a bad idea. We could form a group of regulators."

"We should get the commandant's permission," Luke said. "That way, if there's trouble, we won't be in the wrong."

A small group asked Commander Wirz for permission to form a group of regulators to counteract the raiders, and he granted their request. Most of the other prisoners joined the regulators. They set patrols and caught some in the act. They set up a trial and brought in witnesses. Eventually, they convicted thirty-two, punished twenty-six, and six were hanged for murder. Mosby was one of the six executed on July the eleventh.

A group of the regulator leaders asked that the six not be buried with the other prisoners, so they were buried off to the side. Violent criminal acts had been curbed, because the prisoners knew action would be taken.

The July heat made the Georgia prison a furnace, and no one could get used to the smell. Being inside a burning outhouse wouldn't have been as bad.

By now the place had swollen to over twenty-five thousand, and they were on top of each other. Without huts or tents, newcomers dug a space out of the ground bigger than a fire pit, lined the shallow hole with pine needles or whatever they could get, and tried to erect a stick with a rag for a little shelter from the sun.

The insects and pests were another big problem. Flies swarmed in the smelly, refuse-ridden compound. There must have been millions, and certain areas sat completely black with them. The mosquitoes, bedbugs, lice, cockroaches, and rats added to the agony.

No mail came here. No one had any paper with which to write a letter either. The authorities were skeptical of correspondence, and Luke doubted they'd delivered any if it had arrived.

Luke had managed to stay relatively healthy for the time he'd been here, but he knew he'd lost weight. He'd never regained all of it from being sick before he left Salisbury, and the food here irritated his stomach as Tippy had told him it would. His body seemed to be processing very little of it, and he often had bloody bowel movements. His flesh dwindled away, and his muscles deteriorated.

Aaron had even more trouble. He'd been in his tent for about a week when he became too sick to get up. He had both nausea and diarrhea. Luke took care of him the best he could.

The hospital here could hardly be called that. It had been set up in an enclosed field south of the stockade and consisted of tents, a small cooking shed, operating tables, and some surgeons. They had no bedding, no clothing, no bandages, no medicine, and very little food.

After weeks of nursing, Aaron recovered enough to get up, but he'd lost so much weight he felt weak and depressed. Luke feared he might give up like Billy had in Salisbury. Many here did. They decided death would be better than living in these conditions.

When Luke began to have similar thoughts, he turned to his Bible and the photograph of Leah. If he were to keep his promise to her to come home, he couldn't give up. If God wasn't finished with him, he had to keep going.

"Do you have a wife or girl back home?" Luke asked his friend.

"No. I was courting a young lady in Charlottesville, but she refused to see me after she learned I supported the Union."

"What about family?"

"I'm the youngest, and my parents are both dead. I had three brothers and two sisters, but I don't know what's happened to them since the war. They're all much older than me."

"Do you have a strong faith on which you can rely?"

"Not really. I believe in God, and I've gone to church some, but I've never been baptized."

"Would it be okay with you if we studied the Bible together? I've read my Bible regularly since I've been in prison, and it's helped."

"Sure, at least it would help pass some of the time."

Luke showed Aaron his picture of Leah.

Aaron looked at it for a long time. "She's beautiful. No wonder you're determined to get back. She doesn't have any sisters does she?"

"One a little older, but Ivy's likely still mourning a husband killed in the war."

"Is there someone else you might know?"

"I have a half sister who'd be about seventeen now. I haven't seen her in a while, but I remember her as sweet and well behaved."

"Tell me about her. It'll give me something to think about besides this place."

"Her name is Maggie, and she hasn't had the easiest life. Her mother has never liked me or her very much, but the woman dotes on Maggie's younger brother. I don't think she's physically abusive to Maggie the way she was to me, but Maggie could never do anything to please her. Father tries to make up for his wife."

"What does Maggie look like?"

"She has sandy-brown hair and blue-gray eyes. She's not a beauty, but there's an attractiveness about her. She's unassuming and has a pleasant disposition."

"I take it you didn't grow up in the same household."

"No. Because of my stepmother, Father sent me to live with my grandparents a couple of years after he remarried. They live in Watauga County, North Carolina, but Father lives in Salisbury."

"I see. I hope I can meet them all sometime."

"I hope so too."

Luke found himself becoming for Aaron what Tippy had been to him. Luke also discovered, when he tried to encourage Aaron and bring him out of his doldrums, he also cheered himself.

When Luke began reading his Bible aloud and studying with Aaron, others began to attend. The men liked anything to break the monotony of the prison. Most had rounds they made each day to sit and talk. No one else around had a Bible, and this was something new to do. Luke prayed God would use him to reach lost souls and strengthen others with the Word.

In August, conditions became unbearable. There were almost thirty-three thousand prisoners, and the stench took one's breath away. The stream had become noticeably nasty with sewage. Death rates hit an all-time high, and almost everyone took sick. Stacks of dead bodies became an everyday occurrence.

"I can't go on," Aaron said. "This is too horrible to live in for even one more day."

"I know it's hard," Luke said. "But surely this war can't go on much longer. The South has been running out of food and supplies for months."

"We've been saying the war's almost over for years, and still it continues." They'd both been sick for days. Luke feared he had scurvy. He had no energy, there were spots on his skin, and his gums didn't feel right. If it turned out to be scurvy, he wouldn't get better until they got some fresh foods. If he continued to get worse, he would lose his teeth, have open sores, run a fever, and eventually die. He felt depression pulling at him. Maybe Aaron had been right. Wouldn't it be easier just to give up? It might be better to go now, before things got even worse.

He took out his picture of Leah and looked at it. He remembered their times together, but he didn't think he would ever have those joyous times again. Even if he went home, he would be going home a changed man, a man who'd lived for over a year in the worst nightmare imaginable. Would he even be the man Leah needed anymore? He clutched the photograph to his chest and prayed. He didn't have the strength to go on, but God did. He prayed that God would take him or get him out of this, hopefully by ending the war.

Ivy wrote Sam back, but she'd have to wait until Mr. Hendrix brought her another letter before she could send it. Now that they seemed to be starting a courtship, Leah didn't feel comfortable reading their letters, but Ivy wanted her to continue.

"I'm so bad to believe what I want to believe," Ivy said. "I'm not sure I trust myself to see things as they really are. I'd like your help."

Dear Sam,

I'm glad my last letter encouraged you. You did seem in the doldrums before, but I'm sure it must be hard to be a soldier in such a war. I hate to think of the killing you've seen all around you. I'd like to always be able cheer you and make you smile.

You understood my letter correctly. I would like very much to see you again. In fact, I'm waiting for that day. I've also felt I've gotten to know you better in your letters. I like what I've learned both in them and your visit here. If you're the man you appear to be, I'm interested in getting to know you better.

I know I'm supposed to be subtle and demure, but I don't think our circumstances warrant that. I'd rather just be honest with each other and not play societal games, because I know this is the best way to build a lasting bond.

I'm assuming you are interested in the possibility of a lasting relationship, but perhaps I should ask what your intentions are. I thought we were planning to marry once before, but I was mistaken. Please don't toy with my emotions. I think I'm too fragile for that right now.

We've also been visited by the Union army here at the farm, Kirk's raiders, to be exact, but Leah handled it well. She showed Luke's enlistment papers and Patsy's freedom papers and talked the colonel out of harming anything. I think they were planning to destroy as much as they could.

Leah says this month is hot, but Moses and I think it's very pleasant. I don't think I'll ever enjoy the mountains the way Leah does. I did survive my first winters here, however, and that's no easy feat. I wonder how many more there'll be.

I pray for you every night before I retire. I pray that God will keep you safe and well. I want you to come back, Sam. I want us to have a chance.

Yours fondly,

Ivy

Ivy didn't have to wait very long to mail her letter. Mr. Hendrix came the first week in August.

Dear Ivy,

I haven't got an answer to my last letter, but then I realized I might need to write you another, before you'd have a chance to mail yours. I need another, because your last one is almost in shreds from where I've read it over and over again. Please send me another just as inspiring.

I've just fought in the Battle of Kennesaw Mountain near Marietta, Georgia. After two months of flanking maneuvers, we blocked Sherman's way with our fortifications on Kennesaw Mountain. Sherman then chose to launch a frontal assault, something he'd yet to do.

We won the battle, but Sherman continued his sweep toward Atlanta. Still his casualties were three times as many as ours.

I'm disappointed. General Johnston has been relieved of his command, because he left northwest Georgia without stopping Sherman. We had to leave to keep from losing too many men. I think the Confederacy has made a big mistake. We need leaders like Johnston more than ever.

I'm now under the command of John B. Hood. He has a reputation of being much more reckless than Johnston. I hope this doesn't bode ill for our men.

I dream of you, Ivy. Please don't scold me, for I can't control my dreams. I long to see you and Patrick. I want to go for a walk with you beside me and hold your hand. Will you embrace me when you see me again? I'd like that.

With growing love,

Sam

The summer seemed to pass quickly, and Leah dreaded the coming fall and winter. Fall would mean harvest and food preparations. Would they have enough? Wood would be a problem too. Leah and Patsy helped Moses cut wood every chance they had, while Ivy stayed home with the children. With all the raids, they were also putting more in the cave. Since they had no sugar to make preserves, they pitted and dried some of the cherries and strawberries. The blackberries didn't dry as well. Dried blackberries seemed to be all seeds.

They made pickles with no salt. Leah hoped the vinegar would preserve them. She added a little honey instead of sugar, although she knew the taste would be different. At least the honey gave them something sweet, although she wished they had some flour for biscuits or yeast bread to go with it, but they used cornbread. She thought of Hawk and how he'd taught her how to keep the bees every time she worked in them or set out some honey. She missed him and Granny Em. The raw pain still stung.

They'd planted more beans than usual, because Leah knew she could dry them for winter. Their meals were going to be more limited, but at least they'd have something to eat.

Rachel ran all over the place now and had begun to talk some. She was a pretty little girl with her black hair and warm brown eyes. She still had Patrick at her beck and call.

Mr. Hendrix brought Ivy a letter. "I'm going to have to quit this come winter," he told them. "With all the outlaws in the area, it's becoming too dangerous, and the winter weather is hard on me."

"Can't you find someone else to take your place?" Leah asked. She knew Ivy and Patrick needed Sam's letters. Leah also liked to have the bits of news he sent them, and she kept hoping she'd hear from Luke sometime.

"I'll ask around, but I doubt it. The winters here are just too rough to be riding this far, even if there's no snow, and not many people have a horse or mule anymore."

Leah followed Ivy into the house. Ivy ripped open the letter on her way.

My dear Ivy,

It thrilled me to get your letter. It's even better than the tattered one I'd been still trying to read.

Your letters, especially the recent ones, raise my spirits more than words can convey. To know you are interested in getting to know me better fills my heart with gladness. I assure you my intentions are honorable. I hope we'll grow close enough you will marry me at some point in our future. I don't want to rush you, however. I want you to take all the time you need to be sure. This war needs to end first, anyway.

I am the man I've shown you, and I totally agree with you. This is not the time for subterfuge, and I've never appreciated social niceties that cause someone to pretend. I strongly believe in honesty. How else is trust possible?

I'm sorry to hear Kirk's raiders came to the farm planning destruction. They have a bad reputation, so Leah did well to talk them out of their mischief. I worry about you there with only one man, and him colored, to protect you. I'm afraid this year is going to be hard on everyone, particularly in the South.

For a whole week in July we launched direct attacks on Sherman. Our casualties were extremely high, but I didn't get shot. I'm just exhausted and bothered by all the blood and killing.

I don't see why the two sides couldn't have worked out something better than this. Why couldn't they have said all new children born to slaves would be free? This would have given the South time to adjust, eventually ended slavery, and I don't think the other issues would have led to war. War isn't a reasonable solution. Sometimes I think the Quakers have the right idea with their pacifism. I'm also beginning to think this is the most unnecessary war ever waged.

I would like to be in your mountain temperatures this summer. Tell Leah Georgia is HOT! To have to fight a battle in this heat is agony. To do anything in this heat is close to unbearable.

I've really not settled on where I'd rather live. I can see advantages and disadvantages to every place. I do like North Carolina, but there are even many choices within the state. I'll just try to seek God's direction.

Thank you for praying for me. I need all the prayers I can get. My faith is what's seeing me through these times, that and my resolve to return to you and Patrick. I need both of you, Ivy. My love is growing. I hope it's not too soon to tell you this. Do you need for me to hold back and give you more time?

Please take care of yourself. I pray for you several times each day. It's all I can do for you, since I'm stuck here in this army so far away. I wish things were different.

Love,

Sam

With tears in her eyes, Ivy set down the letter. It looked as if Sam was working his way into her heart.

Luke heard a large group of prisoners would be herded to the train station. Rumor had it they would go to a processing facility, where they'd be released. Those unable to travel would stay at the prison until they were well enough to travel.

"Come on, Aaron." Luke shook his friend. "We're going, if we have to stumble and crawl. Buck up. The railroad's close. We can make it if it means we can go home."

"I don't have a home."

"Then come to my home. Come meet my wife and little girl. We'll go to Salisbury and see Father and Maggie too."

Aaron remained weak and groggy.

Luke felt some of that, too, but a new determination surged. God willing, he would make it on sheer willpower and the Almighty's strength. "Aaron, I don't have the strength to carry you. You'll have to help me."

"I'll help you, Luke. You helped me many a time, and I'll help you, now." Aaron sounded incoherent, but he struggled to his knees and made it to a standing position.

Luke reached out and steadied him, and they leaned on each other as they tried to walk with the others. Somehow they made it to the train station, where the cattle cars stood waiting.

A guard stopped them. "You boys look mighty sick. I'm not sure if we should transport you."

"We're weak from hunger," Luke said. "If we die on the way, it will be just as easy to bury us there as here."

The guard shrugged and let them move on. Aaron couldn't get in the car, so Luke pushed him. Then, Luke had the same problem.

"Here, I'll help you." Aaron put out his hand, pulled Luke in, then passed out.

Luke didn't know where his friend had found the strength in his weakened condition, but they'd soon be on their way. The guards let them get water at the first stop. The water from the tank tasted much cleaner and better than any Luke had drunk in a long time. Aaron seemed to revive a little too.

They ended up at Lawton Prison near Millen, Georgia. The train depot stood a mile from the prison. Luke and Aaron stumbled along together. They fell several times, but they finally made it. The prison turned out to be a huge stockade, so large it couldn't all be seen from any one point. It had just been built, though, and the stream still ran clean and fresh. The prisoners would have no housing, but discarded scraps from building the stockade had been left for them to use in constructing shelters. Camp Lawton also had an order to it. It had been divided into thirty-two sections by sixteen-foot-wide streets, making it appear organized instead of haphazard.

Although still a prison, Luke could see it would be better than Andersonville. It had plenty of space and no stench. After Andersonville, the rations seemed wonderful. They tasted better and came in more reasonable quantities. Apparently this area of Georgia hadn't been as ravaged or distressed as the area around Andersonville had. The cornmeal here had been finely ground and contained no irritants. Beef came each day, and if it came from the scrappy parts of the cow, no one complained, because it had been so long since they had seen meat of any kind. In lieu of meat, they were sometimes given sorghum, and barrels of it were rolled in to give each man half a cup.

The October weather helped too. The air smelled almost fresh and Luke breathed in deeply. The second week they were there, he and Aaron went to the stream and washed up. That improved their outlook too.

A criminal element tried to take control as the Mosby Raiders had in Andersonville, but Captain Vowles sent in troops. They quickly had the villains arrested and put in stocks. Luke was impressed.

Under the better conditions, Luke's health improved, and so did Aaron's. Yet, this didn't mean the camp had no disease and sickness. Hospital tents had been set up, and details still carried the dead away to be buried, but neither Luke nor Aaron became one of the critically ill ones.

Luke kept asking when they were going to be released, but no one answered. Then, one day in the middle of November, they marched to the station and got back into train cars. They had been at Millen six weeks. Maybe now they would be released.

A cold rain peppered down as they left. As his and Aaron's train car pulled out, the men tried to huddle together to stay warm. This had all the makings of a miserable trip.

Luke noticed not all the men were sent in the same direction. In fact, most of the men stood waiting to load on other trains. Luke recognized the train station where they were unloaded. They were back at Andersonville.

By the end of September, they'd harvested most of the garden at the farm. Only the turnips, greens, and a few pumpkins were left, and the women were working to dry pumpkin.

Moses hunted more, and he usually came back with something. Hawk had taught him well. He had to be careful with the ammunition, but Leah thought it should last through the winter if they tried to conserve. He also set the traps, and those took few of their resources.

The cow had delivered a male calf in the summer. Moses had them both in the big cave for now, but they'd probably have to bring them back to the barn for the winter. The cave would be too far away to get to in a blizzard, and the cow would need to be milked.

Mr. Hendrix brought Ivy another letter and picked up her reply to Sam's last one. She'd already written him that Mr. Hendrix wouldn't be coming any more after the first week in November.

"Sherman finally took Atlanta," Mr. Hendrix told them. "Seems things have turned in favor of the Yanks."

"Have you been able to find anyone to take your place?" Leah asked.

"No, I surely ain't. There's just not that many men around. What ain't off fightin' in the war is in the home guard or something. The ones who are left and are interested don't have a horse anymore."

Ivy and Leah went in to read Sam's letter. He wrote:

My Dear Ivy,

I hated to hear your mail service is going to end. I enjoy your letters so much that I don't think I can do without them. Please write as much as you can before then. I'll write you another, which should reach you by the end of October, and you can send yours back then. Christmas will be bleak without being able to send you anything or hear from you.

I do think this war is about to end. You might know that the United States elected Lincoln to a second term. General Sheridan and his cavalry have driven Confederate General Jubal Early from the Shenandoah Valley, which cuts off our main existing supply line. Things are getting even scarcer than they were. I don't know how much longer the South can hang on, but I keep saying that, don't I?

Thank you for writing me such sweet letters. You've given me hope amid a hopeless situation. Many soldiers are deserting regardless of the consequences, and others are staying and just going through the motions. We're all so tired. Being hungry, tired, and homesick doesn't make for the best soldier.

I know things must be hard for you there, too. I'll be counting the days until we can see each other again. We'll just keep
praying and trusting God to see us through this. Then, we'll
appreciate the good times even more.

I need you, Ivy. I need you in my life. I hope you need me, too.
Keep well and safe and wait for me. I'm coming back sometime.

Love,

Sam

Leah and Moses had tried to hide most of what they couldn't
afford to lose. They'd put most of the ammunition in Leah's salt
cache behind the wardrobe. They loosened a floorboard under
the bed in the downstairs bedroom, where they could quickly
hide the rifles if the number of raiders were too great to make a
stand. Leah repacked the trunks and put one with extra bedding
and one with clothes and homespun cloth in the cave.

They kept only a week's worth of food in the smokehouse and
root cellar. Moses would go to the cave and replace it as needed.
The larder stood almost bare.

Leah had a feeling the raids hadn't ended, and as people became more desperate, the raiders would too. They'd fared well so
far, but she feared that might change quickly.

Ivy had been writing Sam a long letter to have when Mr.
Hendrix came for the last time. She'd written some all along, as
Leah used to do for Luke. She wrote about Patrick, her, and the
farm. Her last paragraph took on a different tone.

I'll miss your letters, too. I've come to depend on them, and
even though you're far away, I depend on you. I'm glad you
need me, and, yes, I also need you. Both Patrick and I need

you very much. I'm growing so fond of you, Sam. I know it's been only a year and a half since Lawrence died, but I know he would approve of you. I know he'd want me to find happiness again. Keep your promise and come back to me. I'll be here waiting for you.

Love,

Ivy

Mr. Hendrix came for the last time, gave Ivy a letter from Sam, and took hers back to mail. He looked remorseful.

"Thank you for doing this for so long," Leah told him. "You've really helped us out."

He nodded, tipped his hat, and rode away. Leah felt as if she were losing her last contact with the outside world. Now she really felt isolated on the farm, and she almost wished it were true, so no raiders would bother them.

Whatever Sam had written, Ivy didn't share it this time, but she appeared happier than usual. She went around humming and smiling to herself.

A large, pretty snow came in November. Leah took Patrick and Rachel outside to play in it. Rachel clapped her hands and liked the snow. Patrick scooped it up and did such antics, he had Rachel laughing until she grew breathless.

"Who's your best friend?" Patrick asked her as they went in.

"Patty." Rachel grinned up at him.

Christmas got slimmer each year, but Leah thanked God for what they had. They'd managed to go together to make Patrick and Rachel new clothes to put under the tree. They needed them, since they grew so quickly. The women would cook a good dinner of rabbit stew and cornbread. Moses had tried to hunt a turkey but hadn't been successful. He'd found three rabbits in the traps, though.

They got up and ate breakfast, and the children opened their presents. They were sitting around talking while the stew simmered when they heard a horse. Moses looked out and held up one finger to say he saw just one rider.

Patrick looked out too. "Sam!" he called as he ran out. "It's Sam!"

Ivy ran right behind her son. Leah followed at a more sedate pace.

Sam gingerly got down out of the saddle, and he reached up and took a crutch. By that time, Patrick had stopped on one side of him and Ivy the other. He dropped the crutch, put one arm around each of them, and pulled them close. He put his head on top of Ivy's as if he needed to breathe her.

"Oh, Sam." Ivy pulled back to look at him. She put her hand up to touch his face. "I can't believe you're here."

"What happened to you?" Patrick asked.

Then Ivy noticed the crutch for the first time, and her face turned to concern.

Sam smiled at her. "I'm wounded, shot in the leg, but it seems to be improving now."

"Come in," Leah told him. "You don't need to be standing on that leg."

Patrick handed him his crutch, and Sam hobbled in with Ivy on his good side, and Patrick on the other.

Sam kept one arm around Ivy's shoulders. He came in and stared at the Christmas tree. "I'm sorry. I didn't get to bring Christmas presents this year."

"Yes, you did," Ivy told him. "You being here is the best present you could bring us."

"I've still got the marbles you sent me last year too," Patrick said.

"Are you home for good?" Leah asked.

"No, I'm home on a medical furlough. I'm supposed to report back on February the fifteenth. I came straight here as soon as they released me from the field hospital."

"Surely you didn't come alone?" Ivy asked.

"No, there were three of us. We rode together most of the way."

"When and where did the battle take place?" Ivy asked.

"In Franklin, Tennessee, on November the thirtieth. We won the battle, but it cost us. There were six thousand three hundred casualties, and six generals killed. Being wounded may have saved my life. Many died in the last hours of the battle while I lay on the field."

"The surgeon didn't want to amputate your leg?" Leah asked.

"He said he needed to in order to keep gangrene from setting in, but I refused. They could have forced me, but they let the flesh wound go, since no bones were shattered."

"We'll let Leah have a look at it," Ivy said. "She's good with medicines and healing."

"I think it's doing okay, although the trip here has made it hurt more."

"Can you stay with us tonight?" Ivy asked. "If you go to Boone, you'd have to leave soon to make it before dark."

"Father is in Stanly County visiting his brother for Christmas, and he may stay there for the winter."

"Then, you can stay with us the whole time," Patrick said.

"You're more than welcome," Leah added.

Sam looked at Ivy. Leah could tell he hoped Ivy wanted him to stay too.

"Oh, please do," Ivy said, and he looked pleased.

Sam shared Christmas dinner with them. It was good to have him there, but Leah longed to have Luke here too. She silently prayed he would be home before another Christmas came. She didn't know how much more of this she could endure. She had no choice but to lean on God, but she also needed her husband.

That afternoon, Sam read the Christmas story from the Bible, and it touched Leah anew. She realized she'd not been giving God enough praise and worship. They still held the family devotions, and Leah had always prayed, but she'd let the situation and trying to plan for their survival occupy too much of her thoughts. God was in control. He would be their main support and provider, not her.

As soon as their worship time ended, she went upstairs, got on her knees, and prayed for forgiveness. She'd not intentionally given God too little of her thoughts, but she'd gradually let other concerns take over.

Someone knocked on the front door early the next day, too early for anyone to make it up the mountain. When Leah opened the door, Raymond Blankenship stood there with his hat in his hand. He and Polly lived up the mountain a few miles away.

"Mornin', Mrs. Moretz," he said.

"Come in," Leah told the man. "It's too cold to be standing outside this morning."

"I truly hated to come, but hit's Polly. She hain't feelin' too good, and I wuz awonderin' iffin y'all had somethan' 'sides meat ya could spare. Ya see, weuns wuz raided a while back, and they've took 'bout everthang we had to et and tore up the rest. I've been huntin', but I 'spect Polly's needin' somethan 'sides jist meat."

Leah sent Patrick to the root cellar. She packed the Blackenships a bag with carrots, potatoes, onions, and dried beans. They might run short if they were raided again, but these were her neighbors needing help, and God expected her to give it. Leah also knew the situation would probably be worse than Raymond had indicated for him to come asking for help.

"I put a bottle of tonic in too," Leah told him. "Have Polly take three tablespoons a day. Tell her it's Granny Em's recipe."

"I shore do thank ye kindly," Raymond said as he left with his bag.

CHAPTER SEVENTEEN

Engaged

THEY'D SET UP THE EXTRA bed downstairs for Sam. Although they had an extra bedroom upstairs now, he'd have a hard time navigating the stairs.

Leah wanted to check his leg the next morning, so she had him take off his pants and get under the covers. Only Patrick stayed to help him do this. Sam really didn't need any help, but Sam just liked to have his son around him and wanted Patrick to feel needed.

When Leah and Ivy came in, Sam had the bottom portion of his wounded leg sticking out from under the covers. Leah unwrapped the dirty bandage. The ugly gash showed the bullet had ripped down his leg in the calf area, and it looked red and swollen. Leah knew infection might be setting up under the surface, where it appeared to be healing over.

She touched his leg close to the gash, and it felt tight and hot. When she touched his forehead, it also felt warmer than it should. "It looks like infection has started to set up underneath the skin," Leah told them. "I'm going to need to lance it, to let it drain. If Sam were still with the army, a surgeon would amputate, but I'm no surgeon, and I can't do that. All I can do is to try to stop the spread of the infection and get this to heal."

"How bad does it look?" Ivy asked with a worried look.

"Bad enough," Leah answered.

"What are my chances?" Sam asked.

"I'm no doctor, but I'd guess about fifty-fifty at this point. Infections like this are hard to get rid of, and if they spread through the body, there's nothing we can do." Leah hated to worry everyone, but she wanted to prepare them. Actually, things looked even worse than she'd explained.

Leah gave Sam the best medicine she had for pain, but she knew it would help only a little with what she needed to do. She had Moses go out and cut a sassafras stick for Sam to bite when the pain grew too intense.

She put a folded sheet under Sam's leg to catch some of the blood and pus, and got a large, shallow bowl too. His leg had swollen so much, she expected a lot. She brought her sharpest knife to the bed.

Sam lay still waiting for the cut. He held the stick in his mouth, and Ivy sat beside him, holding his hand with her back toward Leah, so she couldn't see what was being done. Moses stood holding Sam's leg steady. They'd sent Patrick from the room.

Leah could hardly bring herself to look at his wound, much less work on it. She tried to detach herself, so she could do what Sam needed. She held the knife in her hand and said a quick prayer. She applied pressure quickly and felt the knife cut through the flesh.

She tried to concentrate and make the incision deep enough to allow the infection to drain properly but no deeper than needed. The moment the knife entered his leg, the strongest, foulest odor rose. It smelled rotten.

She quickly made the cut, collected the drainage she could, and poured on the tincture that had helped Luke when he'd been shot by thieves outside of Wilkesboro before they were married.

She'd heard Sam groan when she'd made the cut. She looked at him now in the hopes he'd passed out, but he hadn't. He had his eyes shut tightly, his pale face winced in pain, and his hand gripped Ivy's. "It's over now," she told him as she took the stick from his mouth. He'd almost bitten it in two.

Ivy glanced at Sam's leg and quickly turned away. She had tears in her eyes. "Aren't you going to bandage it up?"

"I think it'll heal better if we leave it open for now," Leah told her. "I don't want the pus-soaked bandages to stay on the wound, either. I'm going to give him a tonic four times a day, and it should help some too."

"Is there something I can do to help?" Ivy asked.

"He'll need to stay in bed as long as there's drainage. Wait on him, keep him company, and pray."

After Sam had slept, Ivy helped prop him up in bed. She took him his dinner, read to him in the afternoon, and talked with him when he didn't nap. Patrick played checkers with him after supper and the devotion.

Leah poured on more of the tincture after dinner, after supper, and at bedtime. She'd changed the dirty sheet, which she'd folded under his leg, and gave him the tonic to help with the inflammation every time she used the tincture. She also prayed.

Sam's infection had progressed, and it worried her. Leah guessed it had been festering under the surface when he'd been released from the hospital, but there'd been no signs of it then. On the trip here from Tennessee, it had flared up and become serious.

Tuesday, Sam's temperature seemed higher, and she made him a tea from dried gravel root and willow bark. Since willow bark helped with rheumatism and influenza as well as fever, Leah hoped it might help with the infection too. Ivy sat beside his bed that night.

Wednesday, Sam slept much of the day. Ivy often sat beside his bed and bathed his face with a cold cloth. Even when Sam remained unconscious, he seemed less restless when Ivy sat by his side.

While he appeared unaware, Leah had Moses hold down his arms and upper body while Ivy held one leg and Pasty the other. She scraped away a little more of the infected area. Then she heated a large knife in the fireplace and put it in the open wound. She applied it to one side first and then reheated it and placed it on the other side. The odor of the infection and the seared flesh smelled sickening, but this would be her last resort. She didn't know of anything else to try.

Sam fought against the pain and those who held him down. Ivy and Patsy had to put all their weight against his ankles to keep him from kicking loose.

Thursday, Sam remained unconscious, but the wound didn't look as bad. Leah took that as a good sign. She made him a drink similar to the one Hawk had given her for strength. She beat up an egg, added some honey, and filled the glass with milk. Ivy managed to get most of it in him for breakfast.

For dinner he drank some of the broth from the squirrels Leah cooked. She planned to make a squirrel stew with milk and butter. They had no flour for dumplings or to thicken it with, and there would be only cornbread for bread. She cooked enough to have for dinner and supper.

Sam ate a bowl full of the squirrel stew for supper. He seemed more alert but weak, so he didn't talk much. He smiled at Ivy and soon fell back to sleep.

Friday, Sam seemed a little better, and Leah began to have more hope for him. At least he seemed headed in the right direction.

He continued to gradually improve as Leah continued to doctor him. In a week, his fever had left, and Leah stopped the tea.

The following Thursday, she put a bandage on his leg and allowed him to get dressed, and he sat on the sofa with his bad leg up. She finally ordered him back to bed, because she could tell he still felt weak. He ate well now, however, so she believed his strength would soon return.

By Sunday, two weeks from the day he came, he stayed up all day and came to the table for meals. Leah gave a prayer of thanks.

Both Sam and Ivy thanked her profusely for what she'd done. They both seemed to understand how close Sam had come to dying.

"I'm pleased too," Leah told them. "I have a feeling Sam's going to become one of the family someday."

Ivy smiled as Sam watched her reaction. When he realized Ivy wasn't going to scold Leah for saying such a thing, he smiled too.

Luke realized most of the prisoners from Millen had been sent elsewhere. Only a fraction returned to Andersonville. "Why have we been shuffled all over the place?" he asked one of the friendlier guards.

"Because of Sherman. You were shipped out of here, because Sherman took Atlanta, and we feared he might head this way. He didn't. Instead, he headed for the coast, so we evacuated Millen, because they lay in that path. Camp Sumter shouldn't be as bad this time. There's going to be only about five thousand prisoners now."

It might not be as bad, but it couldn't be called good either. The rations were still as poor, and the stream had cleared only a little. With more space, however, the men had some choice in their ragged, haphazard shelters.

The Confederates had never had any intention of releasing them, though. They'd probably told them that to keep them from trying to escape. Still, Luke thanked God for their brief time at Millen. He felt better after being in the newer facility. Also, if Sherman had taken Atlanta and marched on, then the war must be close to an end.

———————————

Ivy looked at Sam and her heart quickened. She knew she'd fallen deeply in love with him. She'd admitted it to herself when he lay unconscious and so sick. That they'd almost lost him caused a chill to run through her.

The changed Sam touched her heart with his trustworthiness, honesty, and caring. Those qualities reminded her of Lawrence, but Sam differed greatly in other ways. Where Lawrence had pampered and protected her, Sam would treat her as an equal partner, more the way Luke did Leah. Where Lawrence had been patient and unassuming, Sam had a more direct, assertive manner. Ivy couldn't decide which traits she preferred, but she knew she'd loved Lawrence and now she loved Sam.

Because of her and Sam's personalities, she felt sure their relationship would prove volatile at times. However, it would also be exciting. Now, how did she let him know how she felt, and should she set things in motion now, or wait until he returned for good?

Sam looked at her. "A penny for your thoughts."

"I was thinking of you."

"I hope they're good thoughts."

"They always are when I think of you."

"Really? Do you never think of the past when you think of me?"

"Not anymore. I did at first, but I see you as a different man now."

"That's good. I am a different man now."

That night Ivy put Patrick to bed and came back downstairs. In about thirty minutes, everyone else started to bed, but when Ivy rose, Sam took her arm.

"Do you feel like talking?" he asked.

She sat back down on the sofa with him. She wondered what he wanted to talk about, but his face gave her no clues.

"I wondered if you might consider telling Patrick I'm his father now."

This hadn't been what she'd expected. She had hoped for something more personal. "I don't know. It might not be best with you going back to the war. I don't want him to lose two fathers."

"If something happened to me, he'd still be losing another father." His eyes pleaded with her.

"Yes, but it wouldn't hurt as much if he didn't know."

"Do you think Patrick likes me, maybe even loves me, already?"

"I'm sure he does."

"Then, wouldn't he be hurt, regardless?"

His argument had merit. "I guess so."

"And what about you? How would you feel if something happened to me?"

Fear clawed at her as she replied. "I'd be devastated."

Sam took her hands and looked into her eyes. His own eyes had softened and grown tender. "I love you with all my heart. Might I hope you love me too? I know you told me in your last letter you needed me and were growing fond of me, and you signed it 'Love.' Does that mean you love me too?"

She looked into his bright blue eyes and knew this man had depths she'd not even begun to see, but she wanted to see them. She wanted to explore them all and know every inch of him. "Yes, I love you very much," she whispered.

"Oh, Ivy!" He took her in his arms and held her. Then, he kissed her cheek, and his lips caused a tremble to run through her whole body. Something about Sam drew her to him with a force she couldn't deny. She remembered the first night they'd slept in each other's arms all those years ago. His kisses had left her so weak and rubbery, she'd had no will to resist him, and apparently that hadn't changed.

"Say you'll marry me," he said.

"When?"

"Promise to marry me now, and we'll have the ceremony any-time you want. I'd marry you tomorrow if that's what you wanted."

She laughed. "I'd like to have a preacher available."

"Then just agree to marry me, and we'll have the wedding when I return."

"All right."

"Yes? You said yes? I thought I'd have to wait much longer to win you. You've made me a very happy man." He took her in his arms again, but this time, instead of kissing her cheek he kissed her lips.

Suddenly Ivy became caught in an eddy over which she had no control. She just went with the flow of the whirlpool. She had no strength to do anything more.

When Sam pulled away, they both sat quietly to collect their breaths and their thoughts. Finally, Sam turned to her. "The strong attraction is still there."

"I think you'd better not do that again," Ivy told him.

"Why?" He looked as if she'd just broken off their engagement.

Ivy took a deep breath. "Because your kisses affect me way too much. Even just a kiss on the cheek sends tingles through my whole body. When you kiss me like you just did, I lose all sense of reason, and I want to maintain some restraint until we're married."

Her face grew hot from her detailed explanation, but she didn't think Sam would be offended. Indeed, he looked as if he'd been given a great treasure. "I understand, and that would probably be for the best. I feel much the same way. You know, that first time, I didn't set out to seduce you. You just felt so good in my arms that one thing led to another, and suddenly I couldn't stop."

"And now?"

"Now, I think I have more control, but it would still be better not to place too much temptation before us. For the most part, we'll save the passionate kisses until we're married."

Ivy raised her eyebrows. What did he mean by "for the most part"?

"I would still like a real good-bye kiss."

She smiled at him. "I'd like that too."

He smiled back. "Where would you like to live after we're married?"

"I don't really have anywhere in mind." She paused. "As long as we're together, any place will be okay with me."

"What would you think about Stanly County? I'm sure my uncle's offer will still be good. Could you take farming in Stanly County? It would be much more like the climate you had in Anson County."

"I think I might like that. Stanly is just west of Anson, isn't it? I know I've been through Albemarle several times. What's the name of the closest town to the farm?"

"Stanly is on the western side of Anson County. The closest town to the farm is Big Lick."

"What a strange name!" Ivy laughed.

"I understand it used to be a salt lick for deer. It's not a huge town, but it has a post office, several businesses, and a few churches in the area."

"I think it sounds like a good place for us."

"I'll write my uncle and tell him we're interested. I'll put it into a letter to my father and give him our news. I'd like for him to marry us if that's okay with you."

"It is, and I'll be working on my wedding dress. I plan to make it from the blue silk you sent me last Christmas."

"Perfect. Now when are we going to tell Patrick?"

"We'll tell him about our engagement now but wait to tell him you're his father. If you're agreeable, I'll tell him after you've left. I think it would be better if I told him, and he had time to get used to the idea before he sees you again. That will give him time to work through any problems he might have with it."

"What are you going to tell him?"

"The truth. That you and I acted as we were married when we weren't, and it was wrong. That when I was expecting him, Lawrence loved me enough to marry me, and he loved Patrick from the very first. I'll tell him now you and I want to be a family, and we think he should know everything."

"I wish we could tell him everything right away, so he'll know I'm his father before I ride out, but I'll go along with what you think's best. I'm just happy you'll agree to tell him before I come back."

"I love you, Sam Whitley, but I think we're two strong-willed people, and our road may not always be smooth."

"No, but it's going to be highly interesting and exciting. I love you, too, and our love is strong enough to see through anything."

The next day, Ivy, Sam, and Patrick walked to the barn. The day held a chill, but it didn't seem below freezing for a change.

"Patrick, how would you like it if Sam and I got married like Moses and Patsy did?" Ivy asked.

"I'd like that," Patrick answered.

"Then, that's what we'll plan to do as soon as the war's over and Sam gets back."

"Does that mean Sam will be my new father?"

Ivy heard Sam's quick intake of breath. Patrick had accepted Sam quicker than she thought he would. She knew how close he and Lawrence had been. "He would at least be your stepfather. What do you think about that?"

"I wish he could be my real father."

"Then, maybe I should tell you something else." She reached back for Sam to take her hand for support. "Sam and I met a long time ago . . . before I married Lawrence. We thought we loved each other then, and we did some things we shouldn't have until after we were married. We argued and Sam left, but I found out I was going to have a baby."

"Me?"

"Yes, you. Since I didn't know where Sam had gone, I married Lawrence, because he loved us both so much. I fell in love with Lawrence quickly, and we were very happy together. Lawrence loved you just like you were his own flesh and blood. However, Sam is your real father. Do you understand?"

"I think so."

"I didn't know about you until that first time I met you here, Patrick," Sam told him. "That's why I'd never tried to find you. I'd come here once before to check on your mother, and Luke and Leah told me she was happily married and had a son. I never guessed that son might be mine."

Patrick thought for a minute. "I'm glad you're my father."

"And I'm very glad you're my son. I love you so much." Sam got down on his knees, despite his leg. He put out his arms, and Patrick went to him.

As Sam embraced his son, Ivy felt tears trickling down her face, but these were happy tears.

"I'm going to tell the others," Patrick said.

Ivy could feel his excitement. She didn't tell him Patsy and Leah already knew, and Patsy had probably told Moses. She'd explain to him later the details must be a family secret and not for everyone to know. She watched as he ran to the cabin.

Sam's eyes looked watery. He seemed filled with emotion. "That went well, didn't it? Thank you for telling him now, Ivy."

She reached out and helped him stand. "I hadn't planned to do so, but it just came naturally with Patrick's questions and comments."

"Come here." Sam held out his arms to her, and she leaned into him.

She needed this man's comfort and support so much. She put her face against his shoulder, noticing how well she fit in his arms.

"We always did fit together well, didn't we, darling?"

"You've read my mind."

"I'd like to hold you forever, but come. We'd better get in out of the cold."

CHAPTER EIGHTEEN

Discord

THE DAYS FLEW BY AT breakneck speed. Sam's leg had healed nicely, although there would be an ugly scar left. It seemed a little stiff or sore from time to time, but for the most part, it gave him no problem.

Ivy and Sam spent much time together. Leah had told Ivy to not worry about the chores while Sam remained here, and they should enjoy this time together. Patrick often joined them, but sometimes he stayed to play with Rachel.

He treated Rachel like his baby sister, and Ivy wondered if Patrick wouldn't miss the little girl terribly when they left for Big Lick. They'd face that problem when it came, however. Maybe Patrick would surprise her as he had about Sam. Patrick already called Sam Papa. He'd called Lawrence Father.

Sam left on February the eleventh to make sure he would be back to report on the fifteenth. Clouds hung heavy overhead, and Ivy worried Sam might see bad weather. He thanked and hugged Leah for all she'd done. He said good-bye to Moses and Patsy and wished them and their new baby well. He took Patrick on a horse ride, brought him back, and held him for a long time before he released him. "You take good care of your mother," Sam told him. "I'm counting on you."

"I will," Patrick said, "and you take care of yourself and hurry home."

Ivy smiled at her son. He could act so grown up sometimes. The others went inside to give her and Sam some privacy, and Leah took Patrick with her. Ivy turned to Sam. "This is so hard."

"I know. How well I know!" He took her in his arms, and it felt so right, as if she were meant to be there. He held her tightly for several minutes, and she squeezed into him. "I'm going to miss you so much," he whispered in her ear. He kissed her then, before she could say she would miss him too.

She felt she became part of him, molded to him as mortar to brick. She was the pliable wet mortar, and he the solid brick that held her up. She knew she'd have collapsed if he hadn't held her.

When the kiss ended, he still held her for a long time.

"I'd have married you right away, if there'd been a preacher here," she told him.

"I know." He looked as if he were as unsteady as she. Still, he mounted and looked down at her. "I love you so much, Ivy. You could never know how much."

"Oh, yes I could, because I love you that much too."

"I'll be back soon, darling. The war can't last much longer now."

She nodded as the tears rolled down her face, and she watched him ride away.

Leah let Patrick come out to stand beside Ivy. Sam turned before he rode out of sight and waved at them. They waved back. Then, Patrick picked up his mother's hand and led her into the house as if he intended to take care of her, just like Sam had told him. She smiled at her son through the tears.

Sam had been gone only two days when they hit. A band of bushwhackers, no longer Confederate, Union, or deserter, but definitely outlaw, rode in with enough weapons to launch a war of their own. There must have been around fifty of them.

Moses and Patsy hid the guns under the loose board in their bedroom. Leah and Ivy quickly tangled their hair and smeared fireplace soot and grime over themselves to appear less attractive. They put some on Patrick and Rachel, so they all looked similar, and Ivy said a quick prayer for them all.

Some of the men worked outside. They stripped the smoke-house, the root cellar, and the larder. They led all the cattle away and caught as many chickens as they could. They even took the rest of the hay and feed in the barn and some of the wood, but they didn't have room in their wagons for it all.

Part of them came inside. They snatched all the food they could find, stripped the beds of all the bedding, grabbed many of the clothes, and even took some of the pots and pans from the kitchen.

"Why don't we heist the slaves and sell 'em?" one man asked the leader.

"That'd be hard in these parts 'cause nobidy's got the money, and 'sides, I'm thankin' the Yanks are goin' win this war, and thar won't be no more slaves."

The first one shrugged and walked off.

Ivy breathed easier. She would have hated to see what Moses would've done if the men had tried to take them.

"This here's a nice place you have," the boss said. "Why ain't you got no more food and supplies?"

"The salt, flour, and sugar has done been gone fur a long time, and we couldn't git inny more," Leah said, sounding very country, "and this here's the fourth time we've done been raided."

He laughed. Then, he looked at Ivy and Leah quizzically. "You women wouldn't be half bad lookin' cleaned up a bit, but I hain't that choosey anyways."

"Why, thank you," Ivy said. "It's been a long time since we've had a nice compliment like that, isn't it, Sis?"

"Not since we come down sick. Most men don't want nothin' to do with us now."

The man looked alarmed. "What's wrong with you?"

"Nothin' much," Leah said. "It only flares up now and then."

He backed off, and they left.

The women all sat down and looked around. The stripped cabin seemed to shout at them.

"They sure did load up a lot of our things," Patsy said.

"But, none of us are hurt," Leah said, "and that's the most important thing."

"Do we have enough to make it in the cave?" Ivy asked her sister.

"We won't starve, but we might go hungry some," Leah said. "We'll have to ration things out to make it last. No cows for milk or butter will hurt the most."

"You did a good job of acting with me," Leah told Ivy. "Those men didn't know what to think of our sickness."

"It did work, didn't it?" Ivy replied. "I'm glad you came up with the sickness part. That really scared them off."

About an hour later, Leah and Moses went to the cave to get something for breakfast and some bedding to use tonight. At least they had that.

Wednesday, Ivy and Leah spent most of the day straightening up the cabin. Patsy helped some, but she also had to spend time taking care of Ezra.

They discovered the raiders hadn't been able to catch all the chickens. About a third of what they'd had came back to roost.

Sunday, they planned a little birthday celebration for Rachel. She would turn two.

"Luke will have been gone three years in May," Leah said. "Rachel needs her father home."

"So does her mother," Ivy told her, and Leah agreed.

Ivy admired her sister. Leah always seemed so strong and capable. She wished she were more like her. Ivy had always needed someone to rely on, even her sister. She wondered what Leah would do if something had happened to Luke. Was Luke the only man she'd ever love? Ivy had thought that of Lawrence, and now look what'd happened. Sam Whitley had come back into her life.

Luke and Aaron resumed their Bible study in earnest. They'd done some at Millen, but Camp Lawton hadn't been as boring or depressing as Camp Sumter, and Aaron hadn't always joined Luke.

Luke and Aaron managed to not pick up any sickness until the end of February. Then Luke became sick. He couldn't keep anything in his stomach, and he grew terribly weak. Aaron tried to do what he could to help, but Luke gradually wasted away.

When he looked down, his body looked more like a skeleton. "If I don't make it, please go to my farm in Watauga County and talk with Leah. Tell her how much I've thought of her, and tell her I loved her to the end."

"You're not going to die," Aaron said. "I'm not going to let you. You can't leave me. I'm depending on you, even after the war. You may be the only family I have left, and even if not, I adopt you as my older brother. You can't desert me now, Luke Moretz. You just can't."

On March the twentieth, Reverend Whitley came. Ivy couldn't hide her surprise at seeing him, but then a terrifying thought hit her. Had something happened to Sam? She grabbed the door-frame for support.

"Nothing's wrong," he quickly assured her. He must have read her fear.

They invited him to dinner, and Ivy felt he'd come to inspect her. Sam must have written him about their pending marriage.

"We don't have much," Leah told him. "We're having a rabbit stew, and I'll make some cornbread."

"That sounds fine." He turned to Patrick. "You sure do look like Sam."

"He's my papa," Patrick said.

"So he told me, and that makes me your grandfather."

"You're the only grandparent he has," Ivy told him. "My parents are both dead."

"What about your first husband? Does he have relatives left?"

"None close."

"What was he like?"

Why was he asking her such a question? She could think of no reason he should ask about Lawrence.

"He was a wonderful man, kind and good. I couldn't have asked for a better husband. The three of us were very happy."

"How long has he been dead?"

"Over a year and a half."

"And, you think you're ready to remarry?"

"If it's to Sam."

"Sam says he treated you badly the first time. You don't harbor any bad feelings?"

"No. We were both young, immature, and made some bad choices. Thanks to our Savior, we're both different people now."

"I see you don't let someone intimidate you." He smiled at her for the first time. "Sam needs someone like that. He's always been headstrong, especially in his younger days. He's settled down quite a bit since then, but he can still be strong willed at times.

I'll be happy to marry you when he comes home. I think it may be fitting and proper for you two to wed, considering what all's happened, and I know he's very fond of you."

"Thank you."

"I need to be getting on to Boone," he said after dinner. "I thought I'd stay in Big Lick until spring, but that niece of mine got hard to live with. I don't think I've ever met such a flighty, self-centered girl, and she chatters about all the time."

"How old is she?" Leah asked.

"Old enough to do better. Let's see. Violet should be about twenty-five now. She's never been married, and I can see why. I don't see how any man could ever put up with her for long."

Ivy thought the preacher seemed overly judgmental, but maybe she shouldn't judge him either. Everyone had their faults.

"Oh, I've got letters for you, Ivy. Sam wrote me before I left my brother's farm, and he included one for me to give to you if I saw you before he did. He probably knows me well enough to know I wasn't going to stay there until spring. The other is from Violet, although I can't imagine why she'd be writing, but I gave up trying to understand her long ago."

He handed Ivy the two letters from his pocket, and she thanked him. How exciting to get an unexpected letter from Sam!

"Thank you for the meal, Mrs. Moretz. It was a fine one considering how hard it is to keep something on the table these days."

Ivy went to the sitting room and opened Sam's letter first. She now knew her prayers had been answered and he'd made it back safely.

My dearest Ivy,

I had an uncomfortable and unpleasant trip back, because I had to ride in the wrong direction—away from you. As you can tell, though, I made it back.

I learned that in January, Fort Fisher, on the coast of North Carolina, fell to the Yankees. It had protected Wilmington, and that city has now been occupied since February.

How are things there? I hope you've not had any trouble. There's even been talk here of the outlaw bands who are ravaging the poor mountain farms. I'm praying no harm will come to any of you. I can't stand the thoughts of what you could be going through, but I will put you in God's hands and trust Him to protect you.

I miss you so much. What I wouldn't give to see you now and hold you in my arms! I can't wait until you and I are married, and the three of us can be a family.

I'm very proud of Patrick. He's a wonderful boy, and you're to be commended on how well you've reared him.

General Joe Johnston has been brought back to command a small army in the Carolinas. I've asked to transfer to one of his units. We'll probably be up against Sherman again. He's taken Savannah and is destroying a wide path as he heads back north.

I wrote to my uncle at the same time I wrote to father and sent this for you. I'm hoping his offer is still open, and you and I can make our home there. If not, we'll just try to buy us a place somewhere else. I'm looking forward to that time.

I'm almost thankful for the injury that sent me home, because it brought us together. I love you so much. I think of you all the time. You're the woman I've always dreamed of, and, now that you're mine, it's almost too good to be true.

All my love,

Sam

Ivy read Sam's letter one more time. Then she turned to the one from Violet. After what Reverend Whitley had said, she couldn't help but be curious.

Dear Ivy,

I am very surprised to learn you're planning to marry Sam. You see, I thought I would do that after the war. Things would be so much easier for Sam, if he had this farm and property. It's going to be hard for him in this war-torn country, if he has to start with nothing. Are you ready for you and your son to be impoverished? You need to consider what's best for your boy, too, you know.

Not only do we own hundreds of acres of land, but a large two-story farmhouse, plenty of outbuildings, lots of animals, and the tools and seeds needed to keep the farm going. It's a very nice working farm, and it could all be Sam's, if he marries me.

You see, I go with the farm. Sam isn't going to get all this unless he marries me. Do you really want what's best for Sam? If you do, you'll give him up. How selfish are you, Ivy? Think about all this. Give it much thought, and I'm sure you'll do what's best for your son and Sam.

Sincerely,

Violet Whitley

Ivy sat stunned. She didn't know what to think. Should she talk to Sam about it? No, he'd only give up the farm for her, but would that be best for him? Would it be better if he married his cousin? Would Sam, Patrick, and she live in poverty without the farm? Could she stand to watch Patrick do without things he really needed?

Ivy had been used to fine things on the plantation too. Moving to a farm, where she'd have to do much of the work, would already be a concession. Could she also tolerate a meager existence? She shook her head. No, she wouldn't think of herself. That's what she'd done the first time she'd been with Sam, and they'd argued about it. This time she would think of only Patrick and Sam.

She could ask Leah about it, but she already knew what her sister would say. Leah believed in love. She'd advise Ivy to tell Sam about this. No, Ivy needed to start making her own decisions. She'd be thirty soon, and she needed to start making her own choices. She had some time to think it through before the war ended.

———————————

April seemed too early to be planting most of the garden, but they sure did need the fresh food. Leah hoped they had enough seeds saved. There seemed to be fewer every year. The potato crop would be small, because they'd eaten most of those.

They'd been eating the meat Moses managed to kill, but it would be time to stop that soon when the temperatures heated up. How would they manage then?

They'd eaten all the vegetables, except for a few seed potatoes. The chickens were beginning to lay better, but with their depleted numbers, the family couldn't count on but one or two meals from them a week.

Their clothes had begun to wear out, but they didn't have much to make more from, and Leah didn't have any raw material to spin or weave.

They should be able to make it for this year, but Leah worried about the coming winter. If the war continued, starvation might become a reality.

She worried about Ivy too. Something seemed to be bothering her sister, but she had no idea what. Leah had tried to get her to talk, but Ivy said she had nothing to talk about. Ivy had always talked to her in recent years, but not now. She'd started acting troubled right after she read Sam's letter. Had something come between them? Ivy didn't even act excited about marrying Sam anymore.

The third week in April, Mr. Hendrix came up the mountain again. Leah ran out hoping he was bringing a letter from Luke, but he had another reason for coming.

"I came to tell you the war is over." He caught his breath. "Lee surrendered to Grant on April the ninth, and Johnston surrendered to Sherman a little over a week later."

Leah hoped this meant Luke would finally come home. Surely he could come home now. She looked at Ivy, who didn't look all that happy. What was wrong with her?

———————————

"Luke, Luke!"

Luke thought, *What is Aaron yelling about?*

"The war is over, can you hear me? We're being rescued. We can go home."

Luke didn't have the energy to answer. Everything appeared foggy. He thought someone said the war had ended, but he had probably been dreaming. He'd been doing a lot of that lately.

"Come on, son," someone said. "We'll send you home, and take the old man here to a hospital."

Old man! Was someone calling him an old man? He wasn't old. He was only in his early thirties. This must still be part of his dream. Luke couldn't tell.

"I'm not leaving him."

That definitely sounds like Aaron.

"Where he goes, I go. Do you have any idea what we've been through together? List me as sick too. I doubt if I weigh over a hundred pounds, but I am going where Luke goes."

"Okay," the stranger said, "we'll get you both to a hospital."

Luke felt himself slipping back into oblivion. Was he dying? At first he felt happy to be leaving his sorry condition behind, but then he thought of Leah. *Oh Lord, I don't want to leave Leah. And I need to see my daughter.*

———————

Sam rode up to the farm, and Patrick came running out to meet him.

He picked him up and hugged him. "Where's your mama?"

"She's in the house."

"Is she okay?"

"I guess. She's acted kind of sad lately, but I don't think she's sick."

Sam hurried toward the house. He couldn't imagine why Ivy hadn't come out to meet him. He'd expected a warmer welcome. He went up to Ivy, but she continued with her mending. By the expression on her face, he knew something was wrong. "I'm finally home for good, Ivy."

"I know. Welcome back. You look thin. Have you been sick?"

"No, we just didn't have enough to eat. Don't I get a hug? I had hoped for a kiss."

"I think we need to talk first, Sam."

She would hardly look at him, and Sam had a sinking feeling. She'd changed from the last time he'd been here. Did she change her mind about him? *Lord, please, no!* "Okay. Where do you want to talk?"

"Let's walk outside. I don't want to be disturbed."

Sam followed her across the road to the meadow where the spring flowers bloomed in abundance. He couldn't enjoy the beautiful spot now, though. Ivy had his full attention. "What's wrong, Ivy?"

"I think we may have moved too quickly," she told him. "I'm not sure I'm ready for marriage."

She couldn't mean that. Was she breaking off the engagement?

"I'll wait until you're ready, then."

"I may never be ready, so you need to move on. The war's over now. Go to Big Lick and get your farm."

"I don't want a farm without you. What's this really all about, Ivy? What's happened? Have you met someone else?"

"No, I haven't met anyone else, but I don't think I'm the right one for you."

"Are you kidding? You're exactly the right one for me. You're the woman I love. I thought you loved me too." He put his hand gently to her face to get her to look at him, but she jerked back from his touch as if he'd burned her. Was she afraid of him? "Please don't do this, Ivy. Don't break my heart. I need your love so much. I promise I'll be good to you. Give us a chance. Don't throw our love away."

Tears started forming in her eyes. Maybe she did care.

He put out his hands to pull her into his embrace, but she broke loose and ran for the house. Sam stood in the meadow after Ivy had gone into the house. Never had he imagined anything like this would happen. It felt more like a nightmare. He couldn't even begin to understand what had happened. Ivy had been so happy with him when he'd been here before. She seemed to love him as much as he did her. What could have possibly happened?

He finally went to the house in search of Leah. Maybe she could shed some light on the situation. Apparently Ivy refused to do so.

"I have no idea what it is," Leah said. "I noticed a change in her after your father came, and she got your letter. Did you write anything that might cause this?"

"No. My letter didn't say anything different than before. I gave her a little of the war news. I told her how happy she'd made me and that I missed her and loved her. I'm sure I said nothing that would've upset her. What about Father? What did he say to her?"

"He asked her one question after another. Ivy answered them all, even though some were about Lawrence. Your father then told her he thought she might be the right one for you, and he'd be happy to marry the two of you when you came home."

"Did anyone else come here?" Lines etched between Sam's eyes.

"Just the outlaws who raided the farm and Mr. Hendrix to tell us the war had ended."

"Did those men hurt Ivy or was she alone with any of the bushwhackers?"

Leah shook her head. "No on both questions. In fact, she still looked forward to you coming home then. The sadness didn't come until after your father came and she read your letter."

"Do you have any other ideas?"

"No, I don't. I've tried to talk with her, but she won't talk with me, either." Could Sam tell how frustrated Leah felt?

"Do you have any suggestions?" He sounded desperate.

"Just don't give up on her, Sam. I've seen you two together, and I know Ivy loves you. I don't know why she's trying to pull back, but I'm certain she still loves you."

He looked away. "She's got a strange way of showing it." Was he trying to hide his emotions?

"I'll try to talk with her again. You go on to Boone and stay with your father for now, but come back in a few days to see Patrick. Ivy won't keep you from seeing your son."

"Okay, but something's happened to cause this change in her, and we need to find out what it is." He looked as defeated as the Confederate army.

———————

Leah went to find Ivy as soon as Sam left. "What do you think you're doing?" she asked. "Why are you cutting Sam's heart out like this? He looks like he's been through too many hard times already. I bet he's lost thirty pounds. How can you care so little for his well-being?"

"You wouldn't understand."

"I don't understand, but I'd like to. What's caused you to fall out of love with Sam so quickly?"

"I haven't fallen out of love with him."

"Then why did you break off the engagement? Why don't you want to marry him? He's the same man he was three months ago when he was here. It's you that's turned fickle and changed."

"Stop!" Ivy yelled and burst into tears. She ran to her bedroom and slammed the door. Leah could hear her crying all the way downstairs.

"Is Mama mad at Papa?" Patrick asked.

"I don't know," Leah told him. "Do you know what's been making your mama so sad?"

Patrick shook his head. She gave him a hug. He seemed almost as scared and worried as Sam.

Leah knocked and went into Ivy's bedroom. She just didn't understand her sister's behavior and it upset her. "I'm not going to leave you alone until you tell me what's going on. You've got

Patrick about as upset as Sam. Your son is scared his family is falling apart."

Ivy burst into tears again, but Leah didn't leave. She'd shocked Ivy out of melancholy once, and she hoped she could do so again.

"Talk to me, Ivy. Let me help you."

"I'm trying to think of what's best for others and not only myself."

"You're making no sense. Is it best for Sam to be jilted by the love of his life? Is it better for Patrick to have his mother and father separated?"

"Maybe it is."

"What does that mean? Explain it to me. Make me understand."

"Go away, Leah. Leave me alone. It's time I start making my own decisions."

"If this is the way you make decisions, then you need someone to help you."

Ivy turned her back to Leah and said nothing. Leah had never seen her like this before.

When Sam came again, Ivy wouldn't come down to see him. "I'm very disappointed in Ivy," Leah told him, "but I don't know what to do. I knew Ivy could have a single purpose and be very stubborn in the past, but I thought she had moved beyond that now."

"She didn't say anything to you?"

"The only comment I got out of her was something about her trying to think of others and not only of herself. I think she's confused. I know she's not making any sense."

"She's not thinking of me. What 'others' is she talking about?" Sam spent the rest of his time with Patrick. At least, his son acted happy to see him.

Before he left, Leah took Sam to Ivy's door. Ivy had now started locking it.

"Please don't do this, Ivy," he begged as he stood in the hall and spoke through the door. "Don't be so cruel as to make me think my dreams are coming true, only to snatch them all away. I hurried home to you to find you're rejecting me. What have I done wrong? At least let me know what the problem is. Is this your way of paying me back for the way I mistreated you in the past?"

Ivy gave no answer, only silence.

"Are you sure Ivy hasn't had contact with someone you haven't told me about?" Sam asked Leah right before he left.

"I hadn't thought of it before, and it doesn't seem important, but your father also brought her a letter from your cousin, Violet."

"Why would Violet write to Ivy?"

"I don't know, and Ivy didn't tell me anything. In fact, I'd forgotten all about it, or I'd have asked Ivy about it. Your father indicated Violet could be difficult to be around."

"That's probably putting it mildly. She's always been a troublemaker, and none of the family can get along with her. I'll see what father thinks."

Sam came again in two days. He planned to leave the next day to travel to his uncle's farm near Big Lick. "If Violet has anything to do with the way Ivy's acting, I think I can get it out of her," he said. "She talks too much to keep a secret."

Sam spent the day with Patrick until it was time for him to leave. He didn't try to speak to Ivy.

"Why did you run Papa off?" Patrick pointedly asked his mother. "He came home to us just like he promised, but you aren't marrying him like you promised. Didn't you tell me people should always try to live up to their promises?"

"You wouldn't understand," Ivy told him with tears in her eyes as she left the table and went back to her room.

"Has Sam left?" Ivy asked Leah the next morning.

"So now you're interested in Sam. Yes, he went to his uncle's farm in Big Lick."

Ivy turned pale, but she said, "That's probably for the best."

CHAPTER NINETEEN

Changed Mind

IVY FELT THE LIFE DRAIN from her. She made it to the sitting room and fell to the sofa. Why did Sam's leaving affect her so much? She'd thought this was what she wanted. Yet, the thought that Sam might actually marry Violet sent a panic all through her. What had she done? She may have doomed three or four people to misery.

Ivy had no doubt Sam loved her more than Violet, but could he be happy with Violet and make a good life there? Would things be better for him with the farm? The thought of Sam having children with someone else almost made her sick to her stomach.

And what about her? She'd been trying not to look at this selfishly, but how would she ever make it without Sam? Her heart felt like it had a vast hole in it now.

Perhaps she should go back and check on the plantation, but she wouldn't be able to stay there by herself. She had no way of making a living for her and Patrick, and Fair Oaks would be filled with memories of Lawrence. She soaked her pillow with tears that night.

Sam came back in two weeks. Ivy had never seen him look so determined. She ran to her room and locked the door before he got inside. She heard him come straight up the stairs. "Ivy, if you don't open this door right now, I will break it down."

She could tell by his tone of voice, he meant every word. She felt like she walked to her death sentence, but she opened the door.

"How dare you believe some connived story Violet Whitley told you! I would never marry her, even if she were the last woman on earth! Didn't Father tell you what she's like?"

"You're so-so angry, you're scar-ar-ing me, Sam," she stuttered.

He stopped, looked at her, and calmed down. His eyes softened, and his anger dissipated. He took her arm, moved her to the edge of the bed, and sat down beside her. She didn't know if her sudden weakness came from the situation or from his touch.

"Ivy, if I can't marry you, I'll never marry anyone. Look at me. I'm thirty-three years old. I've never married, because every girl I considered courting couldn't come close to being what you were to me. You're the only one for me. Don't you know that? How could you even consider what Violet said?"

"She wrote you would get the farm only if you married her. She said I shouldn't be selfish and make life hard for you. I've been selfish most of my life. I thought this would be a chance for me to make restitution. I wanted to love you enough to let you go."

"How irrational! Don't you know the hardest thing in the world would be my losing you? Nothing else could ever hurt me worse than that. Besides, Violet flat-out lied. My uncle has never suggested I marry Violet. I just talked with him. Southern landowners are expecting heavy property taxes to help pay for the war. Uncle Grover told me, if I would pay the taxes, I could have his farm. He's too old and tired for the heavy work without his sons to help him. He wants to go to Raleigh and move in with his oldest daughter and her husband, who's an attorney there. Right now, he doesn't have the money for any taxes, but I don't even want to consider the farm if you won't go there with me."

"You're sure about all this?"

"I'm very sure, although sometimes I ask myself why. You can be a handful of trouble, Ivy. Are you through wreaking havoc on my heart? I think you've taken ten years off my life."

"I'm sorry I hurt you. I thought I was doing what was best."

"Well, you'd better let me make those decisions from now on. Your thinking gets skewed at times. Seriously, Ivy, don't shut me out. Always come and talk with me about any problems. We can work them out together much better."

She nodded. "I didn't come to you about this, because I felt you would sacrifice the farm for me."

"If I did have to give up the farm, it would be no sacrifice. Not having you would be torture. Fighting for you is much worse than anything I faced in the war. Are we finished with this mess? Are you going to marry me?"

"Oh, yes, Sam. I'm going to marry you. I've tormented myself too. When you went to Big Lick, I realized how impossible it would be for me to live without you."

"Good. I hope you remember that lesson." He pulled her into his arms, and she knew this was where she belonged. He pulled back and then looked into her eyes. "I want to hold you for the rest of our lives." His lips moved toward hers.

"Don't you dare try to kiss me here in my bedroom." She got up and hurried to the door.

He laughed. "You're right, darling," he said. "That's much too dangerous for us."

When they went down the stairs holding hands, Leah and Patsy smiled.

Patrick ran to them. "Can we be a family now?"

"Yes, we can," Sam told him. "Your mother has finally come to her senses. Again."

Leah and Ivy had made her wedding dress before Ivy had gotten the letter from Violet. Sam seemed determined to rush the wedding, so Ivy wouldn't have a chance to back out again.

They were married in the meadow on a beautiful spring day. The sun's rays sparkled over the late-May flowers, and the sky nearly matched Ivy's dress. Leah had helped her make a wreath of spring flowers for her head, and she carried a bouquet of them. According to the look in Sam's face, Ivy had to be the most beautiful woman in the world. Patrick walked her to Sam, and Sam's father married them. Only the family attended.

When Sam kissed her after the ceremony, she clung to him to keep from crumpling to the ground. Never had she felt such a burning sensation within her.

When Sam's lips released her, he looked at her with a gleam in his eyes, as if he knew exactly how she felt. He put his arm around her waist and helped her toward the house. "It's all right, darling," he whispered. "I feel the same way."

"I don't think so," she told him. "You seem to be standing and walking fine."

———————————

Leah held back the tears as she watched Ivy and Sam marry in the same meadow she and Luke had. It'd been so long since she'd heard from him, she almost felt like a widow. She looked over at Rachel. Their daughter had turned two in February.

Ezra began to cry in his mother's arms. Leah breathed a heavy sigh. She'd let the baby do the crying for her today. She would wait until tonight and leave her tears in her pillow. *Luke, where are you? The war is over now. Come home!*

Sam finally located Leah a milk cow for the farm. It hadn't been easy, because many families had lost theirs too. Leah had the money she and Luke had stashed under the tree root, and Sam had finally located a family with three cows, who were willing to sell one.

Sam, Ivy, and Patrick packed up to leave the first of June. Sam wanted to get as much in the ground for this planting season as he could.

Leah hated to see them go. "Write me," she told Ivy. "Tell me everything. I'm going to miss you and Patrick so much."

"I'll miss you, too, Sis. Thanks for everything you've done for us. Patrick and Rachel are going to miss each other too. Just look at them."

Sure enough, the two children were standing to one side. Patrick had his arm around Rachel's shoulder, and she had hers around his waist.

The farm felt lonely after they left. Rachel seemed melancholic without Patrick, and her laughter and excitement had faded. Leah tried to get her interested in Ezra, who was a year old now, but Rachel wouldn't be distracted. She wanted to be Patrick's little sister, not Ezra's big one. Patrick had definitely spoiled her.

In June, Luke became lucid enough to realize he lay in a hospital bed and not a makeshift tent. He looked over and saw Aaron sitting in a chair beside his bed and looking tired, but better than the last time Luke had seen him at Camp Sumter.

"Where are we?" Luke asked.

Aaron jerked to his feet and stood beside the bed. "I'm glad you finally decided to live. I was beginning to wonder if you ever would. We're at a hospital somewhere in Georgia. You were too sick to move far."

"Is the war over, or did I dream it?"

"The war's been over for about two months now. You've been here for about seven weeks."

"Have you written to Leah?"

"I didn't know for sure where to write, and I thought it might be better to wait to see if you made it first. You've been awfully sick, but even when your body seemed to heal, your mind didn't come back to the present. I've been really worried."

"I'm back now and ready to go home. Where's my Bible and Leah's picture?"

"They're right here. I brought them for you."

The nurses had been spoon-feeding him broth, juices, and liquids, but now they began bringing him solid foods. Maybe he'd soon begin to gain some weight and strength. Aaron already had. Right now, however, he still felt too weak to even get out of bed.

July came before Luke could walk well enough to leave the hospital, and he still tired easily. He was determined to get back home, however, so they boarded a passenger train headed to Morganton, North Carolina, the closest a train went to Watauga County. The Union army gave them some back pay, and they thought they would be able to buy a horse to ride to the farm.

July came, and Leah lost hope for the first time. She knew Luke would have come home by now if he could. Had she totally misinterpreted things? Was he dead? Father said he hadn't been listed on any of the death charts.

She picked up her copy of their wedding photograph. How many times had she done this over the past three years? Too many to count, but she needed the real Luke standing before her.

She had shown the picture to Rachel. She'd taught her daughter to say Papa when she pointed to Luke. Was that all Rachel would ever see of her father?

She, Moses, and Patsy had planted the garden by hand. They didn't have a horse or mule to pull the plow. At least, the soil here didn't pack and become hard like the ground in Anson County had. They planted only half a field of corn, because they didn't have any more seed. She'd had a few potatoes and bean, squash, pea, and pumpkin seeds to plant, but the garden looked skimpy when compared to other years. Leah hoped the stores would soon have more to buy now that the war was over. She couldn't wait to buy flour and sugar. They desperately needed salt too.

Leah and Moses were working in the garden when the two riders came. Leah knew one was Luke, not so much by how he looked, but by how her heart started racing. She almost feared her eyes were just seeing what they wanted to see, but her feet still ran as fast as they could to Luke.

He jumped from his horse, and they almost toppled each other, they met with such force. He held her so tightly he almost squeezed the breath from her. "Oh, Leah, my Leah," Luke whispered.

He took both her hands and pulled back to look at her. He had changed. His gaunt look said he'd been sick for a long time. His eyes were more sunken, and they had the look of someone who'd seen unimaginable horrors. He was so thin he looked nothing like the man who'd left.

He turned and introduced Aaron Carter to her. He looked only a little better. Moses came to take their horses, and Leah introduced him.

"Come," she said, clutching Luke's hand. "You need to meet your daughter."

Rachel sat playing on the kitchen floor while Patsy worked on supper. She stared up at Luke, who bent down to her level.

A smile broke across Rachel's face. She pointed at Luke. "Papa."

Luke picked up his daughter and held her against his chest. "Yes, that's right, Rachel. I'm your papa." Tears were trickling down his face. "She's beautiful, Leah. A cross between you and my mother. Where's Granny and Hawk?"

Leah paused. She couldn't figure a way to soften the blow. "They're both dead. Granny Em died in her sleep. Hawk made her casket and dug her grave. He died the following day."

Luke sat down as emotion swept over him. "I never imagined Granny wouldn't be here when I got back. Granny has always been here for me." He paused. "I need some time alone," he told Leah and walked outside.

Leah knew he'd head straight to the graves, but she felt shut out. Didn't Luke know how much she needed to be with him right now? Didn't he need to be with her after his long absence?

She followed at a distance but kept him in sight. He stared at Granny Em's and Hawk's graves. Then he got on his knees beside Granny Em's, and Leah could tell he was praying.

When he stood, she went to him. "Don't turn from me, Luke. We've spent too much time apart. It wouldn't have been as bad if I had continued to hear from you, but not to know anything made me an easy target for fear. What happened? Where have you been?"

"I was taken prisoner at Gettysburg and transported to Salisbury prison. I tried to get word to Father and a letter to you, but Father's house had been closed up, and I don't think the letters to you were ever sent. Then, they transferred me to Andersonville, where I almost died. Thirteen thousand prisoners died in that horrendous place."

"I'm so sorry." Leah began to understand what Luke's eyes told her. He'd seen and been through unspeakable horrors. He would need time to heal and readjust.

"I'm not the same man who rode off to war, Leah. I'll probably never be. I don't even know if I can be the husband you need anymore. I'm not sure I even remember how."

"You'll always be the husband I need, Luke. You never have to worry about that. I've changed too. Time and the war have changed us all, but you and I still love each other. I feel it as strongly now as ever, and that love won't fail us. Besides"—she smiled at him—"it'll be fun discovering each other all over again."

He managed to smile too. "Was it terribly hard here?"

"We had plenty of challenges, but we made it, and we made it thanks to you. The plans you made before you left saved us. We'd have had everything stolen if it hadn't been for the cave and the place to hide our valuables, and we would've starved."

He nodded.

She could tell that surprised and pleased him. Maybe he needed to know he'd helped them survive and wanted reassurance they still needed him. "Come," she said, "let's go eat supper. You look like you could use some good food. We'll have plenty of time to tell each other what's happened while we've been apart. I may not let you out of my sight for a long time."

Thanks and praise filled the family devotion that night. Luke led it while Rachel sat in his lap, and Leah sat close to his side.

"I understood salvation from our Bible studies in the prison," Aaron told Luke. "I promised God, if you and I made it out of prison in one piece, I would get serious about my faith. That might not have been the right thing to do, to bargain with God, but here we are. I prayed the prayer of salvation when I saw you were going to be all right. I'd like to be baptized soon."

"That's wonderful," Luke told him.

"Sam Whitley's father is back in Boone," Leah said. "I'm sure he'd be happy to baptize Aaron." She went on to tell Luke about Sam and Ivy.

Luke remained tentative and unsure of himself. Leah kept reminding herself to give him time. She slowly got him to talk about prison life. It came out little by little, but it enabled her to understand the man before her, and it helped Luke dispel some of the ghosts from the dreadful images engraved in his mind.

She cooked him the cream of pea soup he loved. He ate until she thought he'd burst. She smiled. He needed to put some meat on his bones.

When she told him what had happened at the farm, he expressed concern over the several raids. "You've handled things here very well," he told her. "I knew you could do it, but I'm sorry you had all the responsibly fall on you after Hawk died."

"I'm so glad Jasper sent me Moses. We'd have never made it if it wasn't for him. I just did what I had to do, Luke. We both did what we had to do to survive."

"Let's go to Salisbury to see Father," Luke said. "Moses and Patsy can see to the farm. They'll probably enjoy having the place all to themselves for about a month, anyway. We'll return in plenty of time for most of the harvest. We may be able to pick up some supplies there too."

———

At the end of August, Luke hooked his and Aaron's horses to the wagon, they loaded up their few necessities, and the four of them proceeded to Wilkesboro.

"The two horses will see us down the mountain," Luke said. "We can get more in Salisbury to get us back up."

At the inn in Wilkesboro, Luke felt the most relaxed he'd felt in years. The memories from here reminded him of his and Leah's past and promised them a future. He began to touch his wife, feeling she wanted him as much as he wanted her. He'd been restrained at first and unsure of what their relationship would be. He feared he'd never be the man she needed.

Leah had understood enough to be patient with him, however. She'd let him take the lead in their relationship, but she'd been eager for wherever he led. He looked at his wife. What a remarkable woman!

She was a good listener too. He'd told her much more about the prison at Andersonville than he'd intended. No matter how gruesome the details, she listened attentively, never winced, and always held him in her arms afterwards. Her reaction had told him, no matter what had happened to him or how he'd changed, she still loved and wanted him. She wouldn't try to make him fit the mold of the old Luke. She could be happy with the new one.

The morning after they'd spent the night in Wilkesboro, Luke slept later than usual. He awoke to find Leah gone, and she had taken Rachel from the trundle bed. He must have slept soundly, if she'd dressed and gone downstairs without waking him.

As he approached their table, Aaron and Leah were so intent on each other, they didn't notice him. He stopped, and a stab of jealousy pierced him. He remembered how pretty Aaron had said Leah was when Luke first showed him her photograph. He tried to calculate how much older Leah would be than Aaron. Probably only a few years. Then, he heard what they were saying.

"You're so good for him," Aaron said.

"He's good for me too. I almost cry when I think of how close I came to losing him. I don't know what I'd have done. Existed, I guess, but never lived."

"You might have married again someday."

"I don't think so. I'm not like Ivy or Granny Em. I've known Luke was the only man for me even before our wedding. I think I'm made to love only one man, and that man is Luke."

"I know he loves you that much too. You and his faith are what got him through his time in prison, and he forced me to get through it with him. We both came out sounder than most. I know some of those men will end up in insane asylums. One even killed his own brother for food and buried the bones underneath where he slept. Neither Luke nor I ever intentionally harmed anyone else, and that's made it easier for us to readjust."

"Thank you for talking with me about Luke. I want to understand and help him. I want to be the wife he needs now."

"You are. I hope I can find a love like yours someday."

Luke joined them then, and his heart jumped for joy at the smile his wife gave him. *Thank you, God. Thank you so much for Leah.*

When Luke arrived in Salisbury with Leah, Rachel, and Aaron, his father held him close for a long time. Then, he gave Leah and Rachel a big hug. Rachel took to Dr. Moretz as quickly as she had to Luke. She didn't know about Maggie or Aaron, however.

"I can see all three of the people I've loved so much in Rachel," Father said. "There's Sarah, Luke, and Leah. She's adorable, and she's going to grow up to be a beauty. You'll have to watch out for her, Luke."

Luke chuckled. "Oh, I will."

Luke watched Maggie and Aaron's reaction when they were introduced. Luke had used Maggie as an incentive to give Aaron the will to live. He didn't know how much Aaron had thought about her, but his friend had made it out of Andersonville. Aaron seemed friendly and watched Maggie carefully, but Luke couldn't tell what he thought. Maggie, on the other hand, seemed definitely interested.

Luke looked at the two. Aaron was indeed handsome, now that he had cleaned up and grown healthier. He had medium brown hair that showed lighter streaks in the sun, hazel eyes, and an easy smile. Maggie had changed since he'd last seen her. She had filled out to a woman's figure, her countenance had softened, and she seemed relaxed. It gave her an air of self-assurance she probably didn't feel, but it also made her attractive. Her blue-gray eyes held a warmth and understanding Luke had never seen in her before. He decided she looked more like their father than she did Frances.

"So, when will we get to see Mrs. Price?" Leah asked.

"She still lives in the cottage, and I know she'd love to see you," Father said.

Something in Leah's and his father's voice caught his attention. What did they know that he didn't? He would ask Leah tonight.

"Why don't we invite her to supper tomorrow," Maggie said. "We can have a family dinner party and celebrate Luke's return, our new visitor, and all our special guests."

"That's a wonderful idea, Maggie," Father said. "You plan it as you'd like, and let me know if you need anything. I know plenty of women who'd love to help out for a little money."

———

The dinner party turned out to be a huge success. Aaron looked at Maggie, and he felt overwhelmed. Everything Luke had said about her appeared true. He'd thought of her often to get him through the agony of Andersonville, and he'd even pretended she belonged to him. After he'd gone to Luke's mountain farm, however, reality began to sink in, and he knew he'd be foolish to think like that.

Maggie belonged to a different class than him. She could handle a dinner party with ease and seemed used to the social life of a town like Salisbury. What use would she have for a poor mountain man from West Virginia? Spending some time at the university might have made him more informed, but it hadn't added much culture to the backwoodsman.

She was lovely in an unusual way. She would never be picked from a crowd for being gorgeous, but she had an inner beauty to her. She made his former girlfriend in Charlottesville pale by comparison.

Aaron didn't know what to do about Maggie. Her eyes told him she might be interested in him, but what could Aaron offer her? It had taken all his money to buy the horse in Morganton, a few clothes, and spend the night in Wilkesboro on the way here. He had just enough for one more night at the inn, and then he'd be broke.

They had such different backgrounds, too, and he would always bear the burden of knowing firsthand what Andersonville prison had been like. He understood a little of what Luke had felt when he got home. Their experiences had placed shadows over their lives that would always be there.

He couldn't really ask Luke for advice. He knew his friend would encourage him to take the chance, but he needed to figure things out for himself in his own time.

"Tell me about yourself," Maggie would say to Aaron, and so he did.

He told her about his deceased parents and the brothers and sisters who were too old for him to know well. He told her of his life in West Virginia, and how poor they'd been at times, but how his mother had taught him before she died. He had even managed to receive a scholarship to the University of Virginia before the war. Through all their conversations, Maggie would smile at him as if she approved.

He asked her questions, too, and she gave him all the information, but she didn't tell him about how she felt. She didn't let him know her childhood had been unhappy, as Luke had indicated. Their relationship remained on the surface.

After two weeks, Aaron became more desperate. Half their time of visiting here was gone, and he needed to push himself to action if anything were to develop between him and Maggie. He told himself, if she rejected him, he would be no worse than he was now, but he knew her rejection would be hard to accept. Could he take such a wound?

Maggie tended to be reserved, so after dinner one day, he asked Maggie to walk with him in the garden. She quickly accepted.

"This is pretty," he said as they entered the gate. "In West Virginia, a garden means vegetables."

"It usually does here too," Maggie replied, "but Father has always enjoyed having this small European-style garden."

"I like it too."

"What are your plans now?" she asked him. "Do you plan to go back to the university?"

"I haven't really made any plans, but I don't want to continue my education. I don't think I want to do anything which would require a degree. I like Luke's mountain farm, so I might like to own something like that one day."

"Are you a Christian?"

"I am. I just recently accepted Christ as my Lord and Savior, and I was baptized right before we came here. Luke had his Bible in prison, and we studied the Bible together."

"My faith is important to me. I don't think I would ever be interested in a non-believer."

"Are you interested in me, Maggie?"

She blushed, and Aaron knew he had been too direct and forward, but he couldn't take it back now. Instead, he continued. "I'm sorry if my question embarrassed you. It's just we're not going to be here much longer, and I need to know how you feel."

"I'm interested."

"I'm certainly interested in you also. The problem is I have nothing to offer someone like you. I am practically penniless."

"You have yourself."

"Would that be enough?"

"It might be. I think there's a good possibility it would."

"Did you know Luke told me about you when we were in prison to keep me from giving up when things became so bad? I thought he'd exaggerated, but you're even more special than he told me."

"In what ways?"

"You can be direct, too, I see. You're very pretty with an inner beauty, and I love your personality. You're easy to be around, quiet, and unassuming."

She laughed then. "I'm not sure any of that's true. My mother found fault in almost everything I did. I could never please her. I grew to be shy, withdrawn, and self-conscious because of it. She died when I was fifteen, and Father started spending much more time with me. He taught me to believe in myself and to have some confidence. Every now and then, however, those negative feelings want to seize control of me again."

"I think you're wonderful."

"And you're so different than any man I've ever met, although you might remind me a little of Father."

"I'm not sure I want to remind you of your father."

"Believe me, that's a good thing. He's been the most positive force in my life. You're like him in that there doesn't seem to be an ounce of pretense or dishonesty in you. You're so real."

"I think being in a place like the prison at Andersonville makes one that way. It strips away all facade and you become who you really are. I've seen big, burly men break down and cry like babies, and little runts have the will to survive and try to encourage everyone else. It changes people."

"How has it changed you?"

"It teaches life's lessons in the most dreadful way. They are squeezed into the span of a war instead of spread throughout a lifetime. I'm not nearly as carefree or as positive as I used to be. I know bad things can happen, and sometimes we're powerless to stop them. I know life's a struggle, and I don't think I'm as much in control of my own life as I once did."

"You shouldn't feel as if you're in control. You should give all that to God."

"You're right. I need a positive force in my life, someone to cheer me up. You do that for me, Maggie."

"I don't think anyone can make another person happy. I feel that we have to be content first. If we can't find happiness within ourselves, we'll look and look and never find it."

He looked at her in a new light. Maggie Moretz certainly wasn't shallow. She was bright, intelligent, and filled with wisdom beyond her years. "How has someone just eighteen years old come up with such profound ideas?"

"I've had plenty of time to read and think through my growing-up years. How old are you?"

"Twenty-three, but prison ages one fast."

"I think we should probably go in soon, but I've enjoyed being able to talk to you on a deeper level. I hope you'll feel like talking like this more often."

"I've enjoyed it too. You're the first woman with whom I've ever had such a serious conversation."

"Have you courted other girls?" she asked as they started inside.

"Yes, but nothing ever came of any of them."

"Do you know I've never had a suitor? The war started and took all the young men away."

"I'm sure there're some single men who've come back in one piece."

"Yes, but only one interests me."

Her eyes were dancing with laughter, and Aaron's heart started doing dances of its own. She became more intriguing all the time.

Aaron spent as much time as he could with Maggie. Most of the time, they were surrounded by others, but they were occasionally allowed to walk in the garden alone or walk up the streets of Salisbury.

Aaron especially liked sitting in the church pew beside Maggie. It made him feel like they were a couple and belonged together. The number of young women who flirted with him with their eyes surprised him. He never gave any indication he noticed them, and when it happened, he always turned his attention to Maggie. She usually looked at him and smiled.

That Maggie liked him and chose him above all others boosted his ego as nothing else had. He didn't understand it, but he accepted and marveled in it. He had to struggle to keep his assessment of her from causing him to put her on a high pedestal, because he knew this would be unrealistic and unfair to her. No one could live up to an ideal.

When their time to leave neared, Aaron didn't know what to do. He wanted to ask for Maggie's hand, but he had no job, no means of earning a living, and nowhere to take a bride.

Luke came to talk with him. "You and Maggie seem to be getting close," he observed.

"We are."

"Are you planning to ask her to marry you?"

"I'd like to, but I have nothing to offer her, not even a home."

"You're welcome to stay with Leah and me at the farm. There's plenty of room, and I'd love to have your help on the farm. I assure you, you'll earn your keep."

"I appreciate that, and I'll think about it."

Dr. Moretz came next. "I hate to see you leave so soon, right when you and Maggie are becoming better acquainted," he said. "Why don't you stay here? I could use a handyman, gardener, and driver. I've been without help during the war. I know you wouldn't want the job permanently, but you'd be helping me out until you can find something better."

"I appreciate the offer, sir. I'll think it over." Aaron would've rather had his own place to take Maggie, but these were two viable options he hadn't had before. Either one of them would allow him to be with Maggie more, but he couldn't decide which would be best.

In the end, he asked Maggie. After all, it involved her too. "I know I love you, Maggie, and I would like to ask you to marry me, but I'm not sure how you feel. Luke has offered for me or us to stay with him and for me to help him farm. Your father has offered me a temporary job, which would allow me to stay here and give you more time if you're unsure. Of course, you could tell me you have no interest in marrying me, in which case, I'll leave you here."

"Well, I don't like the last choice at all. I'd be very upset if you left without me." She added in a whisper, "I love you too."

Aaron could hardly believe his ears. *She loved him too.*

"Of the two remaining options, I'd prefer the first one. That way you'd get to farm, which you said you liked, and we'd get to marry sooner."

"I like the way you think, but what about your father? You'd be leaving him all alone."

"No, I wouldn't. I think he'll marry Mrs. Price. They make a suitable couple, and I know they admire each other."

"Then, will you marry me immediately, Maggie? Can you get a wedding together that quickly?"

"Give me about a week, and I'll be ready."

He took her in his arms, and she felt so right there. He kissed her on the lips and felt her grow supple against him.

"I'll look forward to more of those," she said with an embarrassed smile.

"Any time you want, as many as you want," he promised.

"How would you feel about a double wedding?" Dr. Moretz asked Aaron when he went to get permission to marry Maggie. "That is, if Clara will have me."

"I'd be honored, sir, but you'll need to ask Maggie."

"I know my daughter very well, and she'll be delighted."

"I hope I'll soon know her that well too."

"You will, and it won't take long. Maggie can be quiet and reserved, but when she gets to know someone, she's an open book. She holds nothing back."

———

Leah helped Mrs. Price and Maggie get ready for the double wedding, but they didn't really need her help. She'd never seen two more efficient ladies.

The same shop owner who'd made Ivy's wedding dress made theirs. She'd had it hard through the war, and she seemed overjoyed to have their business. She didn't have as many partially made as before, but what she had turned out to be perfect.

Maggie chose a beautiful pale-yellow satin dress with yards of lace. Mrs. Price picked a dress of dark lavender silk in a simpler style.

Luke told Leah to have her and Rachel a new dress made to wear to the wedding too. She chose an emerald-green one and had Rachel a little one made to match. Luke also paid for Aaron's suit. "Don't worry," he told his friend. "I'll work it out of you when we get back to the farm."

The wedding went smoothly. Father and Mrs. Price wed first, and there were no attendants. Leah would have to remember to call her Mrs. Moretz now.

Aaron and Maggie said their vows next. Father gave Maggie away, and Leah and Luke were matron of honor and best man. Rachel acted as flower girl and took her job very seriously for one so young.

After the ceremony, Father took his wife to her little house. Aaron took Maggie to a cottage Father had been able to borrow from a friend, and Luke, Leah, and Rachel had Father's big house to themselves.

"I had the two most beautiful women in the church today," Luke told them, and Rachel laughed with delight and clapped her hands. "I mean it, Leah. You get more lovely all the time."

"You're not the most objective person when it comes to your wife and daughter."

"Maybe not, but Aaron couldn't take his eyes off you when I showed him your photograph, and he commented on how pretty you are. He was certainly unbiased at the time."

"That photograph was taken at Ivy's wedding. It's eleven years old."

"Has it been that long? Where has the time gone?"

"We've spent too much of it apart."

"Now that you mention it, didn't we promise each other we would spend the time after I got back from the war making up for what we've missed?"

His eyes had that mischievous glint again. This was the first time Leah had seen it since Luke had returned, and she felt like bursting out in joyous laughter. Luke was back—all of him.

"I'm ready," she said. Oh, how she loved this man!

Author's Note

I wrestled with the writing of this novel more than any others in the series. I wanted to show the horrors of the war without the story becoming too dark or gloomy. Most of the historical facts are very accurate, however, occasionally there may be some slight manipulation for Luke's involvement.

All of the author's profits go to a scholarship fund for missionary children.

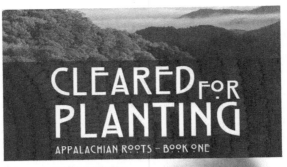

CLEARED FOR PLANTING

APPALACHIAN ROOTS – BOOK ONE

JANICE COLE HOPKINS

Emma has high hopes when her family moves to the North Carolina mountains. Her father appears to have finally quit drinking, and he plans to settle their family once and for all near the Linville River. Here Emma meets Edgar Moretz, an intelligent, passionate, and godly young man. Things are looking up for her, but when she is captured by a Cherokee raiding party, Emma's problems have just begun.

Years later, Clifton has finally finished his medical training and plans to spend some time at his family's mountain farm until he can decide his next step. He also hopes God will send him a special woman to become his wife. But when she arrives unexpectedly, he finds that the road to happiness is not always smooth.

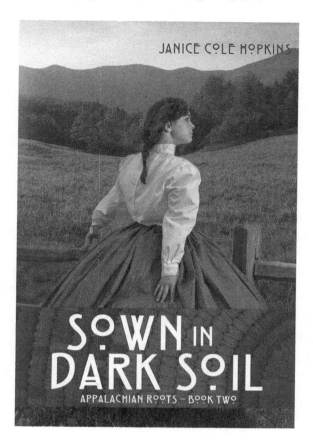

After the death of their father, Ivy and Leah Morgan are suddenly thrust into unpleasant, arranged marriages by their mother. Ivy, however, has other plans. Having fallen in love with Luke Moretz, Ivy insists upon running away to Luke's farm in the Appalachian Mountains to be far from her home and her mother's demands.

Convincing her sister to come along, the Morgan girls leave with Luke. Along the way, feelings between Ivy and Luke become strained, as Ivy's true personality and distaste for the mountains begin to show. Luke must decide whether to follow his growing attraction to Leah or keep his promise to Ivy. Meanwhile, Leah can't help loving all the things about Luke that her sister seems to dislike.

Mixed emotions and the testing of relationships lead to dangerous and unfortunate circumstances that put any chance of future happiness at risk. Will this journey bring the sisters closer than ever or drive them further apart than they could have ever imagined?

For more information about
Janice Cole Hopkins
&
Uprooted by War
please visit:

www.JaniceColeHopkins.com
wandrnlady@aol.com
@J_C_Hopkins
www.facebook.com/JaniceColeHopkins

For more information about
AMBASSADOR INTERNATIONAL
please visit:

www.ambassador-international.com
@AmbassadorIntl
www.facebook.com/AmbassadorIntl